Divers Kinds

Michael G. Casey

ISBN 978-1-9160264-4-5

First edition, 2019

Published by Azimuth Publishing
Dublin, Ireland

Photographic images used in the cover via Wikimedia.

Layout, cover design by iCulture

Please visit michaelgcasey.com

ABOUT THIS BOOK

The first of these short stories, *Epitome*, is about Elvis Presley as you have never seen him before. Elvis is, in fact, one of the most endearing of the characters who people these darkly humorous tales.

There are other fabulous 'Kings', e.g. the Shah of Iran, who feature in some of the subsequent stories, but they are not as charismatic as Elvis.

Neither is Hitler, who appears in another story in reincarnate form.

In a couple of stories, bullies get their just desserts in intriguing ways. In others, bad behaviour in Hollywood and the Vatican is exposed.

One cautionary tale features the obsessive-compulsive behaviour of a 'failed priest' in a refuse and recycling facility.

Another concerns a white-collar criminal who buys the prison he's incarcerated in.

There are a couple of quirky love stories, and others in which characters slide into madness or are driven to murder.

The collection as a whole deals with people in all their splendid, dark-side variety.

"This is a collection of great creativity and play. Some stories give full rein to a what-if idea; others develop protagonists in their unbridled quirkiness. The stories

always entertain, and they always make you think."
—Peter FitzGerald

BOOKS PREVIOUSLY PUBLISHED
BY MICHAEL G. CASEY

Come Home, Robbie, a novel, published by The O'Brien Press, 1990

> "...page-turning urgency ... spine-tingling compulsion ... the sheer quality of the writing lends the story some of the stature of heroic tragedy."
> —The Education Times

Treadmill, an award-winning Chapbook of short stories, published by Tipperary Arts Centre and Start Magazine, 2008

> "...Casey brings to life vivid characters who captivate, amuse and engage ... (He) has a wry observation and quick wit."
> —Mike McCormack

Ireland's Malaise: The Troubled Personality of the Irish Economy, published by The Liffey Press, 2010

> "...(Casey) shows the same Confucian wisdom as his hero, T.K. Whitaker in his brilliant new book."
> —Eoghan Harris, The Sunday Independent

The Visit, a novel, published by The Anaphora Press, 2011

> "…a small Irish town deals with a major event … an interesting addition to the genre … clear-eyed … vivid description…"
> —Denis Fahey, Historian

> "…a lovely clear prose style … some great characters and beautifully crafted vignettes."
> —Stella Kane, Quartet Books Ltd

Broken Circle, a collection of poetry, due to be published by Salmon Press in Spring 2019

> "…very powerful, intelligent poems made their presence known immediately … (Casey) uses casuistry and persuasiveness to rival Robert Browning's dramatic Monologues…"
> —Derek Selen

Michael G. Casey's most recent novels, *Smudged Mascara*, *Maura's Dance with Uncle Sam*, *The Killing of Ros Grenham*, and *Proving Ground*, from Azimuth Publishing, are available in Kindle and print versions through Amazon.

Table of Contents

DEDICATION

For: Saoirse, Orlagh, Cian, Isabella and Darren.

Epitome

THROUGH THE WINDOWS of the neo-colonial house in McLean, Virginia, Louise Staunton watches her little boy, Ed, playing in the back yard. An August sun washes over his neat features as he observes, with utmost concentration, the sickle-shaped leaves of a eucalyptus tree in the boundary hedge. Her heart goes out to him and she smiles, remembering how once she had unsettling thoughts about her ability to bond with him. No such doubts now. Though still some concerns about his upbringing and formation.

Home-schooling had turned out to be successful. Ed showed a remarkable aptitude for art and music and pursued these interests on his own. But, more recently, he displayed signs of becoming a loner, so she had to decide whether to enroll him in a regular school – to help the process of socialization. She was scared he might be bullied even though Uncle assured her more than once that her worries were unfounded. The best bet would be a parochial school where rough play was frowned on. St. John's had a good reputation, was near at hand, and had its own crossing guards at the traffic intersection.

She discussed this with Uncle on a previous occasion when she brought Ed to his clinic in Boston. Uncle thought it was a sensible idea, and agreed to have him enrolled in St. John's. When he finished the clinical tests, he pronounced Ed fit and well, thriving in fact. They set a date for the next check-up in six months' time.

To Louise's relief Ed adapted well to school; he liked the other pupils, joined in their games in the school-yard, was polite to his teachers, including the rather stern Filipino nuns, and was good at his lessons. When he came home from school he would have his evening meal which she prepared – or sometimes a pizza – and then he would get down to his homework. Sometimes she would offer help but it became obvious that he preferred to solve problems himself, even if it took a little longer. She could not have wished for a better son. He was, in short, a credit to her, as Mrs. Kelly, her neighbor, often pronounced.

Sometimes Ed visited the Kelly house after his homework was done. He and Billy Kelly – one of his school-pals – might throw a baseball around in the back yard, or if wet, go indoors and play video games such as Mooncraft or Grand Auto Theft XII. Occasionally their play would become heated but not physical and they never fell out or resorted to mean tactics.

'It's all good,' Louise thought. She no longer resented the fact that she became a home-maker and gave up her research job at the Boston Biomedical Clinic and Research Facility where Uncle was currently Chief Science Officer. She kept in touch with him and occasionally co-authored a research paper.

The last time she brought Ed to the clinic to be examined by Uncle was late fall and the roads of Virginia were quilted with mulchy leaves which made driving hazardous. She compensated by driving carefully and allowing for long braking distances. Uncle ran the tests immediately and the results came back the same afternoon. Ed, who was twelve at the time, was asked to sit in the waiting room.

"He's in good shape," Uncle pronounced. "Developing normally, safely within all the parameters."

"Good." Louise was not surprised. She would have been shocked if some anomaly had shown up.

"Imagine, ten or twelve years ago we were at the front edge," Uncle said with a slight incredulous shake of his head.

Louise nodded, "Yes, it's not so far-out anymore."

"I suppose there were some risks back then." Uncle looked into the middle distance and automatically closed his laptop, slowly squeezing out the flickering light.

"Not really." Louise didn't want to be reminded of that. Back then Ed was nothing more to her than a bag of enzymes, but time had changed everything. Now he was her son, her only child.

"Anyway, it all worked out." Reflectively, he added, "I remember when we replaced the DNA from your egg and replaced it with the donor DNA, the chances were no more than fifty/fifty. Successful fusion of the empty egg and new genetic material was never going to be easy. In the past, as you know, there were many self-abortions and other complications…"

"I guess I had some qualms when the tiny embryo was injected back into my womb. I had to go to Utah for that, remember…? The pregnancy and birth were easy enough though … You really should have won the Nobel Prize for your work at the sub-cellular level."

"We," he corrected her. "Anyway, the zeitgeist wasn't on our side. The so-called ethicists were up in arms. You couldn't afford to shout about that sort of breakthrough back then."

"I guess not."

"And of course, the Nobel Committee itself was constrained by the ethical question." Uncle shrugged but there was something about his expression that suggested lingering disappointment, and maybe even a vestigial desire to even the score.

In the waiting room Ed checked out some music online – Gospel and Country. Good melody and lyrics were making a comeback and he was glad of that. He felt sure that the medical tests had gone well. He sensed that Uncle was pleased with him. He was doubly assured when his Mom came into the waiting room with a broad smile on her face, and when she gave him a high five.

They drove home and soon picked up the Beltway, that anonymous highway – now a seven-lane one – surrounded by the lobbying departments of multinational companies that served the American Empire. No one could ever figure out how political decisions were reached in D.C., but these concrete behemoths – and their invisible occupants – were somewhere in the mix. They passed the multiple golden spires of a church and shortly afterwards took the exit for McLean, and more human-scale, tree-lined roads. Those roads, however, were tough on animals that lived in the woods, and it was not unusual to pass a raccoon or red squirrel that had been hit by a car and squashed flat, their intestines spilling out in purses of startling crimson. As a youngster, Ed had once made her stop to help a prone hedgehog, but it was far too late to save the little creature.

She looked frequently at Ed and smiled; she couldn't have asked for a better kid. He may have started out as something of an experiment but there was now a strong natural bond between them. And why not? She had carried him in her womb for over eight months. She assumed it was Uncle who had donated his DNA but it was a matter of little consequence to her. If Ed wanted to find out later on, then she would gladly seek out the information for him.

On Ed's fifteenth birthday they invited all his friends to a party in the back yard. They all stood around in the sunshine looking a little gauche. One other boy had started out as a frozen embryo and though he and Ed were the odd men out, it wasn't an issue. While not an everyday occurrence, genetic manipulation didn't raise eyebrows, any more than gender reassignment surgery. They were kids together – or rather young adults – and they would probably remain friends for the rest of their long lives. Later in the evening they switched on the karaoke machine and dared each other to sing. Ed was so good he was asked to do several encores. Many friends recorded him on their phones. Passing by with a plateful of iced cake wedges, Louise noticed his natural shyness and how it somehow enhanced his performance. He had a touch of her Boston accent which didn't quite suit the Country songs but still added a certain cachet. It surprised her when he sang old-fashioned, though still quite moving, songs like 'Wichita Lineman' and 'Ode to Billie Joe'.

Shortly after Ed graduated from High School, he enrolled in the Department of Performing Arts in Georgetown University, taking Music Theory and Composition as his major. He also signed up for classes in the History of Rock. His choice of subject surprised Louise, who had assumed that music, or at least singing, would be merely a hobby and that he would pursue subjects that would lead to a safer, more predictable career path. She had often thought that architecture, with its blend of science and aesthetics, would suit him, and whenever they discussed it, he seemed to be on that wavelength too. But she did not object when he made his decision about music. She could understand what it meant to him.

He wrote songs at home with the help of keyboard and guitar, and she was often amused by watching him nod and hum when reading sheet music or scratching his close-cropped hair when composing. He also had a habit of tapping a pencil against his strong teeth.

During the vacations he got internships in the Kennedy Center and Smithsonian Folkways. But he also got part-time work in bars and clubs and occasionally was billed as a warm-up act for some moderately known group. He accompanied himself on piano or guitar; his voice was good with a natural vibrato and it floated on the breath. He could sustain a note for a long period of time and even as it began to fade out he could still modulate it into little riffs. He made reasonable money and had a number of different girlfriends. Louise didn't worry unduly about that, knowing that he used protection. In a way she was glad he didn't get too serious too soon. The important thing was that he maintained a good grade-point average, which he did and, indeed, after his first year he was awarded a small incentive bursary.

She was very proud of him and although she would have preferred if he majored in classical music, for which she had a particular fondness, she was perfectly happy for him to make his own choices. He was creative and self-motivating, and those were the important character traits in her book.

During the vacation of his final year in Georgetown, Ed made surprisingly good money as an Elvis impersonator. He had become, as he laughingly put it, "one of the growing number of Elvi." There were in fact more Elvi than ever – over twenty thousand professional ones – according to the Music Chronicle. Some impersonators were so outrageously unlike Elvis that they became famous in their own right. One in particular, a rotund red-haired Japanese man, had headlined in Las Vegas, but of course it was mainly a self-deprecating comedy act. The majority, however, tried to look and sound like Elvis. The most successful of them were said to have the 'full package' – voice, appearance, facial and body gestures. While Ed was not near the front edge, and wore a cheap wig over his cropped hair, he passed muster in the smaller bars and clubs around McLean. On one occasion he performed in the Crowne Plaza at Tyson's Corner and was offered return dates by the manager.

Louise attended some of these performances and, though not quite her scene, she enjoyed seeing her son come out of his shell. As far as she could tell, he had rearranged some of the classic hits like 'Teddy Bear' and 'Blue Suede Shoes', so it wasn't completely derivative. Indeed, she had the impression that one of the bluesy numbers was his own composition. She was surprised to see and hear the audience grooving to her son; she never knew he had that kind of power. Maybe people had a natural instinct for some form of idolatry – a golden calf, movie star, or singer, take your pick. To her amazement, during the interval of the second show in the Crowne Plaza, she saw Uncle seated on his own a few rows in front of her.

"What on earth are you doing here?" she asked him.

"Oh, Hi Louise." He was a little shifty. "I was here on business ... Just passing by..." He seemed unprepossessing without his pristine lab coat, fawning assistants, and the ambience of science.

"Why didn't you call to the house?"

"Oh, it was just a flying visit. You know how it is." He patted the air dismissively in a nothing gesture. "I just happened to see a poster ... and I came along on the off-chance ... And here we are!" He added in a jubilant tone that blessed the kind fates for this unexpected and welcome synchronicity.

"Quelle coïncidence!" She thought of the slogan she had once seen on a notice board outside a Baptist church: 'Coincidence...? Or is God hiding?'

They joined forces and had a drink with Ed when his session ended and the applause died down.

"I hear you're on course for an excellent degree in music. Well done, Ed." Uncle sipped a dry Martini between nibbles of mixed nuts, cheese sticks and raisins.

"Thank you. I'm enjoying it." Out of the limelight, Ed had reverted to his normal shy self.

"You're lucky to enjoy study," Uncle said. "Music must come naturally to you?"

"I guess so."

"Horses for courses. I couldn't tell the difference between A minor and a hole in the ground ... Well, keep it up, son."

Louise couldn't help registering the last word – and Uncle's self-confessed lack of musical ability. It left an unanswered question drifting in the air.

Shortly after graduating from Georgetown, Ed landed another gig in the Crowne Plaza, but this time as the headline act. He had put together a makeshift combo of fellow students, each of whom was a trained musician. In addition to the usual instruments they had a cello and a piccolo trumpet. The Alexandria Gazette was later to describe their sound as 'a fusion of soul and neo-rock'. But it was his Elvis impersonations that brought the house down. He had that same maple sweetness in his voice, the lip curl, and loose hips. The embellished Karate suit that Louise had helped to bling-up, completed the similarity. This was hyper-reality at its best.

As she watched the performance from her seat in the balcony, Louise could see that something was happening. She was biased of course, but this was a special event. The audience thought so too. She was happy for Ed but she could not dismiss an eerie feeling that forces were already at work which might lead to some kind of separation in the future.

News of his talent spread through the county, by word of mouth, and courtesy of the Fairfax Sun Gazette. More shows followed. Louise went to all of them and was left with the same contradictory mix of feelings – with one addition: he had grown up so fast, too fast, as if his persona came readymade without the anxious searching and casting around of puberty. He was a very decent young man – no doubt about that. But she sometimes had the impression that there were thoughts and memories swimming in his head that she knew nothing about.

After the final concert the Falls Church News Press said, "Ed Staunton is rapidly moving up the Elvi league table and may already have entered the top twenty ... the similarity of phrasing, tremolo and body language give him virtually the whole package. One could quibble about the cheap wig but that is a minor detail. Do not miss Mr. Staunton's next performance as the King."

———————————

One afternoon in August with the air-conditioning on maximum, Louise's cell vibrated and danced a jig on an end-table of glass and steel.

"Hi Louise. That son of yours is going places by

all accounts." It was Uncle with the same gravelly and measured voice that commanded such respect at the clinic.

"Since when did you eggheads in academia become interested in Elvis impersonators?" She blurted out the question which had been building up inside her for some time.

"Well, all knowledge is one," he chuckled, "And nobody nowadays dares make a distinction between popular and high culture. So, it's all good. Listen, I happened to run into a guy at a party recently. An agent. He had seen a video of Ed and was impressed…"

"What kind of agent?"

"Well, I guess he deals with performers – musical, stage, screen … Anyhoo, he'd like to meet Ed … and yourself of course."

"What do you think?"

"Well, I don't really know … There's nothing to lose by meeting the man, I guess. Look, Louise, I know you'd prefer if Ed followed serious music, maybe compose an opera or an overture, but you know, American culture is what it is. For many people Elvis was and still is the King."

On the following Thursday Uncle turned up with AP Klinger, head of the agency of the same name. After some initial pleasantries during which AP distinguished himself as a witty man who didn't take himself too seriously, they agreed that he should represent Ed as a leading Elvi. They signed some forms and had a brief discussion about strategy, especially about the 50th anniversary of

Elvis's death which wasn't far off. AP said he would contact some of the venues in Atlantic City.

"Atlantic City?" Louise repeated with a slight sniff. Sequins came to her mind. Sequins and fish-net tights, and high-rollers with bulging stomachs and white Stetsons.

"Don't be a snob, Mom," Ed said. "It's entertainment."

"He's right," she thought. "He's always right. I can learn a lot from him." The only thing left niggling at her was the thought of Uncle being interested in Elvis Presley. Who knew?

The chosen venue was the Boardwalk Hall in Atlantic City, off Pacific Avenue and a stone's throw from Caesar's Palace. The management had booked bigger acts for the 50th anniversary of Elvis's death, and Ed was one of the smaller fish, due to perform three weeks before that in late July. But it was still a very good gig for a youngster from Virginia. The management provided considerable help in setting him up, facilitating rehearsals with his own group, enhanced by experienced session men.

Ed was given a good-sized dressing room which was equipped with a basket of fruit and a couple of bottles of champagne.

"You're in the big time now, "Louise

marvelled."It's hard to believe."

"I know," Ed said. "This is a step-up from the Crowne Plaza."

After a while she kissed him on the cheek, wished him well and went to her seat in the auditorium which was already half-full. She sat in the semi-dark surrounded by excited people, most of them much younger than her. They were waiting to see and hear her boy. She suffered more stage fright than he did.

Ed put the finishing touches to his costume and make-up and sat back in front of the mirror trying to relax. He could hear a constant hum in the distance and it took him some time to figure out that this swarming sound was coming from the waiting audience. His audience. The ten-minute signal came. He went over some lyrics. When he was collected by the stage manager he walked through winding corridors towards the wings, wearing his cape and jump suit. Nerves were working on him, making him doubt himself. The hum became louder and the lights grew brighter. And then he was on the stage where the blast of energy from the audience rocked him on his heels. It was a transformation. The nervous feeling that had undermined him now suddenly turned into a positive surge of adrenaline that took him over completely. He had planned to start with a down-beat number to help ease him in, but now he went over to the band and told them he wanted to start with 'Jailhouse Rock'. He hit the stage running. This was where he belonged. The hum of appreciation swelled, the lights were blinding. He was ecstatic, standing outside himself.

After the show he couldn't believe it was over. Time had flown. Had he been on stage at all? How had he performed? Judging by the applause and by the jubilant comments of band-members, it had been a great success. He was happy but there was a sense of anti-climax too. Louise met him at his dressing room and drove him home.

"You were fantastic," she said. She too was in a daze.

"It's all a blur," he admitted. "It was over in a second."

"Maybe that's why it was so good."

The East coast music papers were loud in their praises. Entertainment Weekly said he was almost as good as the real Elvis and had to be numbered in the top five Elvis impersonators – the serious ones, not the comedic ones. They advised the public not to miss any of his future shows. Rolling Stone and Billboard also devoted some column inches to praising the new kid on the block.

———————

Louise met Uncle as he flew into Reagan airport. He was carrying a bunch of reviews under his arm.

"Isn't it wonderful?" he said as he sat into her car.

"I thought you were tone deaf," she said.

"I am. Guilty as charged."

She turned to look at him. "Then I don't understand … I always assumed … it was your DNA…"

"No." He shook his head. "Who wants my pathetic genes? Besides, I had no desire to recreate myself. Another me? Oh, God no."

"Then who … Whose…?" She slewed the car onto the hard shoulder and brought it to a stop.

"I'm sorry. I should have told you before now."

"Whose DNA?" she repeated. "I should have asked before." It was her fault too for not asking, but it just had not been an issue for her, not until now.

"I know this surgeon…"

"The DNA came from a surgeon?" She flicked on her hazard lights as traffic swerved to avoid her. Airplanes came flying low over the Potomac to land, one every half minute. The air was thick with jet fuel and the roar of engines, far and near.

"No. The surgeon had kept some tissue after a small procedure he performed on a patient…

"What patient? Who?"

"Oh, come on, Louise. You must know by now."

"No. I don't."

"I think you must know … Half of the audience in Atlantic City sensed it…"

She looked at him and slowly mouthed the first name and the first syllable of the second.

He nodded. "Of course … Who else?"

"My God." She clutched the dashboard. Why

did it come as such a shock? She must have known at some deep level.

"What's so bad about that?"

"My son is Elvis Presley…!" It sounded like a headline from the National Inquirer.

"Well, a clone. But is that not a lot better than being a clone of me?"

"Jesus, I need time … to process…" As a young girl she had listened to Elvis and now, suddenly, she was his mother. She hadn't been a great fan but then she wasn't a fan of Uncle either and wasn't upset by the thought of his genes. But at least she knew him. Or at least she thought she did. She could hardly feel violated since she had been willing to participate in the experiment even though, ethically it was a minefield shrouded in mist. As a young biologist she knew it would help her career, and it did. She still got invitations to speak at conferences and at dinners. OK, she had rented out her womb in the interest of science but at least she might have been told whose DNA had been fused with her egg. There must have been protocols in place. She blurted out these questions to Uncle who answered as best he could. He reminded her that she loved Ed and was more than happy to be his mother. She could not disagree but tried to explain how that wasn't the point. She asked if he had done it for money. He gave a disingenuous reply, adding that money had its uses in the scheme of things. Finally she asked why he had told her now.

"Because it's bound to leak out, Louise. Ed is so

like Elvis that it's uncanny. And there's a good reason for that. He *is* Elvis … The public will not be fooled for long."

And he was right, though there was a possibility that he or AP had set the ball rolling with a judicious leak. Variety carried a philosophical piece on the mass belief that Elvis had not died; this later gave way to a conviction among some fans that he would be reincarnated. It now appeared likely that Elvis had been recreated through the miracle of bio-engineering. The science behind the process was no longer in the realm of fiction. The startling reality was that Ed Staunton was Elvis Presley.

Fortunately, Louise had had a chat with her son before the news hit the street.

"It's OK, Mom," Ed assured her. "I kind of suspected something of the sort. Everything I read about Elvis touched a deep chord in me. It doesn't feel all that strange to me though I can see how you might feel differently. I am who I am. I don't much like the term 'clone' but that's only a word. I am Elvis and I am grateful to have his talent. I knew it for certain that moment when I stepped onto the stage in Atlantic City. And I also sensed it when I met Lisa Marie…"

"That time you took a long week-end in Memphis?" She was a little disappointed that he had kept it secret until now.

"Exactly, I wasn't sure whether I should tell you at the time, but I'm glad I made the trip. Lisa Marie is a lovely person, full of charm…"

"Your daughter who is twice your age." Louise

merely noted the strange fact; there was no implied judgment.

"It takes some getting used to." He smiled "But it's not a problem for her or for me. I also met the siblings of the 'Memphis Mafia'."

"Their Dads loved you. But maybe they could have been ... more protective."

"Don't worry, Mom, I'm not going to go on prescription drugs this time. I've learnt my lessons well ... And I'm not going to ignore Gospel music or religion."

The story was taken up by all major newspapers, radio and TV stations. A couple of them tried to embellish the story by suggesting that it was Elvis's identical twin who had been reincarnated. The more mainstream story spread abroad – first to Britain, France and Germany, and then to virtually every country in the world, including China. It wasn't the first-ever human cloning but it was the first celebrity incarnation.

AP was inundated with requests from impresarios and concert venues around the world. He had to hire ten extra staff to handle the inquiries. It was a seller's market and he was in a position to play one bidder off against another. Extraordinary offers were made, especially for a show on January 8, 2035, the 100th anniversary of Elvis's birth. Bids were made from the biggest event centers in Europe including outside amphitheaters. After much reflection and consultation AP came up with a short list of two: The Colosseum at Caesar's Palace and the Las Vegas Hotel and Casino. He finally decided on the latter because that venue had originally been The International Hotel which Elvis had made famous with 840 sold-out appearances in front of a total of almost four million people.

A marketing bombardment sent expectations through the roof. This was the real Elvis but one who had the benefit of a musical education, plus experience and youthful vigor. The concerts were dubbed 'Elvis Reborn'. Unprecedented numbers of people slept in line outside the Las Vegas Hotel and Casino. Tickets went on sale at 9 a.m. and were sold out before 9.30. The face value of the cheapest ticket was $350 and a brisk secondary or scalping market developed where the basic ticket fetched upwards of $5,000. It was widely rumored that senior politicians and captains of industry had to pay these prices. At Ed's insistence complimentary and cheaper tickets were strictly reserved for those of limited means.

Ed and his Mom occupied a penthouse in the hotel as did Uncle and AP. The band had rooms on the floor below. The hotel management had never seen anything like the ticket sales and, days before the first concert, crowds of fans of all ages and nationalities congregated outside the hotel chanting, "The King is back. Long live the King." Many of them had entered the hotel and casino hoping to get a glimpse of the King. The management advised Ed to stay in his suite; they laid on massive security and decommissioned the elevators leading to the top two floors. They had already begun negotiations with AP for an extended run. AP had also to deal with several requests from biologists and geneticists around the world to meet Elvis. They hesitated calling him a clone.

Ed had to be careful because he had let his hair grow out and now the resemblance was complete. Nevertheless, with heavy disguise, hat and dark glasses, he went out to the strip one evening with Louise before the opening show. They saw pyramids, obelisks, the Sphinx, the Eiffel Tower, Arc de Triomphe, the canal bridges of Venice, and the Colosseum. They saw the fountains in front of the Bellagio. They had a meal in a French restaurant beside the Seine, under a starry sky. It was all so gloriously phoney.

"This is amazing," Louise observed. "Everything here is a copy and is ridiculously clean and well maintained. And yet it is somehow real."

"Just like me," Ed said. "I must confess I do feel at home here."

"Well, you did take this town by storm back in the day."

"I have a vague recollection of that. But my last few concerts were poor. He … I went in for a sort of parody because the energy wasn't there anymore. I can remember that awful feeling of … of … weakness. I just couldn't control my breathing and I slid off the high notes. In spite of that the fans still appreciated the show, but I owe them for that. And I will make it up to them."

She looked at him in wonder. Lights from the Arc de Triomphe formed a sort of halo around his handsome head. She knew now why he had played the karaoke machine in the back yard, why he had studied music at college. He would add technical skill to the raw talent of his inheritance.

On the evening of the opening concert he had a light meal in the suite. The Strip outside – indeed all of Las Vegas – was crammed with fans, mostly ticket-holders but also quite a number of people who were hopeful of picking up a ticket or of catching a glimpse of the returned King. Chanting and applause floated up continuously from the street. Camera crews from around the world were trying to get shots of the crowd and of the wider social impact before moving into the venue to their appointed – and very expensive – spots in the theatre. The police were out in force to keep a semblance of order. Police from neighboring states were drafted in to help out. The sirens of squad cars and ambulances drowned out the usual noises of the Strip. Elvis was back. He may have left the building once but now he was back and that was all that mattered. At one point someone shouted that they had seen him. A cry went up; a couple of people fainted and were helped into ambulances for treatment.

Police were stationed inside the theatre as well and it was significant that agents from the CIA and FEMA were also present, if less visible. Senior figures in Washington were uncomfortable with the kind of mass support that Elvis attracted. Depending on the path he followed he could become a destabilizing force. He needed to be closely monitored.

Religious people of every complexion were also present, strange evangelical types. They prayed aloud and chanted. Some thought the Rapture was at hand. One woman covered her face in a scarf Elvis had handed out to her mother from the stage in the mid-sixties. It was an object of worship. Others tried to take it from her.

Early in the afternoon he was led to his dressing room behind the stage of the theatre. The band was setting up and doing sound checks. He spoke to the sound engineers and suggested more channels for the drums and a slightly different balance of the instruments. The cello he had added to 'Suspicious Minds' needed to be accentuated. So too the strings and wind he had scored for 'Unchained Melody' and 'Always on My Mind'. The technical crew was working on the lights and special effects. They had erected a huge hydraulic hoist which would carry Ed out into the heart of the crowd; from his elevated position he could drop scarves on his adoring public. Three costumes had been laid out for him – one in gold, the symbol of his early years in the late fifties, one in black leather, to represent his comeback, and the third was the blinged-up karate suit with cape, studded with eagle wings, and flared trousers with wide gold belt. There were also a few leis laid out to represent his Hawaiian period. He would wear these costumes for old time's sake but for the more downbeat numbers and his own compositions, he would wear jeans and a white shirt.

He spent some time with the band and the

backing singers, finalizing the running order. He would do many of the Elvis classics in more or less the same order as his last show in 1977, starting with 'Easy Rider' and 'That's All Right Momma'. Towards the finale he would perform 'Wise Men Say', 'Are You Lonesome To-night' and of course 'My Way' and 'American Trilogy'. At the very end he would add a few Gospel songs and two of his own compositions, one of which had something to say about the state of the country. He had been advised against that on the grounds that the Deep State would become an enemy. His popularity would paint a huge target on his back. This concern had not reached Louise's ears but she was a bag of nerves anyway, almost afraid to ask him how he was feeling. Performing on such a monumental stage was something she could not do and never could have done. She knew that he was nervous too, but was able to control the sensation. She also had the sense that somewhere at his core there was a stillness that helped him prepare, that would help him give everything to the audience. He was not tempted to let the chalice pass. This moment was his life.

She left the dressing room when he began his meditation. He recalled the years as a youngster in Memphis making those demos in Sam Phillip's pokey 'Sun Studios' and the informal session he was thrilled to have there with Carl Perkins, Johnny Cash, and Jerry Lee Lewis. He was lucky to have achieved success at such a young age. He also reflected on past moments of success, mistakes he'd made and those that he'd managed to side-step or retrieve. His former existence was now somehow more seamlessly linked with the present moment. There were regrets from the past as well as triumphs. He now had a chance to live his life, an extended life, in a better way. It was a rare opportunity for which he was grateful.

He went over the entire show in his mind, thinking the music – lyrics and melody – remembering the new arrangements he'd made. He prepared mentally for each episode of the show, stage movements, use of the hydraulic rig … He visualized every aspect. He didn't have to worry about camera positions because they were everywhere. Saturation filming they called it. But he underestimated the effects of the audience, how the crowd would scream and applaud for over ten minutes when he entered, how the security men who guarded the stage would come under serious pressure, how close to chaos it would come even after he changed the sequence and began with some slow numbers that he hoped would gradually lull the over-excited audience into relative normality. The management would threaten several times to cancel the show and escort him from the building. And the encores … two, three … five … They would just refuse to let him go. Management had to promise them another show. It would be unprecedented.

When they came for him, costumed as he was, they started the procession through winding corridors that led only to one place. Louise followed at a slight distance; she would watch from the wings. As he neared the stage, the noise from the audience became deafening. Ambulance crews and security men carried out people who fainted. One of his assistants draped scarves around Ed's neck. These would be given out to members of the audience in a communion-like act. The stirring music of 'Thus Spake Zarathustra' came on, growing in intensity. Then the feverish drumming and the three strident trumpet notes repeated over and over. Elvis took several deep breaths, and murmured, "For you Mom and Dad, Louise and Jesse Garon." The procession to the stage continued. Dry ice swirled around him, rising slowly upwards, conjuring ghosts from the past. Lights and thunderous applause struck him at the same time and forced his head back. He smiled with the joy of new life. Elvis was on stage again.

Dreamers and the Judas Goat

I'M NOT PROUD of what I do, and I've been called a Judas Goat more than once. But we all have to make a living. Right? We're entitled to that much. Anyway I'm not the one who sends these people here to Columbia. The traffickers are mostly to blame. They get the *plata*, the big bucks. I just get a cut. And it's not prostitution either, or slavery. Is it really trafficking if the people want to come, and have the *dinero* to pay? I don't rightly know. You decide.

Anyone who watches TV knows that the main route for *migrantes* to the West is across the Mediterranean sea. A lot of people do not know that there is another way – for those who want to go to the USA – and that is through the Darien Gap between Columbia (my country) and Panama. This route to the 'West' is probably as dangerous as the way into Europe in leaky boats. Some say, much more dangerous. Sometimes it seems to me that the population of the world is willing to take huge risks to be somewhere else. I don't get it. I spent some time in the US and was treated like a dog. I couldn't wait to get back to my village.

To get to Columbia these migrants have to pay the traffickers to put them on flights to Brazil or Ecuador where border controls are weak. How much is the air fare from Africa to Brazil? I don't know but it can't be cheap. The truth is, despite all my experience, I don't fully understand what drives them to take such risks to get to Europe or the United States. And why risk climbing Trump's wall when they are going to be undocumented and always living in fear. I guess I don't have to know their reasons as long as they keep coming.

So, I'm hanging around my village, Biao, in the heat of the day. Kids and dogs are playing in the dusty street, running between the stilted huts. I can see that there are a few migrants in the main street with bulging backpacks. Two Bangladeshis and three Nepalese, I'd say. But not enough to make it worth my while to guide them through the Darien Gap. I need about twenty to make a decent profit. I can't wait too long of course because there are other guides and they could steal my migrants from under my nose. I decide to round them up tomorrow. I heat up the crocodile stew and backbone broth and have my evening meal. Then I go to bed and sleep soundly despite the music that the teenagers play for most of the night.

By noon the next day I notice that a larger group has arrived. Going by appearances, I would say some were from the west coast of Africa, others were from around Ethiopia while a few were Arabs. All told there's now about twenty, so I approach them in the street and offer my services. One of the Nigerians, John, acts as spokesman. He complains about the weeks of travel they have already done, buses from Brazil to Bogotá, then hitch-hiking from there to here.

"That has nothing to do with me," I point out.

"And then," he adds, his voice going higher, "we all thought we could take a bus along the Pan-American Highway, straight to the US border."

"Did no one tell you that there is a gap in that highway, the Darien Gap?"

"No," he says. I can see the others nodding their heads.

This doesn't surprise me. The traffickers who take money from these people paint a rosy picture. I suspect they're mainly *estafadores* … conmen. I tell him that that has nothing to do with me but he keeps on complaining. I can't really blame him but it is unsettling the others.

"Look," I say. "The gap exists. I didn't create it. But it is what it is." In my mind I christen him *El Demandante*. He will have more to complain about before this trip is over.

I never fully understood why the authorities left that one gap in the great highway. Maybe to protect the rainforest or to slow down the drug trade into Mexico and the US? Who can tell? I could see *El Demandante* doing mental calculations. But I know he has no intention of going back, not after the effort and money he's already put in. I inform him and his colleagues that my fee for guiding them through would be $100 each. He and a few others try to bargain so I remind them that there are no maps of the area and that they wouldn't stand a chance of reaching the Panama border without a guide. I let them know that I will be using my own canoe for the river part of the trip. I also tell them of the hazards they can expect, from jaguars, Guna Indians, The FARC, drug-runners and of course snakes. I lay it on a bit and it takes a while to sink in. I'm a little sorry for them; they had probably expected to be lying back in plush coaches being whizzed north on a four-lane highway. That's probably what the traffickers told them.

I then inform them about supplies that will be needed for the five-day journey – rice, a cooking stove, rubber boots, and canvas sheeting. I tell them where they can purchase these items – a store further up the street, run by my brother. We arrange to meet at sun-up the next day.

We start upriver by boat. I fire up the outboard motor and hold the tiller. The boat is low in the water due to the weight of twenty odd souls, all young men. I am disappointed to note that *El Demandante* seems to be the spokesman still. I had hoped that one of the Nepalese or the guy from Cameroon might have taken over. I keep my machete close to me. No one looks at their surroundings. Their minds are fixed on America only and the future. Are they all dreamers? I wonder.

At one point we meet some floating trees, the result of storm damage. We have to take the boat out of the river, carry it beyond the blockage and put it back in the water. One of the guys from Ethiopia starts to complain, not to me but to the spokesman. I intervene.

"Get something straight, guys. This journey is not going to be easy. If you don't cooperate then you won't make it. Understood?" There is a sullen silence but I can see clearly that there will be little team-work with this group. Each man is out for himself and has his own dreams. This is often the way.

When we reach the next village I tie up the canoe in a safe inlet and announce that we must now proceed by foot. I lead the way, hacking at the foliage, vines and tendrils where necessary. There is a trail of sorts but the rains tend to wash it out and the mud can be treacherous. As we get deeper into the jungle I can hear *El Demandante* tell the others that he's never been in such thick jungle before. He says a couple of prayers to Allah. I can tell by his soft hands that he's never done much hard work.

Thank God for the Nepalese. They help more than most in preparing camp that night. Following my instructions, they cut down big palm leaves to be used as groundsheets, tend the fire and build a makeshift roof of fronds – because I think it will rain soon. The others don't do much although *El Demandante* does stir the rice from time to time – and samples it regularly. There is some discussion as we eat our rice around the fire. The young guy from Togo wants to know if the drug mules use this trail for smuggling their product into Mexico and the USA.

"They do," I say. I had spent some years doing exactly that, but it was a fool's errand; the slightest mistake could easily result in a bullet to the back of the head. At least now I'm an independent trader. I'm not prepared, however, to tell them the story of my life. In the first place, they have no interest in me, only their dreams. And, secondly, I have to keep my distance. In this business it does not pay to become close with the clients. I broke this rule once and lived to regret it, but that is another story.

"What if we come across them?" He persists.

"Just keep your eyes down and hope for the best," I say.

It begins to rain heavily. The rain sounds like drumbeats on the leaves of mahogany and cedrela trees. But everyone is tired from the twenty-five kilometer trek and sleeps well.

The going is slower the next day because the rain has turned the trail into soft mud and because we have to climb over hilly terrain. Most of the migrants are younger than me but they are breathing very hard and find it difficult to keep up. We encounter a few snakes and the rubber boots do the trick. We also come across items left behind or discarded by another group of migrants who used this trail. Maybe they had to lighten their loads. I had a quick rummage through but didn't find anything of value.

The next day, *El Demandante* complains of fever and asks the others to help him carry his pack. No one will. As I already said, it's every man for him-self. Then he says he's dehydrated and has no water left. No offers from anyone. I let him have a half-liter bottle for $20. He's in no position to haggle. I can see from his eyes how much he hates me. I wonder how he would treat me if the situation were reversed? Later that evening we have to cross a river and I have to get them to hold hands so that the current has less chance of sweeping them away. In this sort of situation they do cooperate, especially when the word 'crocodile' is spoken. When we get to the bank some of them remove their rubber boots and empty out the water. The sun dries them off fairly quickly.

"Dry your feet well," I advise them. "If not … *ampollas* … blisters."

We proceed along a muddy riverbank, carefully, because it is not unusual for people to slip and fall into the river. A couple of years ago, I lost a young Angolan that way. But not today.

I think it was during a break the next day that I had a chat with one of the Arabs, an Iraqi. He offered me a cigarette but I declined. He told me his life was in danger in Iraq ever since he became a Christian. That explained why he was here.

"You became a Christian?" I inquired.

"Yes," he replied. "And my life is threatened. So, I need asylum."

"But Brazil was the first country you landed in," I said. "You could have sought asylum there."

"America better. Good life."

"Will your story be believed?"

"Yes … Good story."

"OK, explain the Mystery of the Holy Trinity." I felt that this was the type of question he could be asked by the officials in his host country. In other words, I was trying to help him. But he became quite agitated and I didn't say any more. I had seen him face east and mouth a few prayers. He might have been a good Muslim but he was no Christian.

Sometime later we reached the top of a hill and had the first view of Panama stretching out in the distance. This raised spirits but not for long. When we descended to the valley we were assailed by a strange sight, a skull on a pole. I halted the column.

"What does this mean?" *El Demandante* asked. He had obviously recovered from the fever.

"Not good," I replied in alarm. "The FARC rebels may be around here. Into the bushes quickly!"

"What's FARC?" One of them asked in a whisper.

"*Fuerzas armadas revolucionarias de Colombia ... terroristas*, very dangerous," I added.

"Allahu Akbar ... Allah, saeiduni..."

"Quiet."

After a long period of silence, I said that I hadn't signed up for this, and didn't want to go on. This bombshell was greeted with alarm.

"You can't abandon us here in the middle of nowhere," *El Demandante* said in a trembling voice.

I told them that I had not allowed for this kind of danger in my original price which covered natural hazards but not man-made ones.

"How much more?" the Iraqi asked nervously.

I said that I needed an extra $200 from each of them, but in the circumstances would settle for half of that. There is little bargaining. They hand over the money, and we proceed cautiously. They're eating out of my hand now. The skull has done the trick. They had probably all seen the movie 'Predator'. What drove these young men to leave family and lovers behind, take on these terrible odds? What was I missing? Did they know that after Panama they would have five more countries to get through? Maybe they had money to bribe the officials. I still, to this day, can't figure it out. Maybe they had some crazy fantasy about America and Europe, the Statue of Liberty or Eiffel Tower welcoming them to a perfect new life? Each of them lived in his head, driven by images. If they only knew the truth.

A couple of days later we can see the border post up ahead, and the Panamanian guards dressed in fatigues. I assemble the group and give them some tips for dealing with the guards. Then I wish them luck with the rest of their journey.

"Are you not coming to the border with us?" *El Demandante* wants to know.

"There's no need. You can see the border now. I have brought you this far. My job is done."

The other Africans have already gone on ahead. Only the Nepalese shake my hand. I stay in the Darien Gap until they reach the border guards – who don't like me much. Then I turn around and begin to make my way back, moving more quickly now. When I reach the skull I give it a little pat on the head. It worked well as usual.

I pick up my canoe and am back in my village after three days, having a beer with my brother in his shop. It is possible that the migrants of my group did not get across the border into Panama –

because of pressure from the Americans. They may have been sent back into the Darien Gap, this time without a guide or boat. Some may have bribed their way in. I don't know for sure, and if the worst happened is it my fault? You decide. I have a bath, a meal and a good night's sleep and get up early the next morning looking for prospects from the window of my stilted hut. I see Africans, Arabs and Asians begin to assemble in the street, looking around them as if checking their dreams against the dusty reality of my village. No doubt they'll need a guide. I'll bring them on a different trail to make sure we don't bump into some of the others on the way back.

Stuff

DIANE WASN'T UNHAPPY that the game was over or that she'd lost. Her opponent, Avril, was so competitive she sometimes barged into her or hit her with the racquet to claim a 'let'. And there was no need because she was far and away the better squash player, well able to place the ball deep into the corners and dominate the 'T'. She brought the same competitive instinct to her profession – buying for the fashion department of a large clothing store. Both young women removed their protective goggles, shook out their pony-tails, headed for the locker-room and then hit the showers.

"Good game," Avril said, pouring a handful of shampoo into her scalp and scratching vigorously with her finger nails.

"You didn't have to be so fierce. It's just a game."

"But I did … Nature … Remember the scorpion and the frog?" Her figure was as slim as it had been in school though, as Diane noticed, it was becoming a little angular, like her personality. The soapy water tended to slide quickly off her body as if there were no purchase to be gained.

As a lab technician, Diane did not have to be so conscious of her appearance and while she hadn't exactly 'let herself go', she didn't agonise over adding a centimetre to her waist every few years.

Back in the locker-room, Avril carefully folded her Nike skirt and placed it on top of her Black Knight squash shoes. She slotted her Wilson ultra-light racquet into a zippered pouch at the side of the bag. A thought occurred to her, "By the way, did you get an invite from Patricia … what's her name … Mahon?"

"I did. It surprised me. I haven't heard from her for months, maybe even a year."

"Are you going to go?" Avril switched on a hair drier and watched, in the mirror, her long blond tresses dancing sprite-like in the heated air. The roots would soon need touching up. She might even go for champagne highlights.

"I thought I would go. To tell you the truth I feel a little guilty about the tricks we used to play on Patricia in our last few school years."

"Well she kind of asked for it," Avril replied. "Some people are like that, you know. Born victims. Bit of a sneak too. She told the teachers about our booze sessions. I'm sure of it. I don't know if our denials were ever believed. Course they couldn't prove anything … It wasn't our fault that her pic went viral…

"Well, an image of a plump gal in her standard-issue knickers with the caption 'Fat Pat' … It was cyber-bullying I suppose." Although it had not been Diane's idea, she had gone along with it.

"Oh, come on … You sound like a safe-space snowflake … We may be Millennials but we live in the real world…" She thought for a while as she applied make-up. "No plus-ones though."

"What?" Diane sprayed a lemon-scented fragrance under her arms and put the cylinder back into her rather used-looking bag.

"Partners … On the invite."

"Oh right. You'd probably like to bring Philip as your 'Plus one'. It's not a problem for me though. I'm celibate at present, as you know … But you should come, Avril. I have a feeling that Patricia is making a gesture … she wants to put all the bad stuff in the past where it belongs."

"Maybe you're right. But I'm not going to apologise." She snapped the tortoise-shell lid of her compact shut with a loud click.

Diane gave her a sidelong glance as they left the club, carrying their sports bags.

———

Avril drove her Audi Sports along the coast road, looking like a celebrity in her skinny jeans and aviator glasses. They passed suburban houses of numbing sameness. At least there was an attractive sunset and a few small boats out racing in the bay. It struck Diane, who sat in the cream leather passenger seat, that the mellow rays of the declining sun acted as a sort of glaze that improved the mediocrity of the landscape. They parked outside a modest terraced house, formerly an artisan dwelling.

"Are you sure this is it," Avril asked. "I think

these are Council houses."

"This is the address on the invitation." Diane rang the bell and Patricia came to the door almost immediately.

"It's great to see you after all this time." Her face was flushed with excitement. The others responded in kind and it was all a bit false and forced since they had hardly been bosom buddies in school or at any other time.

As they gradually descended from the peaks of feverish greeting to the lowlands of civility, Diane observed how nice the house was and Patricia remarked that it was quite good for the North side of the city. As a civil servant with a steady, though not stellar, income she had little difficulty getting a mortgage. During the year she spent as a nanny she had no hope of borrowing from a bank.

Avril noticed the embroidered cushions and wall hangings – all predictably sewn by this rather boring homebody. She also observed that Patricia had lost some weight. As if on cue, Diane said, "You're keeping trim I see."

"I make the effort," Patricia replied with a grin. She led them towards a small dining area with a kitchen at one end, and bade them sit.

They sat on bentwood chairs around a restored pine table. Overhead, there hung a paper lightshade in the shape of a sphere – the kind that used to be popular with students. Patricia busied herself in the kitchenette and then served a vegetable soup and poured Pinot Grigio from a Tetra Pak which she had chilled in the fridge. She used a baize-covered card table as a sideboard.

"Mmmm, this soup is really good," Diane enthused, looping a strand of loose hair behind her left ear. "But then you studied Domestic Science at school, didn't you?"

"Yes, while you and Avril were off doing PE in the gym ... or nipping from hip flasks." Patricia went over to the kitchen area to switch on the extractor fan; she had noticed some condensation forming on the walls and work surfaces. She turned down the gas under the main pan, and put the naan bread into the microwave to warm.

Avril couldn't contain herself any longer. "We ... I was surprised by your invitation..."

"Oh, why?"

"I don't think ... we were very nice to you at school." Diane hoped she wasn't rushing her fences but she had a desire to clear the air sooner rather than later.

Patricia smiled on all cylinders as she resumed her place at the table. "That's all forgotten. Anyhoo, I thought it was time for a catch-up."

"It was very nice of you," Diane said. "Incidentally is that chicken curry I smell?"

"Chicken korma, almost the same."

"You remembered?"

Avril was impressed. "God, it was the only dish they served in that canteen that was half-way decent. You're good to remember." She noticed how her hostess regularly tidied up crumbs that fell from the bread rolls. Was it a sign of OCD? She wouldn't be surprised. In her opinion boring, meticulous people tended to like repetition and ritual.

Patricia modestly suggested that 'her' korma would probably be better than the school's since she had added ginger, and garlic, and crushed peppers and long-grain brown rice, and yoghurt of course. She also let the dish simmer for far longer than the dinner-ladies ever did.

"It sounds delicious." Avril seemed to be thawing out at last.

"Of course, I prefer plainer fare." Patricia said.

"Oh yes, I remember," Diane lied diplomatically. "So what will you eat?"

"Meat and two veg. I have a lamb chop on for myself. But I really enjoyed the opportunity to do something more exotic for you."

"That's so … thoughtful…" Diane began, then faltered, recalling how nasty and mean-spirited they had been to her, "bearing in mind how we…" She stopped as Avril kicked her under the table, and she deftly changed the subject by reminiscing about one of their more colourful teachers.

"I always thought there was something unusual about her," Avril confessed. "Possibly a lezzie."

"You probably thought she fancied you because you were so irresistible." Diane went on to note that the teacher in question had never bothered her.

The conversation turned to relationships but didn't last long since Avril was the only one who had a boyfriend at that moment. She said that he was a good guy though not the passion of her life. And, no, she didn't hear wedding bells tinkling in the future. As a fashion-buyer she got around to many high-end shows. Unfortunately, most of the buyers, designers and male models were gay.

"If not gender-fluid," Diane put in.

"Apparently, there are seventy-eight different genders at the last count," Patricia said.

"Can anyone name even three?" Avril asked.

They all felt old-fashioned and way behind the curve when they could only name three between them: binary, pangender, and autigender.

Patricia served up. She offered cold beer to go with the korma but they decided to stay on the white wine.

"Absolutely delicious," Diane enthused. "The seasoning has imparted a special flavour to the chicken."

"I agree," Avril said. "It's some kind of super-chicken, definitely organic."

"It could be the cilantro I sprinkled on. If anyone needs more yoghurt or anything else, just yell."

As the meal progressed they chatted and reminisced about their schooldays, teachers, subjects, competitions with other schools. They recalled Avril's prowess on the hockey field and Diane's success at quizzes. There was little enough to say about Patricia, who had not made much of an impression at school except possibly in Domestic Science, aka cookery. Her legacy might be: 'She made a good chicken korma'. At one point Patricia excused herself for using her fingers to pick up the bone of her chop and gnaw on it.

"Well, the nearer the bone, the sweeter the meat." Avril spoke with her mouth full.

As they neared the end of the meal, Patricia went to the kitchen area and assembled the coffee things. She used a ground Ugandan variety of coffee that appealed to her.

"That was a fabulous meal," Diane said. "I used a spoon for that superb juice."

"Really good." Avril patted her stomach in confirmation. It was no great surprise really. She always figured Patricia as a homebody.

Patricia plunged the cafetière, poured the coffee and distributed the cups. "Of course you two never had to worry about your weight."

"I wouldn't say 'never'." Diane recalled a couple of the different diets she had tried; none of them had worked. There were a lot of snake-oil salesmen in the diet business.

"Some of us aren't so lucky." Patricia placed a bowl of sugar cubes with silver-plated tongs, and a jug of milk on the table, and sat down.

"You're actually quite … slim … now…" Diane regretted adding the last word. She went on tilt, guessing that the conversation was beginning to enter choppy water; and her instinct proved right.

"Remember that photo of me that was posted online?"

"Y-e-e-s." Avril sat up straight.

"That really upset me. I became bulimic for a while. Needed counselling." Her voice was matter-of-fact, too much so. It fortified the surrounding silence.

"I'm so sorry," Diane said. She didn't want to blame Avril though it had been her fault. "At that age kids can be thoughtless and foolish."

Patricia ignored her. "It really affected my body image. The bulimia worried my mother into an early grave."

"Oh my God, that's awful." Diane went pale and looked to Avril to step up, without success. "We didn't know." So this at last was the reason for the invitation. To clear the air. She had expected something of the sort, though not quite this.

"Youngsters don't understand consequences." This was as far as Avril would go by way of apology. "We were all wet behind the ears."

"I had liposuction recently," Patricia said as she stirred milk reflectively into her coffee.

"Oh, there was no need, I'm sure," Diane spoke by rote, unsure of where the conversation was headed.

"I felt – and looked – a lot better afterwards."

Still keen to appease, Diane nodded her agreement and surreptitiously nudged Avril to confirm.

"Anyway, I'm glad you enjoyed the korma." Patricia looked steadily at them.

"Oh we did. We most certainly did."

"It wasn't chicken by the way. It was my belly-fat."

"You're what?" Avril responded sharply.

"You heard me. Belly-fat. Mine. The stuff that was sucked out of me. The stuff you used to laugh at. I saved it for you." Patricia directed a forced smile at each of them in turn.

"Jesus Christ, I don't believe you…!"

"You should believe." Patricia stood up, went to the fridge and returned with a Tupperware box labelled, 'St. John's Clinic, Adipose Tissue'. She prised open the lid with both thumbs and showed them the contents. "There's some left if you would like to be reminded of the taste. It was so easy to cook. In its own juices. No need to add oil."

"You're crazy…!" Avril began to gag. Diane sat frozen in shock, her gag-reflex immobilised for the time being.

"Use the bathroom if you want but I doubt if you'll get it up. It takes a while to master the finger-throat technique. I should know. Even if you get some of it up there will always be that little something of me as a memento in your guts."

"You mad bitch!" Avril stormed out, followed by Diane who wept loudly even when she got into the car. They hadn't gone more than a hundred meters when she vomited all over the cream leather upholstery.

Patricia carefully closed the Tupperware container and put it back in the fridge. A trace of a genuine smile played over her features.

Infallible in my Kingship

I REMEMBER THE CELEBRATIONS held in 1971 – a year that in my view had a borderline personality. I landed with my retinue at Shiraz airport, suitably refurbished for the occasion, at 5 p.m. local time, and my pilots brought the jet to a standstill in a designated slot. The Mercedes limousine met me and whisked me out to Persepolis. My aides got on one of the official buses and were brought to their accommodations with my trunks.

The road from Shiraz to Persepolis was newly paved and glistened like black glass in the relentless desert sun. A heat haze rose from it so that sand dunes close at hand as well as distant mountains shimmered in a sort of mirage. My accommodation proved to be reasonable – a small house covered in silk, more or less in the middle of a tented city near the ancient pillars of Persepolis. The designers of the tents had, apparently, been inspired by the Cloth of the Field of Gold where King Francis I of France met Henry VIII of England in the Summer of 1520.

For domestic reasons too complex to describe here, my Queen could not travel with me. I quickly settled in to my temporary abode, had a shower and dressed in casual clothing suitable for desert conditions. One of my aides phoned me to say that the Shah had asked to meet me on the last day of the celebrations to seek my advice on affairs of state. I said I would be glad to do so and conveyed my good wishes to his majesty. Then I went out to the little patio in front of my tent/house which I immediately christened a 'Yurt', lit a cigar and continued reading my book, 'Come Home, Robbie', which I found enchanting. I noticed that others followed my example by emerging from their yurts, not to read but presumably to watch the sun set behind the pillars of Persepolis in this gilded desert encampment.

"Hello, old chap. Roughing it like the rest of us, I see"

I looked up to see the Duke of Edinburgh give a languid wave in my direction. He was having a pick-me-up at his patio table.

"Hi there, Phil," I called back. "Is Betty here?"

"No. She didn't fancy it. But Annie's here." He then pointed to some of the fluted columns rising in the background and inquired if they had something to do with the imminent celebrations.

"No," I replied. "They're remnants of the beautiful ancient city of Persepolis – after that Macedonian vandal burnt it to the ground out of spite." At least, I thought, the carvings of nobles bearing tribute were extant as well as the human-headed flying bulls with the impossibly curled beards. I had visited the site long before I ascended the throne.

"What vandal?" Phil asked.

"Alexander the so-called Great."

"We probably have some of the stone carvings

in the British Museum. Safe-keeping, you know. Can't always trust Johnny Foreigner to care for his own traps."

Another voice intruded, that of Haile Selassie. "Good evening, gentlemen. This promises to be a good celebration." With his high forehead and curly beard he looked like one of the bas-relief figures walking up the slope to the Gate of all Nations. Philip and I politely agreed with him. He had four or five serving girls waiting on him, one waving a large plumed fan. We would learn later that he had brought over eighty courtiers and servants – including, according to Olav of Norway, his groom of the stool.

After a while the royals of other countries ventured out and we all greeted each other with pleasantries and good wishes. We felt free of protocol and let our hair down with each other. It was more like a school reunion or a scouts' jamboree. Of course we knew that our own security people as well as SAVAK weren't far away, but they were discreetly invisible. Naturally, no photographers were allowed, since they could have made us all seem rather less than majestic in the tabloids of each country.

"This sun is too hot for me." Olav said. He rubbed his face. "Fair skin, you know. See you chaps later on." He disappeared into his yurt like a badger into its burrow.

"Haile doesn't have to worry about the sun," Phil piped up. "And neither does Juan Carlos, or those sultans over there." Everybody smiled but cast their eyes to heaven when Phil called it a day and went into his yurt.

"I wouldn't mind," Juan Carlos said, "But he's only a prince, and not very princely at that."

"I think he would temper his language," Carl Gustav put in, "if Betty were here."

Gradually the crowned heads disappeared indoors. I waited for a while to watch the blood-orange sun go down behind the ruined palace of Darius the Great, then I too retired. Though missing the luxury of my palace, I enjoyed a light supper of figs, rare Shiraz grapes, sheep's cheese and Champagne.

I slept well and rose early in the morning around 10 a.m., woken by songbirds. An aide had informed me that 50,000 of these creatures had been brought in by the Shah to occupy the thousands of trees and shrubs newly planted in the desert. I wondered where these birds would drink and whether they would last until the end of the three-day ceremony. I heard shots and went out to investigate. Security men were scurrying around but they had nothing to worry about. Victor Emmanuel of Italy was standing outside his yurt in monogrammed long johns firing his shot-gun at the sparrows, many of which were falling from heaven. The security men melted away but Olav shouted from his yurt. "Vic, put that damn gun away. Some of us are trying to sleep. We have this commemoration to go to in the evening. Some of us need our fifteen hours."

"The birds woke *me* !" Vic shouted back in a

disgruntled way, hammering an exculpatory finger against his sternum, but he didn't reload, and peace reigned once more.

Well, we all turned up in proper regalia for the homage to Cyrus the Great at his mausoleum at Pasargadae. Most of my fellow potentates wore sashes with various orders and decorations pinned to them. Needless to say, these badges and honours had been awarded to themselves by themselves. Haile wore so many that, even though used to heat, he felt faint on a couple of occasions and had to be helped into an upright position. The Shah himself was well bedecked and kept walking into the sword that hung from his belt. His epaulettes were too large for his shoulders and looked like yellow sea creatures with tentacles. I, myself, had little time for such ornamentation and wore on my blue sash only a medal I won for life-saving when a lad. It was, at least, a genuine award.

He, the Shah our host, was introduced to us on the steps of the mausoleum as the King of Kings and heir to the Peacock throne of the Achaemenid Empire of 2,500 years ago.

"King of Kings," Olav whispered in my ear. "What are we … chopped liver? His bloodlines are way less impressive than mine."

Sofía of Spain must have overheard because she added, rather inappropriately, that the Shah was merely a puppet of the Americans. This observation caused many of us to glance over at Spiro Agnew. We could only guess at the reasons for Nixon's non-attendance. Agnew was taking the whole thing most seriously, probably because America had such little recorded history of its own. He seemed to be impressed by the trumpeters and marching of Iranian troops all got up to resemble the soldiers of Cyrus. To be honest, I felt a frisson when the Shah told Cyrus the Great to "sleep well because we are awake." But on reflection, I wasn't sure what it meant.

It was very hot and I think everyone was glad when the ceremony was over. A curious thought came to mind as we walked back to the waiting limousines, and I expressed it to Phil, with whom I had been chatting. "Imagine if Themistocles had not defeated Xerxes at Salamis we'd all be speaking Farsi now."

"I don't know what you're talking about," was his brusque reply.

"Well, you see the Greeks were…" I began to explain when he raised a long finger.

"And I don't want to know."

Sometimes I think that bloodlines provide good seats for horses but not for thrones.

Princess Grace then told me how much she was looking forward to the feast, since the Iranians had flown in the food and chefs from Maxim's in Paris. She raised an elegant eyebrow and added, "Naturally, caution is needed. I've seen the huge blocks of ice, but I still have to wonder about proper refrigeration in the desert. Don't you think it's all a little *de trop*? I mean," she lowered her voice, "the Shah does carry himself well, but where would he be without oil?"

"A good question," I replied neutrally, thinking about where any of us would be without birth-right, power, or marrying up. My coronation was blessed by church and state but there were other kings who had little legitimacy. I thought of the French Revolution, the lopping off of crowned heads, and of how Napoleon became Emperor within a small span of years. People need kings just as they need religion, but a good king should never become arrogant or remote.

The banqueting tent was large and full of what ordinary people would regard as luxuries. There was, however, a logistical problem. We monarchs were to enter first, naturally, before presidents and prime ministers. Many crowned heads turned up at the same time so that there was a jam point or Venturi effect. Now if there's one thing that monarchs do not do, it is queue. This is a law of nature. Some tried to avoid the receiving line altogether while others went back out to their limousines and drove around the desert. The Shah stood in the receiving line, glistening with personal ornaments and tension. Fortunately, his large eyebrows ensnared the drops of moisture rolling down his forehead and prevented them pouring into his eyes. He could hardly speed up the process of welcoming potentates, most of whom had made a pact in 'yurt-land' that, while their consorts could curtsy, they themselves would merely nod curtly, and not at all if the Shah did not nod first.

Eventually, most of us were received and seated. There were some queens and princesses whose elaborate coiffures, despite the restraining effect of tiaras, had been disturbed by sudden sand-spirals while getting out of cars. They went with their ladies-in-waiting to the toilet facilities. From there Grace, Ingrid and Fabiola made grand entrances; they looked elegant against the silk background of the banqueting tent, though I do not have the skill to describe what they were wearing. I must confess to another flaw: whenever an elegant lady is superbly dressed, I tend to disregard the outerwear and imagine instead what lies inside.

Rumours had spread among the yurts, earlier in the day, that sheep's eyes were to be served but that, happily, proved untrue. We started with quail eggs stuffed with golden caviar from the Caspian. I noticed that the Shah, who sat at the head of our table, had artichokes instead, and I remembered that he was allergic to caviar, which had been forced on him as a youth when he believed the little eggs were mouse droppings.

Juan Carlos nudged me and asked if I knew what the 'cylinder' was that the Shah had referenced in his tribute to Cyrus the Great. He thought it might have been an early form of commode.

"It was a pottery cylinder on which Cyrus had written out a constitution of sorts. It was well over a thousand years before the Magna Carta…" I would have explained more but I could see Juan's eyes glaze over.

The Champagne and other vintage wines began to thaw us out as we made a start on the lamb with truffles. Just then we heard a loud commotion coming from the kitchen area. A door flew open to reveal a group of French chefs bent over a fallen comrade who had apparently suffered a seizure from all the pressure placed on him. The door was quickly closed but the sight lingered in our minds, especially as the chefs were half naked due to the additional heat of the kitchens. I noted that Grace pushed her plate away from her. I have to confess that the sight of several hairy French chefs quelled my own appetite to some degree.

"I say, that's a bit much," Phil said.

"Well, it is rather warm in there," I pointed out.

"They could rub themselves against one of those big blocks of ice." Then he changed the subject. "By the way, old man, did you bow in the receiving line?" He didn't seem to care that the Shah was seated only four places away.

"I did."

He sucked in his breath and shook his head as if to suggest that I should not have done that. It was obvious that he had not done so. I felt like telling him that a prince should bow to a king but I bit my tongue and then tried some more of the lamb. He looked around, had a word with his daughter, Anne, and then said, "All this ... it's all a bit *nouveau*, don't you think. I believe they spent $700 million on it."

"Well, they do have oil," I explained, "and," I added *sotto voce*, "in my opinion, the OPEC countries are likely to quadruple oil prices in a few years."

"OPEC countries?" he queried. "Haven't heard of the blighters."

We all sat back while the peacock stuffed with foie gras was being served and the Mouton Rothschild was being poured. Frederick of Denmark leant forward and asked me if we were likely to join the Common Market.

"I believe we will join, certainly by 1973."

Phil cut in, "I doubt if the UK will join. Europe is not really our cup of tea…"

"Daddy!" Anne protested, though she didn't have to because Olav of Norway dealt himself a hand, "Of course, De Gaulle gave you a bloody nose a few years ago, when he said 'Non!'" Olav had a wide grin on his face and, since there was no reciprocal smile, he tried to make amends by praising the way Anne was growing up. He added that he had a handsome son of around the same age and wondered if something might be arranged.

"Remind me," Phil said. "What is your house."

"The royal house of Glücksburg," Olav replied.

"Glücksburg?" Phil repeated in a surprised tone. "Glücksburg?"

"Yes," Olav said. "It would be a good fit with the house of Saxe-Coburg-Gotha."

"But we are Windsors."

"From where come these Windsors," Vic asked, from further down the table, and I was sorely tempted to say that in my country the Windsors were people who auctioned used cars.

Needless to say, Anne was looking mortified during this exchange, but worse was to come.

Konstantinos chuckled loudly and reminded Phil about his Greek heritage. He added that he too had a son approaching marriageable age. A dynastic liaison with the Greek throne might be even more suitable. Poor Anne was by now in such distress that Grace had to come to her rescue. This she did by observing that a significant number of dictators were present at the table for Presidents. We all looked around and were forced to agree with her upon seeing Tito, Ceausescu and several others. Olaf then asked provocatively whether monarchs were not also dictators by definition. Carl Gustav and Juan Carlos wouldn't hear of it and went on at some length about bloodlines and constitutional democracy. Phil did not seem to be very interested in the discussion.

"Let me pose a question," I said. "Where major affairs of state are concerned which one of us is not consulted by our respective Presidents or PMs?"

There was much harrumphing and a grudging acknowledgement that such consultations did in fact take place.

"And when you give your views," I followed up quickly, "are they not always embodied in subsequent legislation?" After considerable throat-clearings and sips of brandy I added, "I rest my case. We are not merely titular heads. Olav makes a good point."

"But you see," Vic observed, "Democracy can be quite flawed." He nodded in the direction of Spiro Agnew. "Bought and paid for by big business in the States—and what about Nixon?"

Fabiola took that ball on the bounce. "That is the great advantage of monarchs. We have enough wealth of our own and are, therefore, incorruptible. The advice we give is objective and not influenced by special interests."

This was followed by a general murmur of agreement, which in turn led to a discussion of civil lists in different countries and the danger of populist politicians demanding that monarchs be brought into the tax net. It could have been a meeting of trade union leaders, so heated did many of us become. Marina of Italy observed, "Parliaments have no idea of the expenses we incur or of the contribution we make to civil order." I couldn't help noticing that she was wearing nail polish which, for a princess, was a flagrant breach of protocol. In any case her argument was greeted with general assent.

During the meal, Mohammed Reza Shah Pahlevi sat at the head of our table and spoke with the monarchs seated close to him, one of whom injudiciously complained about a snake that had popped its head up through the plug-hole in his shower. Mohammed apologised and said he would have the problem seen too. He didn't seem fully relaxed and his restless fingers played with one or other of the decorations pinned to his sash. I wondered what he wished to discuss with me, and why he had singled me out. It was odd that he hadn't referred to it in the receiving line.

At one point, Olav said with a slight slur, "King of Kings. Well he's not the king of me." He had a strange sense of humour that did not impress very many people.

"A rum cove," Phil murmured, a little in his cups. And it wasn't clear whether he was referring to the Shah or to Olav.

When dinner was over and the speeches done, we exited the dining tent to our waiting cars. I couldn't but notice that a considerable part of Limoges Dinnerware, Porthault linens and rose-and-myrtle flower arrangements had disappeared from the table at which we had just dined.

I decided to give the son et lumière display of Persepolis a miss on the grounds that the site looked better under ordinary sunshine and would be cheapened by artificial light, so I also missed the fireworks display but that didn't bother me either, given my reservations about all shows that attempt to be spectacular. I went back to my yurt, where one of my aides informed me that he had been caught reading a book by George Orwell, until a SAVAK agent had confiscated it. I wasn't entirely surprised; some monarchies are more oppressive than others. I took the matter under advisement but did not wish to cause a diplomatic incident. My people depend a lot on imports of fossil fuel.

By mid-morning some of us were again breakfasting on our yurt patios and, again, there was that boyish giddiness between us. I don't know why the distaff side did not appear; perhaps they were having a lie-in.

"You know," Olav informed us, "Konstantinos played the damn balalaika for most of the night.

And he doesn't know A-minor from a hole in the ground."

"Tell me about it," Vic said. "I would have sent an aide around to complain but an aide cannot speak to a king."

"It's a real problem," Carl Gustav chipped in. "We can't complain like ordinary folk. That's why we need large palaces to insulate us – so we don't have to complain."

Phil emerged from his yurt just then and enthusiastically endorsed this sentiment. No mention was made of the attempted match-making the previous evening. A car approached, and I recognised the pennant and the uniformed outriders. As I went back into my yurt to receive the Shah I could see the surprised look on the faces of my fellow potentates. The Shah was in military attire. The large epaulettes gave him the figure of an American quarter-back. We went through some pleasantries and then sat down in the main room of the yurt. An aide brought us coffee. I was keen to know what was on his mind, and didn't have to wait long.

"Before you leave our country, I would like to ask your advice on a matter that concerns my people. You are the wisest of all the kings, even though that advantage is not too difficult to achieve."

I let the mixed compliment pass and craned to listen to his low monologue. He informed me that he had received a threatening letter on the eve of the celebrations from a former Iranian cleric, named

Khomeini, who referred to the Shah's kingship as 'a disgrace before God'. Furthermore he referred to the Shah as 'a pathetic usurper'. He maintained a straight-backed posture as he unburdened himself.

"That's a bit strong," I said.

"And it's not as if he favours democracy. Oh no. He is a dictator, albeit a religious one. And he has no charisma."

I thought there was a slight suggestion that he, The Shah, had oodles of that quality. When I took in those puffy epaulettes, ceremonial sword and corseted back, I had the distinct impression that he was rather full of himself. However, I also knew kings who seemed narcissistic, and yet were shy to the point of modesty. So I didn't judge.

"I see." I knew something about the intertwining of secular power and the Islamic religion.

"He, Khomeini, called this celebration of ours 'the Devil's Festival.'" He seemed upset despite his strait-laced manner.

"He sounds quite outspoken," I replied.

"Far worse than Mossadegh ever was. I responded by sending commandoes to storm the religious schools of Qom."

I had read about that incident in the newspapers. There was much loss of life. "I wonder if that was wise, Mohammed?"

He looked at me in surprise. "You have to send a strong message to people of that ilk."

"I wonder if you might have inflamed the situation." I knew only too well how hot-headed religious types could be.

"Perhaps you don't fully understand the precise nature of the difficulties facing us."

"I'm sure I do not. I can only rely on general principles. It would not surprise me if you had a popular revolt on your hands in a year or two."

His handsome face grew dark. "How can you suggest that? We have just memorialised 2,500 years of monarchic rule. Kings rule well because they have to."

I peered further ahead, seeing religious fundamentalism in the ascendant, seeing also the rise of the Mujahideen, spurred on by the coming revolt in Iran, the invasion of Afghanistan by the Soviets and the predictable Cold War response of the Americans. I could glimpse, as through a glass darkly, the election of a dictatorial president of the US at some time in the future. I conveyed some of this to the Shah.

"None of that will happen. And if it did, it could not be laid at my door." He seemed rather petulant.

"I'm trying to help, Mohammed."

"You're not helping." He stood abruptly, tugging down the hem of his tunic. "I don't know why I came to you."

I knew then that he had come to me for sympathy rather than advice. But he had no awareness of that. Suddenly I knew he, and the world, were heading for disaster. I tried to tell him so but he turned abruptly and patted out imaginary creases in his attire. He walked quickly out of my yurt and out of my life.

The new runway at Shiraz airport was badly congested with private jets. I sat in mine and sipped a champagne cocktail, trying to get the taste of desert sand out of my mouth, and possibly the taste of failure. I felt a profound sense of foreboding; the Peacock throne would not last much longer. Even the words of wisdom inscribed on the cylinder of Cyrus the Great would be rescinded, and the world would never be the same. But what can we do when kings do not listen?

Three Letters to Meryl

First Letter to Meryl

DEAR MS. STREEP,

I first saw you in 'Sophie's Choice' and was profoundly moved by your performance. (Nowadays, one might say, 'blown away', though, in my view, that phrase is better applied to spectacle and pyrotechnics.) I sat in the cinema in disbelief that anyone could act like that or produce such a powerful effect on an audience. It was mesmeric, the only performance I had ever seen that went into the realm of the transcendental. In a way it was frightening not just because of the tragic content of the story, but because you had such shamanistic power at your fingertips.

'Sophie's Choice' was the only film I ever went to see twice. Indeed, I went a third time, to see if your power waned. It didn't; it was even stronger. Knowing the story – the 'reveal' – only deepened the pathos because I knew what was going to happen.

I was born long after the war and your performance brought it home to me better than anything else I'd read or seen, including Jewish Museums in several different countries.

Years later, a friend said out of the blue that 'Sophie's Choice' was his favourite movie of all time and your performance would never be equalled. We had an amazing discussion even though we were in perfect agreement! It was said that Picasso was cursed by facility; you were blessed by it.

The reveal in that movie was staggering, never to be forgotten. The sympathy we felt for Sophie was without limit. Tears could not be held back. The fact that Nathan was also a broken angel made it worse because that inability to cope with reality had become so much a part of Sophie too. The scene which showed both of them in bed was like a Renaissance painting. And Stingo's recitation of Elizabeth Bishop's poem, 'Ample Make this Bed', was heart-rending, though there was a note of hope, in that 'Judgment Day' would be 'Excellent and Fair'.

You were, of course, surrounded by excellent actors; the direction was perfect and the music and writing so sombre and beautiful. The Nazi at Auschwitz who forced Sophie to make that awful choice should have looked like a monster but he didn't; he had soft brown expressive eyes that somehow made him evil incarnate. So, one could say that it was the ensemble that worked. Nevertheless your role dominated everything else. You were light and frothy, like Zelda Fitzgerald (lovely smiling face and floating dresses), and then sunk in a pit of despair. Sex and rows with Nathan kept you from the lowest depths but even in your lighter moments you were able to intimate that escapism would not work forever. A sentient human can only take so much.

When I worked on my first novel, 'Come Home, Robbie', I wrote the part of Sal for you. She too had to cope with tragic loss; in this case it was worse than death. You were the only person alive who could have done that part justice. I sent the book to you via your agent. I waited with great expectation, and then I waited some more. There was no reply. By then, of course, you had become the doyenne of Hollywood, but still, as my mother used to say, 'Noblesse oblige'. Not, regrettably in your case. I'm not accusing you of rudeness; stars don't have to be diplomats.

And now, today, I don't really care (in fact am relieved) for one reason and one reason only. How on earth could you waste your God-given talent in a film like 'Mamma Mia'? It was like throwing a precious gift back in the face of God. 'The Devil Wears Prada' was bad enough, but 'Mamma Mia'...? My God, woman, have you lost it completely?

Did you need the money? I know actors are often insecure about finding work but no one could be that desperate. Did you miss the roar of the crowd, the Hollywood ambience? Meryl, why didn't you come to me? I could have saved you from yourself.

I find it hard to forgive what you did because it

tarnishes the incandescent brilliance you brought to 'Sophie's Choice'. You might counter by saying that your work in that movie stands on its own and that nothing you did later could taint it. You might say that an architect who built a magnificent building cannot affect it by subsequent bad design. That is not a good analogy because the first building is not a part of the architect; he did not put himself body and soul into the structure; he did not act the building. Whereas you acted Sophie; you became Sophie – and you later abandoned her for superficial roles that most assuredly do diminish her. What a fall was there.

Did the Blessed Virgin know Joseph even after the first-born or did she remain pristine? You know the answer to that.

Meryl, although it grieves me to say it, I do not want you to play the part of Sal in my 'Come Home, Robbie'. For years I waited for your reply to my offer. And I spent many months grieving over your non-response. But now the truth is I really don't want to hear from you. Having demeaned yourself, I don't believe you could bring the sublime credibility to Sal. Regrettably, I must now formally withdraw the offer of the part. As soon as I finish this letter I will burn the draft contract I had drawn up. Because the part of Sal was written for you, I cannot in conscience offer it to anyone else; I do not compromise my ideals. It's over between us.

We've all lost something. Why didn't you come to me before making those wrong decisions in your life? You had been the best of the best and you could have maintained that position. If only you had come to me…

Sorrowfully,

A movie-goer and erstwhile fan.

Second Letter to Meryl

DEAR MS. STREEP,

Re. my last letter, you will recall that, some years ago, I had offered you the part of Sal in the movie version of my novel, 'Come Home, Robbie'. You will also recall that I later had to revoke that offer because you had tainted your earlier brilliant record by deciding so unwisely to act – if that's the word – in 'Mamma Mia'. There was also the matter of your impolite non-response, about which we will say no more.

Many readers urged me to reconsider my decision; some felt I had been unduly harsh and should not have fired you. Others believed that you could still do justice to the part – and salvage your flagging career. I have pondered deeply and am now prepared to swallow my amour-propre and accept their pleas. There is of course nothing in this for me. My book is already 'out there' as they say, and it has a cult following in Luxembourg.

In any event, I am now prepared to rescind my earlier revocation, and offer you the part of Sal once more – but only on the following conditions:

First, because of the passage of time, you will no longer play Sal, Robbie's mother, but Sal, Robbie's grandmother. You will of course still be married to Bob who now becomes Robbie's grandfather. I will have to tweak much of the dialogue and I will have to dispose of Robbie's parents – perhaps a car wreck. You should be aware of how much additional work is involved for me.

Second, you must persuade Robert de Niro to play your husband. He made some excellent movies but, like you, he blotted his escutcheon – with such films as 'Meet the Fockers'. (Come on, Bob, what possessed you? – a bourgeois camper van, a cat, a false breast, a foreskin in the goulash.) Nevertheless, in a spirit of conciliation I offer him the part. It will be a stretch for him because the character changes in line with the story. He goes from being a diamond in the rough to being a caring man. I think he can do it but he will need meticulous and mindful direction.

Third, we put together the most talented production team that money can buy, apart from the screenplay, directing and editing which, as auteur, I shall handle. You will understand the importance of direction, especially in a movie like this which touches the soul. My directorial style is not excessively rigid; I am happy to listen to feedback from actors. You (and Bob) are experienced actors but you have picked up habits and mannerisms along the way and are likely to resist change. At a certain age one tends to settle for the familiar, the easy chair in the comfort zone. I need you to think about that because Sal is extremely nuanced, deeply spiritual and yet interested in revenge. She is confident and shy, caring and full of invective – a complex human being, and not a stock Hollywood character. To get you to raise your game I may have to be tough on you. There is likely to be considerable tension between us but it will, I hope, be productive tension.

Fourth, I want you to do this project out of love; can real art exist without that? Consequently, you will have to waive all fees. This goes for the rest of the production team too. The profession has been good to you and it is time, as they say, to give something back. (I'm waiving my fees, and I trust this will set a headline for you and for others.)

I should say something about acting. The most important point, as Stanislavsky said, is to get to the truth of the characters. Whether you use Method or Meisner techniques makes no difference to me as long as the characters are fully realised. You, Meryl, sometimes eschew technique and follow your instincts. In the ordinary work you have done before, that approach worked for you. But in the present case it will work only if your instincts are aligned with mine. You claim that empathy alone will bring the character home. To avoid unnecessary conflict, I have to tell you now that this approach will not do for my characters. I have created Sal and know her better than Flaubert knew Madame Bovary. It would be sheer coincidence if your life experiences could capture her being.

Therefore, you will have to listen very carefully to my notes.

You should realize that I am taking a huge reputational risk. You (and Bob) may suffer from a sort of *taedium vitae* which you might 'justify' on the basis of postmodernism, the lack of guiding narratives and so on. In other words you might not recognize great art any more or, worse still, regard it as meaningless. One week on the set of 'Come Home, Robbie' will rid you of all such unsettling feelings. That is my prediction, but it is not an absolute guarantee. Hence the risk on my part; I am counting on you to give of your best. Will you? Will you do that for me?

This is a chance for both of you to make amends for the mediocre work you have done. You need to demonstrate that you have not wasted your talents on this earth. You owe it to the public and to yourselves to show that you can recreate or even surpass the brilliance you displayed in 'Sophie's Choice' and 'Raging Bull'. This opportunity will not come again. To preserve your sanity do not let 'Come Home, Robbie' be known as the extraordinary film that Meryl and Bob turned down. What a lethal blow that would be to your work and legacy. Do not let that happen.

I look forward to drawing out your latent talents,

Your Director.

Third and Last Letter to Meryl

DEAR MS. STREEP,

As you know, we had our differences in the past. I had to withdraw my offer to you of the part of Sal in 'Come Home, Robbie'. You gave me no choice because your appearance in 'Mamma Mia' would have damaged your credibility in that role.

That decision did not go down well with fans (mine or yours). There were many appeals to my better nature and I, again, offered you the part – on certain conditions, e.g. we would all waive our fees, and you would persuade Bob de Niro to play your husband. This was an opportunity for both of you to redeem your lapses of judgement so grossly displayed in 'Mamma Mia' and 'Meet the Fockers'.

In essence, I was offering you a way of preserving the legacy of your earlier work in 'Sophie's Choice' and 'Raging Bull', respectively. To my consternation, you didn't even give me the courtesy of a reply even though I was putting my reputation and career on the line for you.

To make matters infinitely worse, it has recently come to my attention that you have just done a sequel to 'Mamma Mia'. Not only had you the temerity to do this, but you didn't give me any warning. Fool me twice … no, I'm afraid not. Moreover, this production is reputedly more glitzy and kitsch than the original which grossed over

$600 million at the box office. (What do they say about fools being easily parted from their money?) I understand that an aging pop singer, called Cherie or Cher plays your mother. Dear God, woman, have you lost it completely? Did you not listen to a single word I said to you in my earlier letters? Have I been casting my margaritas before porcos?

I had offered you nothing less than a new lease on your artistic life, but you have deliberately and with full awareness chosen to participate in this discordant, porn-lite, lowbrow, shag-fest that is anathema to most right-thinking people, including the LGBTI community. I can only assume that the talent you once showed has deserted you. I don't deny that it must be painful to hear every day the steady drip of your substance leaking away, and I can understand how such a loss might lead to desperation. In a way, a terrible *tristesse* overhangs this entire affair, and there are times when I weep for you and for all those who made a similar Faustian pact with Hollywood.

But sympathy can only go so far, and you must understand that actions have consequences. Unfortunately, you are now typecast as a daft woman, cackling away to herself on a Greek island with her even dafter, pop-singing mother who clearly doesn't understand the law of entropy. You have left me with no alternative. I mean how could you possibly play the complex and layered part of Sal and expect an audience to suspend disbelief? You couldn't – nor do you deserve to. I must now permanently withdraw the offer to play any part in the movie version of my novel, 'Come Home, Robbie'. This is not negotiable, and I will not allow myself to be pressurised by fans on this occasion. Not even the job of dolly grip is open to you. Please note that you have also deprived Bob de Niro of an opportunity to restore his legacy. It's all such a hopeless mess … Are you trying to push me over the edge? I see a darkness in the glass…

You went for the money, as if you needed it, so don't come running to me if and when other directors give you a wide berth. I will not listen to the standard complaint that there are no good parts for aging actresses. You had been offered a once-in-a-lifetime role and you turned it down flat for a movie whose subtitle, 'Here We Go Again', is clearly a triumphalist taunt, designed to throw my generous offer back in my face. So be it. There will be no more opportunities from this source. None. You have played fast and loose for too long. Oh Lord, why did you do it…? What did I do to deserve it…? I coulda been a contender … I can forgive but not forget … or is it the other way around…?

I had expected so much of you … Too much. Perhaps it was my fault all along for believing in you. I have learned the hard way that talent and virtue do not always go hand in hand. But I will not judge you; no, that is Heaven's part. Don't worry about me … I'll go on…

I can't go on. I see dark clouds gathering on the horizon … despite the Indian summer … Light fades over the trail of tears … Oh, the horror…

Farewell,

Someone … who … once … cared – – – –

Angel of Krypton

BETWEEN LACK OF APPETITE and broken sleep, Hugh had to admit to himself that he was smitten as never before. What else could it be? He couldn't even read properly and spent most of the time back-skipping over the same paragraph. He didn't have to search for a diagnosis. It was Carla, or at least his intense feelings for her which he couldn't explain if his life depended on it.

His room-mate, Andy, lay on top of his bed picking at an old guitar. "I know what you're going through," he said, and added unhelpfully, "Most of us go through it when we're fourteen or fifteen."

"I'm a late developer. So what?" Hugh had decided he wouldn't go to the library; he wouldn't be able to study. He might go for a walk later but that would require effort which he found hard to muster. He was wallowing, and knew it.

Andy tuned the A string and then played a chord to see how it blended in. "You know, women," he began portentously, "really aren't all that different. You think Carla is one in a zillion … No, correction … you think she's unique. But she's not. She's very attractive – no argument there – and there's something about her, that *je ne sais quoi,* but she's what … one in a hundred. Don't lose your head over her."

Andy meant well, so Hugh didn't take offence

but the fact was that he had already lost his head over her, head, heart, energy and will; that was precisely what had happened. He was crazy about her, but she was like Kryptonite to him, draining all of his energies and leaving him in a crumpled heap. He had the image of Carla walking up Baggot Street, satchel on hip, long hair falling over her face so that her brown eyes were half-concealed, yet sad and mysterious. Then there was the red mini-dress, long, tapering legs, and small feet that hardly touched the ground. He once saw her walking towards him in the distance; the crowds seemed to part to create a special path for her; only she existed. She often looked soulful, frail yet brave, as if she had to cope with some conspiracy directed at her. He thought of the *Tuatha de Danaan,* a spiritual people who disappeared into the woods when harassed by a more brutish, earthy race. Carla had that sprite-like quality. She never seemed happy as such. Something weighed on her as if she had been wronged in some indescribable way. On their recent date in a café, she refused anything more than a milky coffee and she didn't even finish that; nor did she get any froth on her lip. "I don't have much of an appetite," she'd explained. She said it perfectly, the words issuing from the finely sculpted lips of an angel or even the Madonna.

"It's amazing," Andy said from the bed at the other side of the room. "Once you do the deed they fall off the pedestal fairly quickly. Women, I mean." He kicked his shoes off just in case the panoptic landlady checked on them as she often did.

Hugh was aware that Andy had said something but had no idea what it was. He returned to the miasma of delirious reflection, how they kissed under the elm trees that lined the canal, and watched swans move through the reeds. It seemed wrong to inflict him-self on her like that, her porcelain, Meissen face. It hurt him that she gave no sign of welcoming those kisses. He had to take the initiative all the time and he was afraid of crossing the line, wherever it was. So her fragility was matched by his caution. Their touching was as light and tentative as her feet upon the ground.

The next morning after his lecture on mechanics he met his cousin, Amelia, in the Great Hall. He had confided in her because she was womanly wise.

"I saw Carla in the women's room earlier," she told him.

"Oh Yes?"

"She monopolised the main mirror putting on lipstick, probably for your benefit." She grinned at him, enjoying these little teases. She didn't fully realise how serious it all was for him.

"I doubt that … I don't think she uses make-up at all … doesn't need it."

"Don't be daft. We all do … she more than most. "And, you know something else?" She leant closer to him. "She doesn't seem to have any friends." Amelia intended this as a negative – a sort of indicator – that he should take into the reckoning.

"I know that," Hugh took it as a compliment. It was natural; why would perfection mix with the ordinary? It could only mean contamination or dilution at the very least. He lingered to see Carla going up the curved staircase to one of her lectures in Sociology. He smiled and waved at her. She responded with a minimal movement of her hand. The truncated wave sustained him in the library for a while but then his concentration went. He tried hard to get it back because he was already falling behind in his coursework, but it was no good.

The sorrows of his life were to be compounded the next afternoon when he was walking back to the digs with Andy, who was unusually quiet. Hugh asked if he was all right, and Andy replied that he had heard something earlier that day that he felt he should get off his chest.

"Well, go ahead," Hugh said.

"You won't like it. I'm not sure … I should tell you … It's about Carla…"

"Then you must tell me." Hugh's pulse rate shot up.

Haltingly, Andy told him that he'd met a medical student from Carla's home town of Belmore, who told him that Carla had been involved in a scandal in the town.

"Ah," Hugh began. "It's just tittle-tattle." The Great Hall was a hothouse full of loafers warming their backsides against the radiators, who had nothing better to do than make up yarns about their fellow students, especially attractive women.

"You're not going to like it," Andy warned his friend. "Apparently she was living with an older man and was cited in a divorce case."

Hugh gave a loud bark of laughter. "That's absolute bullshit, Andy. You should have more cop on."

Andy stopped as they turned into Dartmouth Square, reached into his inside pocket and produced a sheet of Xerox paper. "I went to the National Library and went through back issues of The Belmore Echo ... and I found this."

The colour drained from Hugh's face as he read the newspaper cutting. He read it again and then again. The married man's name was Donal McGlinchey. He crumpled up the paper and didn't say anything.

"Sorry," Andy said. "It's better that you know."

As they walked on in silence, Hugh could not believe how severe the pain was. He longed for a physical wound that might distract him. You could staunch a wound, bandage it, use a crutch if needs be. But with this sort of trauma to the heart nothing could be done, nothing at all. He knew now how literal heartsickness could be. And he was indifferent to everything around him. Summer could have been winter for all he knew or cared. What was that other thing in the newspaper cutting, The Croppy Inn? It sounded like the name of a pub. Had Carla mentioned that her mother ran a pub in Belmore? Maybe that was where she'd met the adulterous Donal McGlinchey.

Andy wanted to put his arm around his friend's caved-in shoulders. Love was such a double-edged sword, he thought. It could be so uplifting – and so damn depressing. Anyway, it – romance – was all a load of bollocks whatever way you looked at it. The perpetuation of genes didn't need all those encumbering frills and folderols.

Over the next few days Andy tried to get him to play a game of handball or do circuit training in the gym, but Hugh wasn't interested. He couldn't muster the energy or the motivation. Everything was meaningless. He felt some anger towards Carla because of her duplicity, but strangely, it made no difference to how he felt about her. She could have been an axe-murderer for all he cared. Indeed, if anything, the recent news made her more attractive because even more enigmatic and less attainable. But the seed of anger caused him to conceive a plan of sorts for their date on Friday.

They met for a drink. That in itself was a mistake because every male head in the bar turned towards her and then, briefly, towards him to see what kind of male would be able to date a woman like her. They probably assumed he had a Ferrari parked outside the door. After a quick drink – she didn't finish hers – they went for a walk along the canal. When they stopped under their favourite elm-tree to kiss, he was more forceful than usual. When he felt her pull away from him, he strengthened his grip on her and tried to force his knee between her legs.

"No," she said. "Please don't."

"Yes … Why not?"

"I don't want to." She detached completely and stared into his eyes. "What's gotten into you, Hugh?"

"I'm confused," he said as matter-of-factly as he could manage. "If you can do it with a forty-year old married man…" He could hardly believe those words came from him, and he couldn't finish the sentence. She said nothing and he couldn't gauge her reaction though the silence said a lot.

"Who told you?" she asked at length, looking down at the ground.

"The Belmore Echo, in the Court Notice section. Your name was up in lights and so was his … Donal McGlinchey, I believe…"

"I see." She continued to stare at the ground as if she were so honest she could find no way of eschewing guilt. Her demeanour filled him with sadness, and he hated himself for putting her in this position.

"Is that all you can say?" His heart was pounding. It was as if he were fighting for his life. "Why with him … and not with me?" It was a brutish question but one he had to ask.

"We go back a long way." She stroked back a strand of hair that had fallen over her sad eyes.

"Do you love him?" His voice shook because he knew he could be signing his own death warrant.

She didn't hesitate very long. "Yes, I suppose so. There's a lot of history."

Badly gored, he tried to rally, "Jesus Christ, why are you fooling around with me then? Am I just a distraction until you get your degree … and then you go back to him?"

"Don't put it that way, Hugh. I'm … I'm very fond of you."

"Fond? Fond? Oh, Christ!" He was going to add, that he was head-over-heels in love with her but he had to salvage a tiny bit of pride. Maybe it was some kind of survival instinct. He knew the break-up had begun. He was still fascinated by her even though he didn't have a clue who she was and he never had. The mystery was how he could love her so much without understanding anything about her. He tried to be adult about it. He kissed her lightly on the cheek, "Goodbye, Carla." Then with an effort of will, he added a massive understatement, "I'll miss you."

"Goodbye, Hugh. I'll miss you too."

He thought she might have stammered a bit as if taken a little by surprise, but he couldn't be sure. She went one way and he the other. He turned and watched her walk away with that slow, perfect gait and the ethereal feet that barely touched the ground. The moon cast her shadow onto the silver water of the canal. She didn't turn because that would have meant a slight leaching of her mystique. He wept silently and was glad the trees shielded him from moonlight.

Andy did his best for him. Since distraction was the only therapy he knew, he brought him to the handball alley, the tennis courts at Belfield, student hostelries. After a while they graduated to student hops. At first Hugh went through the motions but his heart wasn't in the activities. However the most extreme side effects of the infatuation gradually faded away, such as the inability to read and concentrate.

Some months later it was learned – probably via the grapevine which originated in the women's room – that Carla had quit college and gone home to Belmore, presumably into the arms of Hugh's bête noire, Donal McGlinchey. By this time the edge of Hugh's pain had been blunted. His cousin, Amelia, used her second-year Psychology to reassure him that getting through a rite of passage could only make him stronger. Hugh, who by now was recovering his sense of irony, said that he was grateful for that nugget of wisdom and would take it under advisement.

———————————

Hugh graduated, landed a good job in IT, said goodbye to his friend Andy, who decided to go to Australia – with his guitar on his back even though he had only mastered five chords – married for love, not calf love, and had a daughter and a son. Shortly after his forty-second birthday he was invited to present a paper to a conference in Cork.

On the drive down he listened to the radio and went over the paper in his head, trying to anticipate questions he might be asked after he delivered it. Suddenly, he saw a sign for Belmore. Something lurched inside his chest cavity. Without thinking, he took the off-ramp. He slowed the car as per the town's speed limits and kept an eye peeled for the pub Carla's mother ran. What was it called? The

Croppy Boy? No, The Croppy Inn, that was it. It surely didn't exist anymore, especially after the drink-driving laws had been tightened some years back? He drove on and suddenly there it was, right on the main street. Should he? No. No, ridiculous thought. God in heaven, imagine raking all that up again? He drove on.

And then, as if by magic, he found himself in the pub's car-park. He looked at his watch, hoping it would deny him the time. But it did not. He had always been on the right side of punctual. Wait now, what if McGlinchey now owned the pub, and was in there? Did he really want to meet the bastard? Well, if there was a sixty-ish old geezer behind the bar he could suss him out while keeping his own identity a secret. What if Carla was there? Oh God, was he up for this at all? Would his heart stand it? He looked at his watch again, hoping time had flown so as to restrict his options. It hadn't.

The interior of the inn was gloomier than he'd expected, given the strength of sunshine outside, and it took a while for his eyes to adjust. The only person behind the bar was a girl in her early twenties playing with a smart phone. She slid off a stool and moved towards him with a welcoming smile. He ordered a coffee and then heard himself asking if Carla was around.

"Carla McGlinchey?"

"Y-e-es." So she'd married the shit. He reminded himself to act his age, remember his perfect family and leave the past where it belonged. In a way, though, he was glad she didn't have a different surname because that would have indicated that he'd been beaten by more than one rival. And it meant she wasn't promiscuous; she'd stuck to that forty-year old bugger.

"Well, she lives just across the street." The girl offered to phone her.

"Oh, there's no need." Hugh's blood ran cold. It was all happening too fast.

"It's no problem." The barmaid seemed interested in the situation. She picked up her phone and gave him a questioning look. He didn't say anything but allowed it to happen. "Who shall I say?"

"What? Hugh … Hugh Montgomery." In for a penny, he thought. After his name was transmitted there seemed to be a long silence. Would Carla even remember him? Then the phone was put down. "She's coming over."

Hugh sat at a table in a corner as far away as possible from a group of locals who seemed, by their glances, to have some interest in him. What had he started, he wondered? The surge of adrenaline was increased when he thought of Carla walking up Baggot Street with her hip sway and red mini-skirt, cutting through crowds with her doleful authority. Would she recognise him? Oh God, what had he done? He had an instinct to bolt, run to the car and speed away. But it was too late. The door opened.

It had to be Carla. But it wasn't. It couldn't be. This was a large woman with glasses, wearing brogues and a wax jacket pulled over her shoulders.

"Hugh!" she called out. "Hugh Montgomery, as I live and breathe. God Almighty! How the hell are you?" She embraced him, pumped his hand and sat down heavily. Carla was never this loud. This was a horsey woman, probably a farmer. Her hands were strong and weathered; they probably milked cows and delivered calves. This woman had grown around Carla, absorbing her in some strange biological mutation. Where was the frail beauty, the astral personality? This new woman was handsome in a rough-hewn way that could never have been predicted.

"Hello, Carla," he forced out. "It's … good to meet…"

"Shit, we should've got married!" She laughed and slapped him on the shoulder. "That other fella became a right pain in the butt."

"You're…?" Conscious of the interest of the barmaid and the people at the other table, Hugh minimised the conversation. But Carla was unconcerned.

"Divorced. Oh yes, years ago. He wasn't much good. Anyway, I have three kids and half a farm, and," she waved around, "this palace of debauchery." Her laugh sounded like a snort or even a honk. She held up a hand and the barmaid brought her over a large gin and tonic. Despite her strenuous offers, Hugh refused to have anything because he was driving. Carla took a long sip. "Drinking the profits," she explained. "Now tell me all about your life." She gave a thumbs-up sign to the men at the far table.

Hugh told her about his wife and family and job, all very conventional stuff, he realised in the narration. In the middle of his recitative two farmers came into the pub, tipped their caps at Carla and referred to her as 'Ma'am'. They ordered two pints of Guinness.

"Would I have known your wife," Carla asked.

"No, she was a few years behind us." He thought it a strange question for Carla to ask. She hardly knew anyone back then. But where had the lonesome mystique gone? He had to get to the bottom of this. Maybe the direct approach would work with this new Carla. It was worth a shot.

"Carla, may I ask you something?"

"Of course, Hugh, as long as it's not for money."

"Well, what I mean is … back then … you were sort of … introverted … And now … Well, it's a bit confusing…"

"The difference between me then and me now? I get it. It's simple really. Back then I didn't know my ass from my elbow, so I kept my powder dry. It takes a long time for personality to gel. It did for me anyway."

He was only partly satisfied by that explanation and probed for more clarification. She told him that before she went to Dublin she was as wild as a March hare and, because of that, got involved with McGlinchey. But once in Dublin, she decided to change her ways. "We all have to experiment, don't we? Try on different outfits to see which fits best. Besides I had a feeling that you were looking for a *spéirbhean,* an *aisling…*"

"So all that ethereal stuff was an act?" Christ, how well she had read him.

"More an experiment. Trial and error." She smiled at him as she sipped her drink.

So she wasn't 'the full person' when he knew her. This phrase was what the Vatican used when granting an annulment. If one of the parties hadn't, for whatever reason, revealed their true selves, then there had never been a real union. The church believed that love and knowledge were much the same. But he had loved her to distraction without knowing her at all. It was weird.

"But why did you bother when you knew you would go back to McGlinchey?" There, he'd got it out.

"Oh I think I knew deep down that the *aisling* thing wasn't really me. So, I knew you loved me for what I wasn't, some image of your own that you projected onto me. That could not have lasted. It became a strain too. You had very high standards, you know."

"I did?"

"Oh yes. I knew that if I bolted my food or belched in front of you, the spell would be broken." She laughed loudly but it was an honest laugh without any judgment in it. "I'm sorry if you were confused."

"Oh, it's OK." They were both nineteen, still wet behind the ears. He appreciated her honesty now. And she probably didn't fully appreciate the pain she'd put him through. How could she? He looked at his watch; it was time to leave. She walked him to the car park where they hugged each other firmly and promised to keep in touch. It was as if they were old friends now.

He drove away, thinking of those tender years of unformed characters so vulnerable to pain. He thought of Amelia and Andy and others who shared in the fraught project of growing up. They'd all made it. Some paid a bigger price than others, especially those who tried on the most experimental costumes, and who depended too much on appearance and constructs of imagination. But, as far as he knew, they'd all arrived at their destinations in reasonable shape. He rolled down the window and breathed in the pure country air. In a perverse way he missed the magic of youth, however painful it had been. But he had no complaint about the relative serenity of middle age which was something like a safe harbour that had been waiting to welcome them all along. But never, in his wildest dreams, would he have guessed back then that the sprite-like Carla would end up as a divorced farmer and a pub-owner, fond of gin. He wished her all the luck in the world.

Letter from the Curia

TO: THE HOLY FATHER
From: The Congregation for the Institutes of Consecrated Life and Societies of Apostolic Life, The Curia, Vatican City
Date: 17 March, 2019

Most Holy Father,

I write to you about the matter we discussed recently during a stroll in the gardens of the Apostolic Palace, concerning the possible annulment of a gay marriage, and the complex issues arising therefrom.

As you know, Mr. Thomas O'Meara of the Parish of Ferns, Ireland, 'married' his 'partner', Mr. Sean Graham just short of a year ago. Naturally, the Church did not recognize the 'marriage' or sanctify it in any way. Last Spring Mr. O' Meara approached his local Bishop by registered mail, formally requesting an annulment of his 'marriage' to Mr. Graham. The Bishop believed rightly that the matter went beyond his authority and he referred it to my Congregation via the Papal Nuncio in Dublin. (The protocols were all followed in a proper manner.)

Subsequent discreet inquiries on my part have clearly shown that this request is genuine and not a hoax. Indeed the Bishop has confirmed that both homosexual men have become quite abusive towards one another in their home, in public, and even, on one most embarrassing occasion in the church, during a sermon from the pulpit.

I inquired from the Bishop why these men do not simply separate or seek a civil divorce through the courts as they could do, given the peculiar legal situation of that country. He informs me that both men are devout Catholics and would not feel entitled to 'marry' again without an annulment from the Church. They are, apparently, *de conscientia bona,* despite their aberration.

As you are aware, this is the first such request we have received and it is difficult to know how to proceed, even though I have had my staff search through all of your relevant *Motu Proprios.*

The main argument in favour of becoming involved, i.e. agreeing to adjudicate on an annulment, is that it might bring forward other similar requests and thereby undermine the abhorrent notion of same-gender 'marriage' with its cavalier approach to the sacraments.

The main argument against is that it would be very difficult, in logic, for the Church to consider an annulment of a 'marriage' which is not recognized as such since there is no sacral element.

The second argument against, bears on the question of non-consummation. This is a difficult topic in a homosexual context since the act itself is inherently barren and a grave moral disorder.

In summary, if we were to accept this challenge

we would essentially be adjudicating on an institution which does not exist and on the performance or non-performance of an act which is in itself a serious moral disorder. How, for example, could we grant an annulment on the grounds that a sinful act had not been committed? And yet if we refuse to be involved we may lose an opportunity to spread the Gospel as it pertains to marriage. In either case The Vatican is likely to be the centre of strident and vociferous attention.

I have sought the advice of the Prefect Emeritus, Consultor, Definitor, Judicial Vicar and, of course, the Devil's Advocate. Their advice differs in several respects and no clear course of action has emerged.

I would be most grateful for your opinion and advises. I will continue to pray over this problem.

Yours in faith and love,

Meo Cardinal Buttafuoco. (Signed)

Post Scriptum: Your Holiness, it has just come to my attention, *per varios modos,* that the above-mentioned Mr. Graham may be transitioning from male to female. The transgender issue may well be the source of the conflict between both men. In the context of annulment proceedings, Mr. O'Meara might well claim that his 'partner', Mr. Graham, did not reveal his 'true self'. As you know, this is one of the grounds for annulment. However, the entire matter is now so complex that I doubt if the Church should get involved at all. I await your observations.

In fide fortis,
M. Card. B.

Backpedaling on Recycling

MARISE AND BRENDAN KNEW they were approaching the Municipal Refuse Facility when they saw plastic bags beginning to appear on the shrubs lining Brennan Road. Their Toyota Avensis was full to the brim with assorted rubbish they had swept, ripped and extracted in one way or another from the apartment they had just rented. An awkwardly shaped tree branch protruded from an open back window and a couple of discoloured mattresses were tied to the roof.

Just at the open-gated entrance a group of Travellers, who camped nearby, peered into the car to see if they had anything of value. It didn't take them long to decide that the trash on view was of little use. One of the Travellers waved them on with a cheeky grin – as if he had any right to stop them in the first place.

"This reminds me of that Attenborough show about those small animals…" Marise began. "I can't remember what they're called. Anyway the females follow the males and study their droppings. If they see that there's a lot of good insect protein they may start courtship proceedings. If it's all just cheap herbivorous shit, they'll walk away."

"So, you married me for my droppings. Lucky for me I had the protein." Brendan slowed the car and turned into the refuse facility and immediately endorsed his friend's description of it as 'Trash Heaven'. The smell was atrocious, organic, probably rotting matter infused with oil and grease. Seagulls swooped overhead and if the wind was in the right direction you could hear the squeak and rustle of well-fed rats.

He stopped at a sort of box office where the official queried what he had brought to dump.

"Mainly garden waste. Clippings. Oh, and the mattresses on top."

She stretched her neck out of her window, peered into his car and pointed to something in a black sack on the back seat.

"What's that?"

Marise craned her neck. "Aluminium," I think. "An old window frame."

The result of that discovery was that they had to pay an extra 20%. The charge for green waste was the lowest, the base from which other costs rose. The tariffs for different materials were displayed on a large glass-covered notice board in the form of a spreadsheet.

"Just as well she didn't see the other shit," Brendan said. He believed in the environment as much as the next man but this obsessive emphasis on recycling, and the burden it placed on ordinary householders, was excessive. And probably even counterproductive. He had often seen women drive there to dump a few cardboard boxes. The drive there and back probably put ten times more carbon into the air than burning the damn boxes. It was ridiculous – all thanks to that idiotic Green politician, known as 'The Rubbish Minister'.

They were lucky to get a parking spot not too far away from the waiting skips, each one labelled with the different types of material that should go into each skip. They were very fond of taxonomy in this facility. Marise and Brendan jointly dumped the mattresses first, in a skip labelled 'Bedding'. Then they decided to do the garden waste. They dragged the plastic bags out of the car as carefully as they could. Some of the cut grass had been rained on and was inclined to leak all over the upholstery. They noticed that a lot of the other recyclers were grandfathers; this was obviously one way granddads had of paying for their keep in the homes of their children. Most of them worked slowly, limping and holding their backs. Marise made a mental note never to put her father through this torture – assuming he came to live with her and assuming the planet hadn't self-destructed by then.

Each time they emptied the green contents into the garden-waste skip they folded up the plastic sacks and put them in a special plastic bin. Every now and again, employees in hi-vis jackets passed them by, checking that the correct material was going into the correct skip. They moved slowly, yard-brush or shovel in hand, tidying up debris that inevitably fell between car and skip. One man, a Pole called Bolek with fair balding hair seemed to keep a particularly keen eye on Brendan, as if he were more likely than most to break or bend the rules.

When they had finished with the green waste,

they split up. Marise brought the aluminium and other light metal to the relevant skip while Brendan looked after the broken electronic and electrical stuff. He was just about to throw in an old toaster when Bolek stopped him.

"No. Not here," Bolek said. He pointed to the toaster. "Electric, not electronic." He pointed to another skip hundreds of yards away. "Electric over there."

"I see." Brendan carried the toaster and threw it into the distant skip. He looked over his shoulder and there was Bolek right behind him.

"Electric toaster in electric skip," Brendan confirmed. "OK?"

"Correct," Bolek said. "Logical."

There was something about him, Brendan thought – a whiff of something that seemed familiar – an ambiance of floor polish, institutional walkways, coloured windows. Something a little authoritarian too, despite the grubby yellow jacket.

"Aristotelian?" Brendan took a chance.

"Yes." Bolek gave a wide grin. "*Per genus et differentiam.*"

"Seminary?"

"Yes. Gdansk. You too?"

"Maynooth. But didn't last."

Bolek drew down the corners of his mouth. "Me neither. Faith … difficult…"

"Yes," Brendan agreed and then, as if to salvage some aspects of spiritual life, contrasted it with the noxious materiality that surrounded them, by waving his hand across the acres of trash.

"Tak … Yes," Bolek said. "Komodyfikacja … Excuse me," he added as Marise came back from the light metals area. He moved aside to get on with his duties.

"Have you made a new friend?" she asked, waving away a seagull and rearranging a strand of hair all in one movement.

"You won't believe it. I'll tell you later." He lowered his voice to give her the short version to keep her going. "A Polish immigrant, ex-seminarian like myself."

"It's a shame," she said "that this is the best job he can get."

They split up again. She went off with a few rolls of carpeting and he went in another direction with a few bags of rubble, gypsum and broken pieces of wall-board. He had most of it perched on the side of the skip signed 'Building Materials' when Bolek appeared at his elbow. He looked carefully into each bag as if he were a customs official at Sydney Airport. If Brendan expected that he would turn a blind eye to a fellow seminarian he was badly mistaken. There was no collegiality here, and certainly no cronyism. They were both 'failed priests' but they may have failed for entirely different reasons. Eventually Bolek nodded. Brendan wasn't sure, but he thought he detected a hint of disappointment in the man's face. He threw the rubbish in and walked back to the car to see what was left. He was relieved to see that all that remained was an assortment of tiles, some broken, some still intact but rejected for one reason or another. Marise returned and helped with the tiles. Without giving the matter too much thought they carried them towards the 'Building Materials' skip. Brendan had just thrown in a few of the broken pieces when Bolek came running over.

"No," he called out. "No ... Building materials only ... No tiles..."

"Tiles are used in buildings," Brendan pointed out.

"No, not buildings ... decoration only..."

"Buildings are decorated inside," Marise said in a voice that teetered on the edge of laughter.

Bolek waved his arms. "No." He pointed to the sign. "This mean ... materials for *structure* of building ... Not decoration..." He pointed to another sector of Trash Heaven. "Over there ... sign for decorative material ... You go there..."

Marise uttered a snort of laughter and was about to set off when Brendan put a restraining hand on her arm. Two could play at that game he thought. He wagged a finger under Bolek's nose. "You're wrong. This sign here says 'Building Materials'. It does not say 'structural'. The term, 'structure', does not appear. These tiles are used in buildings. Therefore, this is the correct skip. Q.E.D."

Bolek interposed his body between Brendan and the edge of the skip. "No, Not Q.E.D. Not correct. Building mean the process of building ... not building itself ... Tiles not used in *building* buildings."

"Of course they are. What about bathroom sinks and toilets? Splashbacks? They're fittings and fixtures."

"No … not hold anything up in building … No."

"The building profession would not agree with you. I'm an accountant and I'm telling you we include tiled goods when we depreciate buildings. What about roof tiles? Do you understand?"

"Tiles no relation to building," Bolek said flatly. He formed a triangle with his hands, fingertips touching at the apex, to illustrate the pitch of a roof.

"Oh yes they do have a relation," Brendan retorted. "Anyway, these tiles are porcelain not ceramic. Do you understand the distinction? You're making a category error."

Bolek waved his hand. "No distinction … No category error … Dresden, Meissner … figurines porcelain as well as ceramic … all decoration, not structural…"

"You're a materialist. That's your problem. What if matter is in the eye of the beholder? What then?"

"Matter real," Bolek threw back. "Molecules … protons…" He smacked the back of one hand into the palm of the other as if smashing atoms.

"Oh come on," Marise said. "What difference does it make?"

"It makes a lot of difference," Brendan said in a low voice for her ears only. "I've met these fellows before in seminaries. Rigid to a fault … They have scruples and try to impose them on everyone else. They're a disaster area."

Bolek had heard the word 'scruples' and it

struck a chord. "No scruples … Logic. You hear, logic. You go in skip … take out tiles!"

"Do I understand you correctly? You want me to go into that filthy 'Buildings Materials' skip and remove a few broken tiles that actually belong there?" A faintly enteric smell drifted up from the floor of the receptacle, making Brendan think that there was far more than building materials in there. It was probably kitchen waste that someone had tipped in when Bolek wasn't looking, or was off duty.

"Yes. You make mistake. You must correct it."

Marise, who was wearing an old pair of jeans, offered to hop in but Brendan wouldn't hear of it.

He turned to Bolek. "Why don't you get into the skip if you feel so strongly about it?"

"Oh, because I am immigrant I have to do it? No! Immigrant not mean slave!" Bolek prodded his chest with a stubby finger. "I refuse-disposal officer."

"Oh Christ … You're really beginning to annoy me now," Brendan said loudly. He went to throw the remaining tiles into the skip but Bolek barred him and raised the yard-brush, holding it as a weapon. While they confronted each other, Marise got hold of the remaining tiles and put them back in the car. She got behind the wheel and began to reverse. Brendan gave Bolek a push, half-hoping he'd fall into the damn skip, and jumped into the passenger seat, breathing hard.

"What a fucking maniac. I should have asked for his supervisor."

"Oh look, let's put it behind us." She drove out the gate and headed for home. After a while she started to grin.

"What?" Brendan asked.

"Oh, I don't know. The sight of two failed priests fighting over definitions in a skip."

"We weren't in the skip."

"Oh, Sorry ... Another distinction. More angels dancing a jig on a pin. The Jesuits have a lot to answer for ... From where I sat, you might as well have been in a skip." She drove on in silence while he observed with distaste the micro debris that was left and the fresh stains on the relatively new upholstery of the car. The desire to save the environment had become a religion and brought out obsessive-compulsive behaviour in some people that had nothing to do with ecology.

"Turkey vultures," he said, "those birds that clean large parts of Africa by scavenging..."

"What on earth are you talking about now?"

"Those animals, you know, where the females of the species study the droppings of the males."

"No. They weren't birds."

"Yes, they were."

"No. They were mammals ... You not correct. I correct. Q.E.D. Enough said. End of." She held up a hand, and gave a bark of laughter.

Just before they reached Brennan Road, Brendan asked her to pull over. She did so, thinking he might be feeling sick – despite his good genes and rich droppings. As soon as she stopped, he threw the remaining tiles into the adjoining field.

"You can't do that," she said, startled. "That's fly-tipping."

"No it's not," he replied. "Not fly-tipping. Just relocating what may or may not be matter."

A Confusion of Roses

EDDIE WAS IN A PICKLE. Margot, the den mother and larger-than-life office manager who had trained them in when they were raw recruits, was retiring. The office as a whole had made a presentation to her – a state of the art plasma TV with all the bells and whistles – but it was decided that each of her protégés, Eddie included, should give her something of a personal nature on this, her last day. She had been especially kind and helpful to him from the moment he joined the firm, and he owed her a lot. Her sense of humour rubbed off on the whole office and had the effect of keeping the tension level at the lower end of the gauge. The fact that her parents had come from Cork also strengthened the bond between them.

But he had not as yet come up with any ideas about appropriate gifts. The others didn't seem to have had any difficulties; he had picked their brains but all of the good ideas were taken. The stationary press was already full to bursting with beribboned silver and gold packages. Eddie was between girlfriends and had no one to advise him. What on earth would Margot, a young-at-heart sixty-something, appreciate? How was he supposed to know? He gave his own mother vouchers on her birthday – she was happy that he remembered – but that wasn't an option for Margot. It had to be personal; judgment and taste were required. The thought wouldn't just count; it would be the linchpin of the whole exercise. And of course he'd left it all to the very last minute, putting himself under the cosh.

He skipped lunch and braved the humidity of Washington DC to search for something. He tried the local drugstores just on the off chance, but they were too cheap and impersonal. It hadn't really occurred to him before how much junk was on offer. He hailed a cab and went to the nearest shopping mall where at least there was adequate air-conditioning. He rushed around various stores and gift shops, looking, browsing at unnatural speed, raking his mind for ideas, asking for assistance.

"She's around sixty," he would say. "It's a retirement gift … small … personal…"

He was hoping that some kind matronly type would take him in hand and teach him the rules of this strange realm. But it was not to be. Many of the shop assistants didn't seem to hear the word 'small' and their suggestions tended to run to hundreds of dollars; they were on commission and seemed to enjoy making him feel cheap. On more than one occasion he had to add "…more of a token really…"

And in a way that was precisely what he was looking for, a token or symbol that would speak for him. He wondered why a 'Thank You' card on its own wouldn't do the trick. No, it had to be an object, something tangible, mute though full of meaning. The word 'personal' was also fraught. It did not imply intimacy, but merely an acknowledgement of the recipient's personality as perceived by the giver. It wasn't easy, however, to convey that to shop assistants. They didn't seem to understand the subtleties.

He considered paperweights, vases, cuddly animals, even fridge magnets and bumper stickers. It was a minefield; some of the stuff might even be considered tacky. A lot of it carried romantic if not erotic implications which would be utterly disastrous. A former girlfriend had apprised him of some of the rules and conventions. No item of clothing that touched the skin, no jewellery, certainly not a ring, but not even a watch because that could be interpreted as a pre-engagement present. It occurred to him that if etiquette was a product of civilisation then civilisation had a lot to answer for.

However well-meaning he might be, he could end up making a dog's breakfast of it. A gift that was worse than no gift at all. The wrong gift could be an insult. Oh God! How about a bottle of vintage wine? Did she drink wine? Brandy? Despite the air-conditioning he began to perspire. Time was running out; he had to be back for a meeting at three – a wealthy client who hadn't filed a proper tax return for years. Big mess, big bucks.

He was racing along one of the main drags when an ad in a window caught his eye. 'Amazing Valu'. Leaving out the 'e' of 'Value' didn't make it much snappier but he was impressed by the merchandise and the price. Roses, twenty dollars a dozen. From what he could tell it was exceptional value – with or without the 'e' – and someone had told him that you couldn't go wrong with flowers. Women didn't seem to mind that they withered and died as long as they were fresh when they got them, and as long as they weren't purchased from the forecourt of a filling station.

The manageress of The Bloomery assured him that there was no age limit when it came to the appreciation of flowers. They were the universal gift. She smiled hugely showing teeth that were almost too perfect, florist's teeth.

"But wait a minute…" Something niggled at him. "Roses, romance … Don't want to give the wrong signal."

"Oh, you don't have to worry about that," she said. "These are short-stemmed. You're confusing them with long-stemmed ones. These are not the romantic variety."

"Are you sure?"

"Oh, yes. Absolutely."

Further down the counter a man was buying a wreath of lilies. White for a funeral. It was all most complicated. Even dandelions meant something. And what about pink carnations? One had to tread warily. He thought of the video game where the little digital man had to cross over a pond using crocodiles as stepping stones. Having sorted out the semiotics of stem lengths he bought two dozen which were wrapped in a huge cellophane cone trimmed with a white lace design. He dictated the card: "To Margot, Have a wonderful retirement. With every good wish, Eddie." Safe enough, he thought, as the card was placed inside the large bunch of scarlet petals.

The scent was overpowering, especially when he left the shop, and he became quite self-conscious about carrying such an obvious bouquet. Two dozen red roses made a huge splash. He tried to appear nonchalant but couldn't quite carry it off. He got some appraising glances from mall-cruisers and he was almost certain that a teenager hanging around Swenson's Ice Cream Parlor called him a fag. The roses lit him up like a beacon. A passing Marine pursed his lips and made a kissy-kissy sound.

Eddie reckoned that the sooner he got back to the office the better. He would just go straight up to Margot, give her the flowers 'as a small token of esteem' and wish her well in her retirement. A hug might be necessary and a cheek-on-cheek, French-style, but he could manage that without putting his foot in it.

On the way back the cabbie peered at him through the rear view mirror and said,

"Someone's gonna get some tonight."

"It's not what…" Eddie decided not to explain himself yet again. Besides, the cabbie obviously couldn't see that the roses were short-stemmed and there seemed little point in explaining the difference to him.

In the lobby of his building he had to rummage for his ID card. One of the security guards was openly grinning, another smirking covertly. What was it with flowers? Was a man not allowed carry them without being regarded as a sex fiend or a wimp?

The elevator stopped at the fifth floor and a well-built African-American woman got in. She seemed totally mesmerised by the display of roses, looking from them to him and back again.

"Man, you gonna be luckier than you think."

"They're for my secretary..."

"She's one lucky gal."

"No ... no ... It's not..." He stopped for fear of babbling.

"If she don't appreciate them honey, you can find me on the fifth floor, Cornel's Realty. Unnhh, ummmmm." She got out on the eight floor, blowing him a kiss.

A slim blonde woman got in. She breathed deeply through narrow nostrils and said, "Two dozen red roses. And what a beautiful scent. This restores my faith in men."

He wondered how she knew there were two dozen; she must have had a trained eye – or was it some natural instinct women were born with?

"And I thought romance was dead." She gave him a sweet smile.

Women didn't normally speak to him in the elevator; in fact, nobody spoke. What was it about flowers that broke the ice? He was vulnerable. Oh, God, that was it. Vulnerable and romantic, maybe even foolish.

"You don't understand. These are short-stemmed, not long-stemmed." He pushed the bouquet slightly in her direction though there was obviously nothing wrong with her sight – or with her sense of smell.

"Oh, that distinction went out years ago," she said. "Roses are roses. They mean what they say. And those beauties speak volumes."

He felt as if he'd been viciously punched in the stomach. "But the florist said…"

"Oh, don't mind florists." She smacked him playfully on the arm. "They're like used-car salesmen. They'll say anything to move stock. But those are sweet-looking roses. Fresh too, some still in the bud. Look at those tiny buds! Your girlfriend will be delighted. My husband is afraid to be seen carrying flowers. He sometimes has them sent but he won't carry them. So congrats to you. Well done." She smiled as she stepped out of the elevator, making him feel like an ardent swain – and a harmless idiot.

Eddie was in trouble. He'd been conned about the stems. He also felt annoyed for another reason. If someone had only told him about the power of flowers before now he'd have been far more successful with women. It was just his luck to find out about this secret weapon at the wrong time, in the wrong place.

He went straight into the bathroom on his floor and locked himself into one of the stalls. He sat on the toilet seat looking at the flowers. God in heaven, they were just flowers, a form of vegetation like … carrots or lettuce. No, they weren't; he was trying to delude himself. They were symbols or maybe even metaphors; they spoke a language he didn't understand, not the words or the grammar. He couldn't help noticing the folded petals exactly like … Don't go there. Stop it right now!

A thorn pricked his thumb and a tiny speck of blood appeared as if by magic. As he licked it away the image of a crown of thorns entered his head and, what used to be called, 'the Passion of Christ' – a term he had never understood.

He knew that if he had a different personality he could make a joke of the whole thing with Margot and avoid any embarrassment. But he didn't have a relaxed soul and that was that. It would be entirely a matter of her interpretation, and, since he didn't know the language, he had absolutely no idea what that interpretation might be. There was no time to go out to the shops again. It was the roses or nothing. With some reluctance, he decided it would have to be nothing – combined with some excuse or other. He would have to junk the damn flowers but he couldn't very well leave them in the toilet. There was a trash chute further down the corridor and that was where he headed – at some speed, keeping close to the wall.

"For me? You shouldn't have!"

Oh God, it was Margot – with glasses perched on her nose. He came to an abrupt stop and stood frozen.

"They're beautiful, Eddie. What a wonderful surprise! I had no idea … you know what I mean…" She began to simper.

"Well … eh … eh…" What could he say? He didn't know if she was being serious or not. His voice was drowned out by those shrieking, voluble petals of operatic crimson.

Margot reached forward and relieved him of his burden. She held the flowers to her face and read the card. "They are beautiful, Eddie. I love them … If I were thirty years younger I might read something into it." She laughed, and after a little while, so did he. She put her free arm around his shoulders and walked him back to the office where they and the roses received a burst of applause.

The Baggage-handlers are on Strike

OVER THE BREAKFAST TABLE Mrs. Cantwell reminded her husband that after she dropped the kids off at school she would be visiting her mother who was in bed with a tummy upset.

"So I won't be home until about five this evening … are you listening?"

"Yes, five. That's fine. Enjoy your day." Jim went back to the newspaper and continued chewing the rather limp toast. There was, however, plenty of rind in the marmalade.

"I'm visiting my mother," his wife repeated with emphasis.

"I know." The nuance escaped him that a day spent in such a way could hardly be described as enjoyable. She wasn't exactly going on a skite. "Give her my regards."

She left shortly afterwards and Jim brought the newspaper with him to the downstairs cloak-room. He continued to read while he sat on the WC. There was plenty of time to get to the office – his first meeting wasn't until nine thirty. After he washed and dried his hands he pressed down on the door handle but realised that, out of long habit, he'd locked the door. Irritably, he turned the key sharply, but it broke in the lock. There was a moment of disbelief followed by a berating of the self. He stood there holding half a key in his hand.

He assumed the solution would come to him fairly quickly, but after a minute or so he began to realise that he was in a fix. Even if he pushed out the broken bit of key and dragged it back under the door it would be no good to him. He wouldn't be able to turn it because the shaft had broken off, and he didn't have a wrench. Consideration of rougher tactics got him nowhere; it was a robust door, not one of those modem plywood ones.

He sat on the toilet and considered his options. He didn't have a mobile phone, partly because of inverted snobbery but also because he felt there might be something to the brain-damage theory. There were no tools in the cloak-room, not even a screwdriver. Even if he found a hairclip or something like that he wouldn't have a clue how to pick a lock. It gradually dawned on him that he would have to wait for his wife to return that evening. What time had she said? Five p.m. And it was eight a.m. now. God, he would be stuck there for nine hours at least. He ground his teeth. How had he been so stupid?

He wouldn't be able to tell anyone to cancel his meetings. And what excuse was he going to give afterwards? He couldn't very well admit that he'd locked himself in the loo; he'd never live it down. Maybe if he relaxed, something would come to him in time. Another question gnawed at him: How could he face his own company for that length of time?

The newspaper gave cold comfort because he'd already been through the main stories and he had no time for the opinion columnists – prima donnas every one of them. They didn't know the meaning of journalism, and had never taken the trouble to break a real story. The crossword was a possibility, the cryptic one, but it might be best to keep that for later, as well as the Sudoku.

He occupied himself for a while by going through the contents of the press under the sink. Labels on bottles of detergent were not of huge interest but were better than nothing. He noted that one detergent claimed to kill all known germs including E-coli. It contained non-ionic surfactants (biodegradable) and was not to be used with other products lest chlorine be released. The house-person was also invited to call the company's hygiene advisors free of charge. So much for that, he thought. Who was it who said hygiene was a Protestant virtue?

The mirror over the sink occupied him for a while. He couldn't be sure but his face seemed to be wearing well for a man of forty-four. There were incipient jowls but no sign of sinewy neck, and the crow's feet weren't too pronounced. On closer inspection he noticed a small nest of blackheads in the flange of his nose, and he set to work on them with his fingernails. The operation was reasonably successful, but it left his nose raw and red. He splashed cold water on it. Some of the water dripped down his chin and went inside his collar. Drying himself off with a hand towel occupied another few minutes.

Then he had a stroke of luck; while rummaging through the medicine cabinet above the sink he found a nail scissors and proceeded to give himself a meticulous and long drawn-out manicure. He got the cuticles back, revealing the lunulae which had remained hidden for the past quarter of a century.

The pedicure took longer. The nails on the big toes had grown very thick and when he did manage to cut them – after considerable effort that left him all but winded – they shot across the room at lightning speed and in every direction. He managed to gather up the errant clippings and flush them down the toilet, although some of them refused to go down, and continued to float around like minuscule canoes. What were nails made of, he wondered. Cartilage or some kind of hard skin? Did they continue to grow after you were dead?

In the process of removing some sprigs of nostril hair, he nicked his nose which yielded quite a lot of blood – eventually staunched by the insertion of a plug of toilet paper. Other hairy places came to mind as candidates for trimming, but he decided to let sleeping dogs lie. Afraid of doing some real damage, he laid the scissors aside and looked at his watch. Eight twenty five. Not even a half hour had gone by. Eight and a half hours to go. Maybe longer because the Red Hot Chilli Peppers were playing in the RDS and that would probably foul up the traffic in the late afternoon, causing his wife to be later than planned.

There was no shower in the cloakroom so he'd

probably gone as far as he could where grooming and personal hygiene were concerned. He sat on the toilet seat and tried to meditate and think some bigger thoughts than trimming nose hair. It was far from easy and nothing came, nothing of a substantive nature. Eventually a few anecdotes seeped into his mind and he felt disappointed because these were recycled and lacking in originality. Maybe he couldn't think any more; maybe he'd lost the facility years ago. One of the anecdotes involved a snippet of dialogue:

A : "We all have too much historical baggage."

B : "We can handle it."

A: "No, we can't. The baggage-handlers are on strike."

The joke played over and over in his mind until it became a piece of nonsense verse.

"No, we can't. The baggage-handlers are on strike." How could he handle his own company?

A half-hour of solitary confinement and he was going mad. He thought of that prisoner-of-war movie where Steve McQueen survived solitary confinement by throwing a baseball against the wall. No, the ground first. Ground, wall, hands – that was the sequence, keeping the same rhythm all the time, the ball moving in a loop that repeated itself over and over. That would drive anyone mad. But then, baseball meant something special to Americans.

He studied the wallpaper; that had been an awkward job. Those little rose-buds were impossible to match up ... Paper ... Papyrus ...

sign of civilisation or decadence? How could any society be regarded as civilised when founded on war, autocracy, conquest and slavery? Hmmm…

And what of the S-bend pipe invented by Thomas Crapper. Before that amazing though under-appreciated invention, life was malodorous even for royal families whose chamber pots were emptied into the moat by Grooms of the Stool. When the hot weather came they bailed out to their summer palaces until the moat was cleaned in their absence by the good fairies. Funny though, because he quite liked the smell of horse manure – possibly due to the extra fibre of the equine diet. The lion house in the zoo was another matter, however. The family had had good times in the zoo, despite the smells…

He was saved from self-indulgent nostalgia by a knock on the front door. Probably the postman. Should he shout for help? No, he'd be the butt of every joke in the neighbourhood for a year. The postman was a dreadful gossip, ferrying tales from one house to another like a busy bee fertilising every living thing in sight. He heard the flap of the letter box fall back and the steps of the postman receding down the driveway. A chance missed. What the hell; he'd done the right thing. Maybe it wasn't the postman at all but the holy Joe who collected the dues for the church, referring to them as 'fire insurance'. Not so amusing after twenty years of repetition. Hell didn't exist anyway, did it? Burning for all eternity. ETERNITY. No, it couldn't be right.

The church had already abolished limbo; hell would be the next to go. Then heaven?

That would be sad. Nothing to look forward to in this vale of tears. No incentive to do good, no jewels in the crown or higher place closer to God.

Even the soul was under attack. Neuroscientists claimed that only matter – in the form of molecules – existed. Could this be true? He would have to read up on the whole subject of Being. He used to worry about those big questions when he was a teenager but later on he seemed to have lost interest in all that reflective stuff. Maybe because there were no answers.

That never bothered the French though. They still sat around in cafés discussing the death of God, the meaningless of language, religion and life. Well, good for them. They had a lot of free time – as he now had.

Back to the minutiae, and wishing his life away. He saw a spider scurry out of the sink hole. He put a finger in front and the insect ran along his finger into the palm of his hand.

Jim grinned at this modest achievement and fantasised about training insects, following in the footsteps of the Birdman of Alcatraz. He tried to get the spider to walk around his hand but it refused and finally spun a thread which it abseiled down. Jim watched in fascination but realised too late that the spider had, unhappily, abseiled right into the toilet bowl. Because it was already half drowned he had no option but to flush it away. The last couple of toenail clippings went with him. Him. How did he know the gender? Could have been a her, a mother who might have left a nest of baby spiders somewhere. It wasn't his fault. Even so it could mean bad luck.

His thoughts were random; he just couldn't organise them. So much for free will. Where had he read that the activity of thinking consumed vast quantities of the body's energy? That might explain why so little thinking was done. Knowledge was a poor substitute. His mind zoomed off again…

What about the prisoners in Guantánamo Bay? It was hard to imagine Americans torturing them by water-boarding and sense deprivation. He still believed all Americans were like Gary Cooper, strong, silent, heroic. The Twin Towers had scarred the American psyche and made them feel vulnerable for the first time. It did not augur well. If you scare a giant you better watch out.

He stood on the toilet bowl and looked through the narrow window at the sky, which was magnificent but uninspiring, at least to him. He noted wet rot in the timber window frames. Another job for him. Damn and blast those cowboy builders who put unseasoned timber into the houses. He'd already gone through a ton of red-lead putty, filling the craters left after gouging out the rotten wood.

He got down with a sigh. Hungry now. Yes, it was close to lunch-time. What a creature of habit he'd become. The well-stocked kitchen was only a few metres away but he couldn't reach it. He contented himself with a drink from the cold tap and sat down again, trying to resign himself to the long wait. He thought a bit about work, the family and then those anecdotes again. The baggage-handlers are on strike. When had he become a magpie, picking up the trinkets of other peoples' ideas and jokes? He knew many of the epigrams of Shaw and Wilde and could use them at appropriate times. It was easier than thinking.

The children came often to mind, their faces seemed anxious and questioning. Had he listened to them keenly enough? Had he been able to meet their needs? He remembered playing Frisbee with them. Young faces and sunlight. Where had the time gone between then and now? Sad ... sad. The Cat's in the Cradle ... He should have done better by them ... They deserved so much more ... Change thought if possible ... The baggage-handlers are on strike...

For a brief moment he felt as if he were someone else looking down at his predicament from a great distance. A little later an unusual torpor overcame him; the sensation was frightening for a while but then he submitted almost gratefully to it...

Almost eleven. Must have dozed off. At least six more hours to go. Buttocks sore now from hard plastic toilet seat. Could murder a cup of tea. Would be having one about now in the office; he could almost hear the tea-lady rattling the cups on her trolley as she came around the corner into his corridor. She often slipped him a Jammy-Dodger or a couple of Fig-Rolls.

What else could he do with a pair of scissors?

Open his veins? The scissors certainly Weren't strong enough to take off the door hinges. He went back to the mirror again and contemplated his sagging face. The sight offered no solutions of any kind. He felt tired and depressed, and lowered himself with a sigh on to the toilet seat...

———————

He awoke to the sound of his name being called out by his wife. It's over, he thought, stretching free of cramp. Over. As he called out he had a faint but persistent sense of having missed an opportunity. He couldn't quite figure it out so he dismissed it. His wife used a screwdriver to push out the broken key then fetched the spare one. When he saw the door opening he felt a surge of gratitude.

He never enjoyed a cup of tea more as he sat in the kitchen with his wife, making light of his ordeal and appreciating her remarks to the effect that it could have happened a bishop. Her mother had recovered well from the tummy bug. Both women had had a pleasant reunion. She had picked up some nice Polish sausage on the way home.

Later that evening – after a substantial meal to compensate for missing lunch – it occurred to him that he had wept in the cloakroom. He wasn't sure but he thought it might have been just before he fell asleep. It was a matter of little significance but he couldn't quite dismiss it, and he went back to the cloakroom to see if something might jog his memory. He saw it immediately, the crumpled toilet paper with which he had wiped his eyes before he gave in to that brief rehearsal for death.

Bernard

BEFORE GETTING INTO BED, Deirdre Lonergan hung the toy spider from the cane headboard, just below the framed photograph of the hotel manager greeting the Duke of Edinburgh. Her husband, Tom, who was beginning to doze off, turned one eye up at the spider — he'd got it for her in a shop in King Street near the Gaiety — and grinned into his pillow. It was one of the best investments he'd ever made. And she'd packed the damn thing and brought it all the way to the Caribbean.

"G'night, Dee." He turned his face to receive the scented peck, redolent of cold cream and Ambre Solaire.

"Night, Tom." She slipped between the sheets and assumed her sleeping position. A large spatulate fan revolved slowly overhead. Since the room had modern air-conditioning, the fan was obviously designed for atmospheric purposes of the other sort. Before Deirdre fell asleep she resolved that before the holiday was over she would put the spider on the pillow, just above her head. Yes, that might be a realisable goal. Tom believed in setting goals, though she doubted if he could really empathise with the ones she set for herself.

Next morning they planned the day over breakfast as the waiter, dressed as a midshipman, poured their coffee. There wasn't much planning to be done. Poolside first (rather than the beach), then maybe into town in the afternoon to do a little shopping – she hoped Tom wouldn't haggle too much with the local traders. In the evening there would be a barbecue in the hotel for all the guests, a limbo night with the island's best steel band, crab races and other sideshows.

"Maybe I can see Cedric Granger sometime today." Tom swept an isolated strand of greying hair across his forehead although he wasn't as concerned about his comb-over as he would have been at home. Granger was also a businessman and could be a useful contact.

"Now, Tom," Deirdre remonstrated. "Holidays, remember? You said I should forget about the kids and you would forget about business. You need the rest." She was being disingenuous, just a little. The fact was that she didn't find it easy to warm to the Grangers. A few nights ago they'd been chatting over drinks in the residents' lounge. Or rather listening to Cedric Granger's monologue: "I was in town today, the market area. Looks good in brochures. But when you're there … Phew, the smell … and those Carib chaps hacking away at coconuts with their machetes … The sugar mill is in ruins needless to say. It's stone-age stuff. You'd wonder if we did them any favours by pulling out. Course we still give them a protected market for their bananas. But the island hasn't developed at all since independence. Makes one wonder … it really does…"

"Mmmm." For the sake of politeness Deirdre

pretended she was prepared to mull it over, take it under advisement. But she disagreed with everything he had to say. In her book, he was a guest of the country and should, if anything, be embarrassed by Britain's colonial past.

"Oh, they get by," one of the Americans said lightly.

At least, Deirdre thought, the Americans could live and let live. All they wanted was good service and value for a buck. But the British just couldn't let go; it was sad in a way. Cameron wasn't the worst but maybe he couldn't undo the legacy of Margaret Thatcher who had rekindled the old imperial fervour with her fierce simplicities...? Both of them had done the groundwork for Brexit, the last throw of the dice.

Tom laid his napkin down on the breakfast table and held up his hands, conceding with a smile, "All right. Business goes on the back-burner."

Later they appeared at the poolside in their recently purchased swimwear. Lacking the courage for French-cut or Bermuda shorts, Tom had compromised on Dunne's Stores' boxers − olive green and patternless − and felt reasonably confident though he was surprised at how bow-legged he'd become. Deirdre wore a one-piece swimsuit − mercifully these were back in fashion, thanks to Jerry Hall. Her figure was still quite good and she'd spent some time on a sunbed before leaving Dublin. Anyway she wasn't interested in competing; it was more a matter of not standing out or of attracting attention for the wrong reasons. She carried a voluminous beach bag of towels, lineaments and lotions and presumably – Tom didn't have to ask – the ubiquitous spider. She had the latest Maeve Binchy book and he had a Dan Brown. Before flopping on the li-lo she deftly hooked her fingers under the elastic of the swimsuit and snapped the fabric into a less revealing position.

"Fairly crowded already," Tom observed. His gut seemed a lot flatter when he lay on his back, but he was far from ripped.

"It's going to get very hot today." Deirdre was smearing on sun-block. Melanoma was all the rage that summer. She passed the plastic bottle to him. They wanted a tan – that was the proof of a good holiday nowadays – but had to be careful how they acquired it. Tanning without tears.

They settled back into their own worlds, sharing the sun, the mattresses angled so that they could see from hooded eyes what was going on. Several people were in the kidney-shaped pool while a couple of kids were diving from the higher of the two boards, pedalling in mid-air and laughing their heads off.

Over by the bar, thatched with tropical leaves, a knot of drinkers had formed. As Deirdre gazed at the still palm trees, the shrubs of hibiscus and the terracotta hills beyond, it all seemed too perfect somehow, an artificial backdrop against which they all posed. She was also conscious of a sense of exclusivity. The hotel stood in its own grounds completely surrounded by stucco walls and gate lodges, the same cordon sanitaire that once protected the Governor General of the island. Indeed, from where she lay she could make out the white crenellations of the colonial HQ behind the eucalyptus trees at the perimeter of the pool area. The locals who sold batik, string beads and straw hats on the beach were not allowed in here.

As the sun got up the activity seemed to slow down. Eventually there was just one person in the pool and he was simply lounging on a rubber inflatable. People they vaguely knew waved even more vaguely towards them through the shimmer of heat. It required an effort of will to raise a glass of iced tea to the lips. Speech was laboured and phatic: "…but at least not humid…"

"Yes … a dry heat … Need the sunscreen though…"

Surprised, Tom woke from a short nap and immediately fell to thinking about business. If he did hire a manager he wouldn't have to do all the on-site inspections himself. He could extend the business into Rathfarnham, where the houses were generally older and where there was already a pent-up demand for replacement windows. Could he import the window frames already made up? China perhaps? Cedric Granger might have a view on that. Forget it for now. Deirdre was right. He read a page of Dan Brown but the effort was too much; symbology was too challenging in the slothful circumstances, and his sunglasses didn't reduce the glare enough for comfortable reading. Maybe a leisurely swim now that the pool was almost empty? No, the person he'd noticed earlier on the inflated li-lo was still hogging the middle of the pool. Was this the reason or was he trying to justify his inactivity?

"Where did this come from?" Tom referred to the drink by his side.

"The Robinsons sent them over," Deirdre said. "Margaritas," she added with little relish, her lips stretched in anticipation of a sour taste. She raised her glass in the direction of the Robinsons before taking a sip.

Tom beckoned a waiter and asked for rum Daquiris to be sent to the Robinsons. This was poolside protocol in the morning. There was an informal round system but guests didn't actually mingle until the sun went down. Besides which there was the barbecue that night.

Deirdre applied some more sun-block to her throat. She still hadn't developed any sign of neck wattles but there was no point in tempting fate. Some months ago she'd been helping her oldest daughter with her make-up and caught both their faces side by side in the mirror. The contrast set her back. She couldn't exactly pinpoint how or in what particulars her own face suffered by comparison, but there was a general heaviness of feature, some absence of definition; not even the deep brown of her eyes escaped that grainy shadow. Soon hot flushes no doubt. Ah well, could be worse. The family still revolved around her and she was making progress with her phobia. Small mercies, not to be discounted. She turned on her front and lowered the straps of her swimsuit. Her timing was not the best, however.

"Hello you two. Relaxing eh?" The Grangers were passing by en route to the palm-fronded bar.

"Well … you know…" Deirdre fumbled with the straps and made to turn.

"Don't disturb yourself…" Mrs. Granger said. "We'll see you tonight at the limbo bash?"

"Yes…"

"Absolutely," Tom added, lying back again after this contribution. A sky-writing plane passed overhead: Eat at the Wharf.

Thinking of a swim, he glanced again towards the pool. The young man was still there, motionless except for the gentle bobbing of the ribbed raft; he must've fallen asleep, lulled by the minuscule waves. Tom lay back, too lazy to read. The harsh blue of the sky was beginning to get to him; it was unforgiving. It made him feel as if he had a fever. To his shame he wished for an Irish cloud or Atlantic breeze. Mid-morning now, the guests were probably beginning to think about lunch if only to break up the relentless day. His own thoughts were becoming vague, amorphous, hardly anything more than the contemplation of the pink reredos behind his eyelids and the occasional red or yellow floater. He could doze off again. God, it was ridiculous, this inactivity, as if they'd all regressed to some neonatal state. Oh, let it be. No, he would have to have at least one swim before lunch. He shaded his watch with his right hand 1:45. Maybe in ten minutes or so…

"Tom."

"What?" He felt Deirdre's hand on his arm.

"That man in the pool…"

"What about him?"

"There's something unusual … He's a local man."

"So?" Tom propped himself up on an elbow, surprised at the effort involved.

"Well, none of the guests … I mean … no one else is…"

"Maybe he's one of the staff." Tom shrugged, "You're beginning to sound like Granger." It wasn't his most felicitous quip and he regretted it.

"He's been out there a long time," Deirdre pressed.

"Who're you telling? He's been hogging it all morning. Right smack in the middle of the pool." He wondered if he wasn't protesting too much. Turning more fully towards her, the sun glanced off his chest hair which was beginning to turn grey.

"Do you think he's all right?"

"'Course he is. He's on one of those li-lo things."

"Yes, but…" She removed her sunglasses and craned forward. "Tom, I think his face is in the water." Her voice had dropped to an urgent whisper. "I think you should do something."

Tom sat up and looked around. No one else seemed remotely interested. Surely someone else would have noticed if…? Unless, of course, they all felt as he did, tired from too much sleep. Still, it was inconceivable, in this charmed garden …

Shading his eyes, he focused again on the floating figure; the head did seem to be slumped. And it extended over the front of the li-lo. With a spurt of anxiety and not a little embarrassment, he got to his feet and dived into the pool.

"Way to go, Tom!" an American guest yelled.

As he swam, a sense of dread crawled over him. By the time he'd covered half the distance the knowledge had seeped into him that the young man was dead. He raised the head from the water and saw the rictus, the grey discolouration of the skin. He towed the li-lo towards the shallow end. It was his own exertions that saved him from shock. He called out to Deirdre, who was standing at the edge of the pool.

"Get the manager ... and an ambulance. Quickly!" The peace of the poolside was suddenly shattered. Most of the guests had roused themselves and were rapidly coalescing around the staff who had come running out.

"Please let us through," the manager pleaded. Two of the security staff knelt at the edge of the pool and with Tom's help lifted the body out. They laid it on the turquoise tiles under the diving board and tried to prevent the quests from getting too close.

"It's Bernard," the manager said. "He shouldn't have been..."

"First aid. Who knows how to...?" Cedric Granger pushed through the crowd.

"He's dead," Tom said.

"Take him round the back." The manager

looked scared.

"Wait now," Granger interrupted. "The police. Shouldn't we wait till the police arrive?"

"It makes no difference," the manager said abruptly. "Take him to the staff quarters. Quickly." Using the li-lo as a bier, the security men bore him away. Some of the guests made to follow but the manager asked them to go back. He whispered something to Cedric Granger, who took charge of the situation and ordered brandy for the ladies. They stood around uneasily, shocked, having been so abruptly roused from collective torpor. The animated buzz of conversation seemed unnatural at that time of day; its pitch varied from sympathy to excitement. Here was an experience which, like a tan, could be brought home.

"Who was he?" someone asked.

"I don't know," Tom said, though he had the strangest notion that he'd seen him somewhere before.

"We noticed him in the pool," an American said. "But we had no idea … How did you…?

"I didn't," Tom replied. "It was my wife who…"

Deirdre felt all eyes turning towards her but she couldn't say anything. She just stood there, a towel around her shoulders, clutching the beach bag. The manager returned with a couple of maintenance men who immediately set about draining the pool. He spoke in apologetic tones to the guests, regretting the incident, and inviting them indoors where aperitifs would be served, courtesy of the hotel. They followed him into the lobby where a free bar had been set up. Some of the guests took their drinks upstairs where they reappeared on balconies looking out.

Tom and Deirdre went to their room to change. They heard the sounds of an ambulance arriving; they didn't hear it leave, presumably because there was no need for a siren. Tom offered her a drink from the mini bar but she declined. It was rare for her to clam up like this and he knew how out of sorts she was.

Later, in the dining-room, she pushed her plate away and held her forehead.

"What is it, Dee?" he inquired.

"I think he was our waiter." Her face wore a wretched expression.

"The dead man...?" It hadn't struck Tom before, but it was a possibility.

"I don't know for sure."

"I'll ask," he said idiotically, leaning back to summon help.

"You can't."

"No. You're right." He recalled the face in the water. He would never forget it. But he just wasn't sure if it was the man who had waited on them for the last several days. The tall youth, dressed as a midshipman, who placed a vase of hibiscus on the table and unfolded the scalloped napkins with a snap. For their very first meal on the evening of their arrival, the waiter had greeted them in Irish, using a phrase he'd obviously picked up from other Irish tourists. He certainly wasn't in the dining-room this lunch time. Maybe it was his day off; in which case he wouldn't have been near the pool. Tom hoped that was the case. But that meant hoping that some other mother's son had drowned. Was it important to know who had died? It wasn't as if they'd have really known him anyway. He wondered why Deirdre was so upset and so quiet. At the next table the guests were not so reticent; they discussed it openly and with a certain vigour; one of them mentioned the name, 'Bernard', more than once. But no one knew whether their waiter was called Bernard.

Rumours abounded. The young man was on drugs, he'd had a row with his boss, he had simply asphyxiated, he had committed suicide. But how, Tom wondered, could you kill yourself by holding your face under water? Surely the survival instinct would take over?

They returned to their room; Deirdre lay down for a while and Tom sat in a shaded corner of the balcony.

Confused thoughts raced through her mind, none of them making sense. But she was angry, perhaps beyond reason. Angry that it had happened, angry that it had happened in that fools' paradise in full view of all the pampered guests, angry at the efficiency of the manager in whisking the body away and protecting his patrons from inconvenience, angry at her own blindness and at the fact that she had allowed herself to be cast in the role of a self-indulgent, wealthy, fun-loving moron who was afraid of spiders. She was almost certain that Bernard had been their waiter and she was angry at herself because she didn't know for definite. Her head throbbed as she joined Tom on the balcony. If she had any lingering doubts they vanished when she saw, from the balcony, the steel band setting up at the side of the freshly-filled pool, now surrounded by Chinese lanterns. The barbecue was proceeding as planned. She imagined going down to dinner or breakfast and wondering if their waiter would appear or not. Her face was mottled as if a phobic reaction were setting in. This was one anxiety that would not respond to therapy.

"I think we should go home, Tom."

He looked across at her and nodded.

Be Bold Again

THERE HE WAS AGAIN on the platform, trembling, a small elderly man with decent coat and hat, waiting for the train. Trembling and chain-smoking.

Six months previously he had shuffled in my direction and asked if he could talk to me; it was good for his nerves. His voice shook and he frequently removed the crush hat to wipe his narrow damp skull with a handkerchief. Over the following weeks I managed to piece together his predicament, or at least the broad outlines of it. Every day he got the 8:50 DART at Dalkey and travelled the two stops to Dun Laoghaire where he went for counselling in a clinic which specialised in nervous disorders. He hated and feared that clinic. The nurses and therapists did their best to break him down, reduce him to tears. He was humiliated every morning of his life.

And, according to him, the staff of the clinic were in league with his wife behind his back. They would tell her if he missed a session or even if he stayed quiet and didn't bleed on the carpet as they expected him to do.

His wife would tell them what he did at home – or rather didn't do. She had told them that he made no attempt to give up smoking, that he wouldn't do any gardening or go with her to the shops. His biggest sin of commission, which was duly reported, was that he took his medication in the early afternoon, instead of at night, and often knocked himself out for the rest of the day so that he was oblivious to her advice.

Every morning on the platform he could hardly move for fear. He shuffled because he was afraid to lift his feet off the ground. He was a walking panic attack, and felt completely trapped by his forced routine, by the therapists and by his wife. He worried about everything, not just the forces ranged against him or the prospect that his over-worked heart might burst, but small things too, like whether the train would be late, why the signal hadn't turned green, whether he would get a seat, whether he would be in a fit state to walk the final two hundred yards to the clinic.

His overriding fear was that they – presumably the authorities – would decide to put him in hospital. They had done so before when he was a younger man, and he nearly lost his reason. On one occasion he found himself in the 'wet brain' ward, but not for long. He jumped through a window and clambered down a drainpipe onto a flat roof. The police caught him some days later in a B and B in Enniskerry and brought him back to the hospital in a Black Maria. This colossal fear did not, however, in any way mitigate the smaller fears which came at him from all sides. He seemed to have an infinite capacity for fear and could 'entertain' several at the same time – or rush from one to another – so that the cumulative effect was paralysing.

One morning when the train reached Dún Laoghaire, he lost his nerve completely, and I had to help him out of the carriage and support him with a hand under the elbow en route to the Clinic. He dismissed me before we got there because he didn't want to be seen getting a hand from anybody. But he was seen, and the staff informed his wife that a strange man had helped him up the street.

"They've got me," he said over and over. "They've got me now. I'm caught out. I've nowhere to turn." Tears rolled down his face. I couldn't understand why his wife or the therapists would take such a poor view of the incident. Maybe he exaggerated their reaction, but it didn't matter. He was in extreme pain. That was all too clear.

Worse was to come. Some days later he shuffled towards a stranger on the platform and asked if he could talk to him. The stranger told him to fuck off, that he should be in a loony bin not out in public bothering people. By the time I arrived he was in an awful state and said he was going to throw himself in front of the train when it arrived. He didn't go that far but I could see that it was more than a cry for help.

Some time later, I told him I didn't believe that, in this day and age, anyone should have to suffer like he did. Since group therapy clearly wasn't working maybe he should go to a psychiatrist and see about more appropriate medication. He recoiled from this suggestion on the grounds that the doctor would put him straight into hospital. I made some other suggestions which he also rejected.

Everything seemed to be a dilemma or a trap. I had read somewhere that depressed people could not believe in any solutions; even hoping for some cure could bring additional torments raining down on them.

I began to wonder if he wasn't inventing those traps to punish himself. In his mind he had to endure this inexplicable pain every waking second of every day. I felt like asking if he really wanted to get better, but I didn't have the diplomatic skills to be so personal with a man I barely knew. If he wanted to continue suffering, then the question arose: What was he punishing himself for?

Surprisingly, he partly answered that question on Monday morning the following week. He made a throw-away remark to the effect that he never really missed the drink.

I saw an opening, "So, you were an...?"

"An alcoholic. Yes. Drank two businesses ... I've been on the wagon for seven years but..."

How had his wife survived those bad days? The poor woman must have suffered as she watched not one, but two businesses going down the drain, and God alone knew what other alcohol-induced incidents had affected her. There may even have been young children caught in the cross-fire. Her strict treatment of him now was probably based on a fierce determination to keep him well.

During the next week he seemed a bit better than usual, at one point cracking a joke with a doleful, apologetic expression on his face that matched the sagging punch line. But a few days later he was worse than I'd ever seen him. He shook so much he couldn't speak properly and I had to strain to hear him. Because of the shakes he couldn't light a cigarette but didn't really want one since his throat was dry and his stomach bilious and heaving.

He had overheard his wife on the phone having a conversation with one of the therapists. She said that he refused to do the garden or even the lightest household chores. He would not accompany her to the shops or to bridge games. She insisted that the time had come to have him packed off to hospital; the doctor would concur, and they had St. Patrick's in mind rather than John of God's.

"St. ... Patrick's..." He could hardly get the words out. This was the original insane asylum – founded by Jonathan Swift – for the poverty-ridden lunatics of Dublin, many of them in the last stages of syphilis, and its name had a terrible resonance. He couldn't get on the train and I waited behind with him on the platform of Dalkey Station. He was in such a dreadful state I suggested that he should take some of his medication there and then but it turned out that they only gave him the tablets on a daily basis. He had to turn up at the Clinic every morning to get them. His wife insisted on that procedure.

I got him to sit down and wait for the next train. He had begun to moan and whimper, and when the next train arrived he couldn't get on that one either. He was paralysed. Whatever his past sins, he didn't deserve such punishment.

I wondered if his wife might not also be indulging in a little revenge; after all, this was probably the first time in their married life when she had the upper hand. And he was so riddled with guilt about his past life that he was virtually asking to be punished.

I quickly banished such unworthy thoughts from my mind – in any case it was none of my business.

Two more trains passed and by now he'd be so late for the Clinic that he'd get dogs' abuse, and the matter would be reported to his wife. He looked at me with hopeless eyes. He was unable to speak but all the time this high-pitched moan escaped from his throat while his whole body shook, and sweat streaked his face. It was the sound of the whimper that finalised the decision that I had been turning over in my mind since the first day I met him.

I couldn't stand that sound any longer and I brought him in a taxi to the nearest pub where, without much thought of consequences, we got as drunk as we could as fast as we could. When, after about a dozen drinks, I eventually heard his laughter, which was surprisingly raucous, given his gaunt frame, I knew that we would both remain under the influence of strong drink for a long time to come.

———————

The trembling man's name turned out to be John.

We had many good years, all of them spent under the influence of alcohol. Our typical day in the pub fell into a sort of pattern: the first phase was self-medication, otherwise known as the hair of the dog. John's potion of choice for this phase was brandy, large and several; mine was neat gin, also large and several. He would usually have difficulty in raising the first glass to his mouth and I often had to lend him a (slightly) steadier hand. After the first couple of glasses, out would come the cigarettes.

The second phase was the beginning of feeling all right. It was a miracle every time. We could look at the sunlight coming through the window − our version of smelling the flowers. It often felt good to be alive. We tried to make that phase last as long as possible because we knew that if we went too quickly into the third (manic) phase we would end up in hell the following morning.

Despite our best attempts, however, we usually plunged into the third phase as if we were driven by a desire for ecstasy instead of just contentment. We sometimes ended up on the street and occasionally in a cell, with the morning hell waiting for us with no antidote in sight. But we never once regretted the choice we'd made, despite what the wise therapists might say.

We often mused about whose liver would give out first. It wasn't whistling past the graveyard; neither of us really cared. Our commitment to drink was complete. Normal life wasn't an option, for him or for me, and we weren't ready to shuffle off the coil. So there was method to our madness. We loved the barmen. Though they were well paid – and we tipped abundantly – they did put up with a lot from us and they often cajoled the cops into turning a blind eye.

John kept a safety bottle in a water butt at the gable end of his house. One night he woke up desperate for a drink. There was none in the house – his wife used to go around pouring it out – so he slipped out to the water butt for his emergency bottle. It was the middle of winter, but he probably didn't feel the cold. However, the water in the butt was frozen solid and the bottle of booze was entombed and beyond reach. He scratched and clawed at the surface and eventually took a lump hammer to the ice, waking the neighbours and his wife who slept upstairs. She called the police. Maybe it was the last straw for her, because shortly after that she poisoned him.

I was with him the day he died. We started in the back bar of McDermott's and had safely reached the second phase when he started to complain of cramps.

"Maybe it's the liver packing up at last," the barman quipped. He was right as it happened but not for the reason he thought. John's wife had, the night before, unusually left a meal out for him – a pork chop. He should have smelled a rat but he was in the third phase and scarfed it down. It was this decomposed swine flesh that he threw up all over the bar that morning. The spew took the varnish off the mahogany; imagine what it did to his innards. He was dead by mid-day.

There was an autopsy and I suppose I could have given evidence that would at least have done his wife out of the insurance money. But for good or ill – or maybe sheer laziness – I decided to let sleeping dogs lie. John had stopped trembling at last; whether he was at peace, as they say, is another matter but he was at least remembered fondly in a couple of the pubs we frequented, and that is probably better than the eulogies of those who live their lives in a more normal way.

After the funeral I had a bad morning, a real fugue. I was afraid to sleep. There were demons all around me, not funny critters but real demons, mean, threatening bastards. I had a family once, a wife and two daughters, and suddenly I realised the loss. Where were they? Had I really abandoned them? I drank because they suffered; they left because I drank. There was no way out of that and never was. C'est la vie. I am, therefore I feel. Enough!

I threw back neat gin with a vengeance and couldn't move from the edge of the bed until the start of phase two began to seep into me – or I into it. I realised then that it wasn't John I tried to save that morning on the station platform. It was myself. And I knew that 'save' was the wrong word. I'm sure the wise people would call it avoidance, extreme pot-holing. My least unhappy place was beneath the radar of meddling people and their rude curiosity.

They were nice to me in the pubs that day, probably assuming that I was grieving for John. I was in a way, but only in a way. Fellow booze hounds rarely become very close, since alcohol is, and remains, their first love. I did miss him though, especially that raucous laugh (phase two only) which was in such sharp contrast to the former whimpering as he waited for the train.

I'm not sure why but for a couple of weeks − goodish weather, probably summer− I went on the wagon. It may have been a fluke. I had a fall and broke my arm, so it could have been some sort of medical intervention that created a hiatus which I tried to prolong. During that period I remember making a conscious attempt to reintegrate into society, as the wise people put it. I seem to recall that one of the doctors who dealt with my arm − or was it leg − suggested that one had to be sociable to lead any kind of rewarding life.

Well, after the two or so weeks I came to the conclusion that society wasn't worth the effort of reintegration. Of all the people I met there wasn't one with whom I would have liked to have a drink. Anyway the demons came back and I skipped out of their way and, like a burrowing animal, went back underground to the land of mahogany counters and flashing optics.

But while I was on the wagon I met several members of society, one of them John's widow who was much younger than I expected. It may surprise you to learn that she tried to seduce me and even mentioned the possibility − as if it were a bribe − of a long-term relationship.

"I drink." It was only fair to point this out.

"I know."

"I am wedded to drink."

"And I'm attracted to the addictive personality." She wouldn't quit.

Maybe she liked a challenge but I had already decided to go back to the old ways and I knew she'd try to reform me. Maybe she saw in me another John to kick around. If alcohol had left my libido intact I might have nibbled, but fortunately I was free of such weakness.

"You poisoned him."

"Yes," she said. "We poisoned each other. But one of us had to raise the ante." She went on to explain how exciting it could be, with her terrified of my alcohol-induced exploits, and me enjoying the frisson of never knowing when I was about to be poisoned. Russian roulette would pale by comparison.

Her addiction may even have been stronger than mine and it is quite possible she could have made me feel guilty about my drinking. However, I had a vision of myself shuffling along the platform of Dalkey Station, trembling with nerves. I even heard a faint echo of John's former whimper as if it came from my throat. I bade his widow farewell and headed underground from where I've never looked up.

Cut-to-chase Scene

FOR NO APPARENT REASON Sammy would forget to shave about twice a year. This morning something must have snipped the circuits and changed his routine. Maybe he had put on his left sock first when he got out of the shower, and that changed everything. He was strap-hanging on the subway more dismayed than usual by the uninspired graffiti and laboured filth, feeling with his free hand the unaccustomed down on his chin. He felt hung-over, commuting to work without the absolution of a shave and a splash of cologne. But deep inside was the slight boast of a spirit that could have spent a night on the town with The Rolling Stones.

It was that same spurt of excitement that came with snow in the morning when the whole of Manhattan was snarled up and commuters dawdled in wonder, breathing white whiffs of anarchy into the air. So there was a buzz in his blood but maybe the hint of an omen too, for today was the day he would hear about the promotion. If he didn't make the cut, the confident Ms Susan McAllister would become his boss. It didn't bear thinking about, but he couldn't think of anything else.

Sammy devilled in silence, keeping his head down. His mild manner and weak face gave the impression that he could take instructions well even against his better judgement. But deep-down he disliked authority, especially in the elegant guise of a strong, psyched-up person like Susan McAllister.

As he slotted himself into his knee-hole desk he knew that the Brass on the twenty-second floor were already on his case, deciding between him and McAllister. His teeth nervously chafed the cleft under his lower lip making a sound like a mouse scratching at night. The furniture that cramped his space and style was all moulded plastic, hard and lacquered in radioactive colours, designed to keep the brain cells restless and inquisitive. He was still in the creative section of the advertising agency, stuck in his gaudy little office like a performing flea.

The Brass on the twenty-second floor had different accommodations. From the oak-paneled walls and carved credenzas came the serenity of control that Sammy longed for. Their offices were as commanding as the poop decks of old sailing ships. The Group VPs didn't have to be creative. No, they waited inscrutably, and absorbed in their padded minds and deep-pile carpeting the daily quota of ideas submitted for approval from the floors below. They weighed carefully the splay of ideas, separating the buckwheat from the bullshit. Choice was their calling; that and decision-making. There was no court of appeal.

Sammy had to become one of them because he was written out. Too many of his recent ideas had been rejected, sprats thrown back in the water with scarcely a ripple. He was de-captioned, a copy-originator turned copy-cat, living off the sour milk of old Aha moments. He had to make it to the ranks of senior management before they found him out. He dreamed of having his own corporate accounts, with others to beat their brains for him. That was why he had "thrown his hat into the ring" as he put it nonchalantly to his colleagues, behind clenched teeth.

The Brass were up there right now behind double oak doors deciding between Susan McAllister and himself. The fact that they were writing the script without any input from him was a source of considerable anxiety.

His secretary, Babs, brought him coffee with blobs of condensed milk floating on top. For the first time he complained, "Babs, could you not stir it?" His voice was high and querulous, not far off whining pitch. It surprised him.

She bridled. "For three and a half years you never complained." Surprise muted her initial response which then turned to self-justification. "In any case, my job description doesn't say anything about making coffee."

He didn't want to escalate the situation. "I'm sorry." He rummaged in the top drawer of his desk, and felt he should explain. "I'm looking for a disposable razor…"

"Well, I don't have one."

"It's just that I forgot to shave this morning."

"Oh," she said. "I thought you'd been sleeping rough." Her sarcasm was like congealed grease. She pivoted on a heel and left abruptly. The slam of the door threatened to reduce the hard plastic of his office into its elemental crystals. Her offended hauteur lingered like over-sweet perfume. He felt nauseous because of the unaccustomed altercation, and regretted having started it.

In the bathroom he tried to mulch up a lather out of a palmful of liquid soap from the dispenser. He looked at his inconsequential face in the mirror as he shaved. He contorted his face this way and that to give the blade a draw. Luckily his beard was light and the wispy hairs came away willingly and without pain in the thin furrows of soap. It was more a depilatory than a shave. Goddamn weak triangular face disappeared into nothing at the chin. It just plain ran out like the tapered end of a parsnip. It was a nothing face that would never have character unless kicked by a mule. He replaced his bifocals which put two half-moons under his eyes. His hair was still thick enough; it was his face that was bald, featureless. Maybe he should let his beard grow, but on balance he decided against it; even a patchy fuzz would label him creative. He didn't want that image any more.

He had to get that face deposited safely on the twenty-second floor or he was sunk. Security meant freedom. He could sniff the ozone in the air up there, taste the sea breezes in his mouth, spy out his own horizons for once and test the margins that confined him.

Should he call Susan McAllister? To alibi himself in advance, or try to unsettle her? It was his first decision of the day, a woeful one that augured badly.

"Hi, Sammy," Susan McAllister breezed into his eardrum, then she broke off to toss out some instructions to her secretary, "Put it on the Chamber's file and copy to Bronski with my compliments." She always liked to give the impression that she was being interrupted. Then, true to form, she apologised for letting the brunt of business get in the way of good manners. "What can we do for you? Her authoritative tone implied excellent time-management skills; she could even make time for a chit- chat with him.

"Well, I guess," Sammy regretted his lack of rehearsal, "today is the day." Out of long habit he picked up a pencil to make notes.

"You mean you haven't heard?" Susan's voice was larded with sympathy. She was probably shaking her head at the unfairness of it all. "The news is out. Sorry you couldn't have made it too."

"Wha…?" Sammy choked; ripped from stem to gullet.

"I'll keep an open-door policy though," Susan said. "You can consult me any time." She followed up with another flurry of asides to her secretary.

Sammy's forty-two year old heart, pumped up by bedroom barbells, did isometrics inside his ribcage, until McAllister chose to break the silence with smug barks of laughter. "Got you, didn't I? No decision yet." She laughed again, indulgently, knowing she'd put one over on old Sammy; the spitballs kept coming until she'd struck him out.

Though Sammy began to breathe again, he

covered the mouthpiece to muffle residual gasps. He opened a drawer, spilled some Librium on his crimson blotter pad between the doodles of dead ideas, and gulped down a few, chewing them for faster absorption. Bile came into his throat as though years of Babs' coffee decided suddenly to back up. He could visualise McAllister's liberal mouth neighing into the phone, her equine good looks, long slender hand holding the receiver. She could walk between the raindrops without having to feint or scurry; she had the most valuable asset in the advertising game; she had presence.

Sammy felt like a piece of lint McAllister might flick off the well-cut shoulder of her Gucci suit. There was no way he could compete with her take-charge manner. But he wouldn't give up just yet.

"You almost had me going then." He tried to keep his voice mellow, bantering even, despite the tangle of his larynx. He could take a locker-room gag and a flick of a wet towel, but he covered the spilled pills with a sheet of paper in case Babs walked in. The thought of having to work under McAllister did not appeal. "God, please don't let her win," he prayed. He was back in the schoolyard again at recess, a group of bigger kids advancing on him chanting, "Snitch, snitch." He took his beating then and sniveled back to the dictionary to increase his word power, the blood from his nose dripping on the open pages from Polyanthus straight through to Popinjay.

Sammy cast about for a reason to hang up, but as usual McAllister beat him to the draw, "Must sign off now. Have a call coming through from the Paris office. But let's keep in touch."

"Yeah, I have to dash off to a meet..." Sammy blurted out. But it was too late. She had already hung up.

The final interview had taken place a week previously. Sammy wondered what impression he had left lingering in the non-committal air as the bland gazes of the Brass saw him off the premises. Those whitebait eyes gave nothing away. He had swabbed the decks, cleaned the head, but the Flag Officers reserved judgement. He had fought the equation in their minds: ability plus motivation equals performance, but one without the other means zilch. Naturally, you had to have both. The questioning was standard enough.

"...What do you think..." – the words were patronising with a nice hesitancy – "What do you think..." – they could even afford the luxury of repeating themselves – "were your ... aaahm ... better ideas?" Yes, a predictable question but, due to anxiety, he shot out his answers too quickly. Susan McAllister had probably ruminated for a while, maybe cracked a joke or two, and then gave some prodigious reply.

"Well," Sammy had said, his heart beating against his breastbone, "I did ... you know ... the shooting stick for Bloomingdales," he paused for breath, "and the silver-knobbed cane for Hechts…"

"Yes, you do seem to have an … um … penchant," they riffled through his personnel file, "for sticks."

"Well, you know," he tried to share the laughter, to join in the twenty-second floor camaraderie as coffee was served by a phantom butler. "I do like the idea of a … hallmark … a cachet." Real cream swirled in Blue Mountain coffee that was specially shipped from the Rastafarian hills south of Montego Bay. Everything in the executive suite was real, only the people were phoney. Maybe his stick fixation came from a deep prong of desire to shaft them all. Then he became defensive, quickly rattling off older ideas, trying to make the sparks fly again: the subliminal pudenda in Moyers Spaghetti sauce − the subtle association between fertility and Maxima Sanitary Pads. Then he realised that he had backed himself into the creative corner, all by himself. So, he tried to show his business mettle, how he could advertise the agency itself, how he could strategize. He belonged with them in the wheel-house. Clients on the horizon. Hoist the logo. Sunken treasure dead ahead.

But he felt that he had changed tack too often, giving the impression of a soft-focus ditherer, frayed at the edges. Susan McAllister on the other hand had probably left a huge package of herself carving its shape in the air. In short, Sammy hoped they wouldn't attach too much weight to the interview.

He sifted through his in-tray, but couldn't concentrate. They were up there right now dissecting him, reaching through the loose-leaf pages of his personnel file to grasp his soul. What in God's name were they saying about him…?

"He's bright enough … but I don't know … a feeling…" Vibes, distancing caveats, thoughtful grimaces.

"He has done some good scenarios…"

"True, but it's a pressure cooker up here, as we all know…" A minute's silence, to pay tribute to the burden of leadership. "Has he the testicularity? Can he take the pressure? No doubt about Ms McAllister on that score…"

"Mmmm, and the way he fidgets. And that self-stroking body language. Plus that wan face … Imagine the first impression on clients?"

It was almost lunchtime. Sammy heard the sound of bathroom plumbing overhead. "My God," he thought, "if it spills over into lunch I'll be lost in the canapés." He buzzed Babs, "Any calls?"

"No!" A syllable like a shard of ice. She was still rankling over the coffee. God, why did he have to alienate her on this of all days?

He rushed out of the building into Central Park. Dodging skaters and joggers wired for sound, he bought a hot dog, took a bite, gagged and threw it in a litter bin. "Apathy is my devil," he thought. The work was ridiculous of course and he couldn't quite conceal the fact. Who needed a silver-knobbed cane anyway? But Susan McAllister could play the game. She sometimes criticised the agency even in front of the Group VPs, but would then apologise ruefully. It was a powerful tactic implying that she was prepared to risk their wrath out of the depth of her concern for the organisation; thus she proved her commitment.

By comparison, Sammy's attitude to the Agency was little short of treason. But if the promotion came through then he could be loyal; admirals didn't mutiny as a rule. On the twenty-second floor, self and corporate interest merged into one. His mind needed to rest and graze. Maybe he could even begin to write plays again, turning his proselytising sketches into something real for a change.

He thought he saw Susan McAllister coming out of the Waldorf with the Brass, all belly-laughing after a celebration lunch. It was imagination of course but it reminded him of one of his humiliations in the Agency, when he thought he could upgrade advertising copy and tell the consumer something real about the product, a car in this case. He had proposed a TV campaign using computer graphics to expose the dynamics of the car's design. He had been laughed out of court. "Show the goddam product, not the drawing board. A minute's air time costs half a million. Don't waste it on a bunch of lines..." Susan had joined in the condemnation. Puffery remained the order of the day.

A boy ran across his field of vision trying to get his kite airborne. The kite, a cheap plastic one in the shape of a dragonfly, refused to take off though there was enough wind. The boy's hair flew back from his forehead as he ran, his spindly legs threshing the long grass in worn sneakers probably handed down from his brother; he looked back ruefully each time the kite bit the dust. Something touched Sammy, a farewell tug of memory from his own past. It was a risk to approach anyone in the Park but he took it.

"Why aren't you in school?" He immediately regretted coming on so strong.

The boy wasn't fazed: he gave him a tough look, "What's it to you?"

"Nothing." Sammy enjoyed letting the kid brazen it out. He himself had been no stranger to those sad tactics when he was that age. "Let me help get this thing flying." He noticed the blurb on the membrane-thin plastic: IT FLIES ITSELF! Christ, they had a lot to answer for, all of them.

"I can do it myself," the boy said with the self-sufficiency of all lonely kids.

"Here," Sammy smiled. "I'll hold the kite. You run in that direction as fast as you can. Into the wind."

The boy gave him an uncertain look, then paid out some line and began to run. Just before the line grew taut Sammy released the kite, nudging it skywards. The wind took it from there with a slight gasp; it was airborne. The kid felt the pull and turned around with a sudden smile. Sammy waved and walked back towards his office building.

He tried to occupy himself with some busy-busy

work but his in-tray was sadly depleted. Maybe they were by-passing him, phasing him out? High conspiracy, unlawful assemblies in corridors, covert glances, secret memos to Personnel, or Human Resources as they called it nowadays. Tomorrow, he might find his end-table missing, four pale leg marks on the thin rug. The next stage in the process of being de-hired. Babs would love it; her whittled proboscis would throb to the news.

He jumped when the call came through, the summons. He went crouching to the bathroom, had the fastest dump of his life, splashed water in his face and raced upstairs.

Walking down the corridor of the twenty-second floor, he tried to compose himself, straightening his tie, brushing imaginary dandruff from his shoulders. He thought he saw Susan McAllister come out of the Executive Suite walking in the other direction. Was there a spring in her step, a blue rosette pinned to her lapel, the sound of champagne corks in her head? Sammy waited until the coast was clear. His life seemed to have been spent in corridors, skulking outside closed doors, while he exhausted the options in his head.

"Well, Samuel, we've reached a decision. The best person won." (Naturally, they couldn't make a mistake.) "Congratulations!" They stood to welcome him aboard, hands extended.

"All which thy child's mistake,
Fancies as lost, I have stored for thee at home:
Rise, clasp My hand, and come!
"My God, I made it." He almost passed out.

On the other hand; "Samuel, we decided to keep the post on ice for another year or so. Neither of you is … aaam … quite ready." (Naturally, how could anyone aspire to their lofty wisdom?)

"For ah! We know not what each other says,
These things and I; in sound I speak —
Their sound is but their stir,
They speak by silences."

Fair enough. Misery likes company. At least Susan McAllister was shafted too.

But then again; "Sorry, Samuel, maybe next time. We know you will work well under Ms. McAllister's leadership. It was a difficult decision." (Naturally, they wouldn't earn their fat salaries for making easy decisions.)

"Thank you for your time, gentlemen," OR, "I quit, you pompous puke-heads."

"How hast thou merited —
Of all man's clotted clay the dingiest clot?
Alack, thou knowest not,
How little worthy of any love thou art!"

By the time he reached the double doors of the Executive Suite he was purged of scenarios and was ready. From the west side of the building he could see the tree tops of Central Park and above these he spied a little dragonfly kite sailing in the air. He turned the brass knob and entered without knocking.

The Circle around Peadar and Una

IT WAS ONE OF THOSE painterly autumn days, an unexpected but welcome bonus before the onset of winter. The day had russet colours, mild breezes and the appearance, if not the heat, of a diffident sun.

Peadar let go of Una's hand to throw a stone down the embankment into the sea. They had walked out to the lighthouse at the end of the West Pier and were now almost back to the port town of Dún Laoghaire. In the sea outside the pier there were several youngsters on jet skis, showing off and making a terrible racket; they were out of stone-throwing range.

Una broke the smouldering silence that had enveloped them before they even reached the end of the pier. "Your Aunt Sadie shouldn't have said that to me." *Don't make excuses for her. She knew exactly what she was saying and it's inexcusable. The meddling old cow.*

"She didn't mean anything by it," Peadar said. *Maybe she did, maybe she didn't. OK, she was out of order to say that Una had had enough to drink. But it was a throw-away remark. She was looking out for both of them. She was a kind woman. Who else would have raised him from a whelp after his mother died?*

"Oh, didn't she?" Una watched a motionless grey heron suddenly uncoil its long neck, stab its beak into a rock pool and draw out a small fish the size of a sardine which it swallowed whole. *Old witch. Doesn't think I'm good enough for his nibs here. And he won't stand up for me ... A Mamma's boy, no, an Auntie's boy.* "Why didn't you stand up to her?"

"What?"

"Nothing."

He stopped at the Coal Harbour and stared at the small boats riding gently at anchor. Those with masts gave off a tinkling sound, like Swiss cow bells, as the breeze blew ropes and cables against hollow aluminium. One rowing boat was tied to a plastic milk container; its oars were shipped, like chopsticks on a plate, but the oarlocks had been removed. Clever, because the oars were useless without them.

"Spit it out, Una." *I hate this. Innuendo, hints ... like needles in the eyes. She just won't let it go. What a way to spend Sunday. I'd prefer to be at work.*

"We know she doesn't think much of me ... But she didn't have to call me an alchie…"

"She didn't call you that." He stopped walking for a second as if that would somehow put an end to it.

"As good as." *Balance needed. Don't be too sensitive or offended. Don't give the old bag the satisfaction. On the other hand, must drive the point home. So Peadar gets the message. Have to make him cut the apron strings somehow.*

"You're making far too much of it, Una." He looked at his watch, which had been a present from her for his last birthday. *Almost one already. Meet the lads in Croke Park at three p.m. for the match. Kilkenny and Tipperary. Should be fantastic. Forget all troubles. A few beers after the match. Lovely hurling.*

"You'd defend that woman if she was a serial killer." *Grow a pair ... sometimes wonder ... you, the father of my kids ... maybe, but still ... Prefer a bit more ... what ... get up and go. Can't have everything though. Not getting any younger.*

Peadar forced a laugh as if he believed she had been joking. He changed the subject. "I just realised. I have to be in Croker by three." *No objections, please. Don't turn this into another row, for God's sake.*

"I'm upset and all you can think about is a football match..."

"Hurling." He swung an imaginary stick. *And the ball goes over the bar for yet another point by Peadar Mahoney. He's on fire today ... playing a blinder...*

"I would have hoped for a little more support." *Selfish too. He never had to make a sacrifice for anyone. Spoiled by Sadie. That's why he takes her side ... Spoiled rotten by Sadie. She was probably trying to compensate for the loss of his mother. Still...*

Something caught Peadar's eye. There was a

crowd in the dry-dock area near the old boat crane. *Just the ticket. A diversion. Get her mind on to ordinary things.* "Look, what's going on over there?" He pointed. "A crowd … onlookers."

"Oh, they're probably just launching a boat."

"Or taking one out … or maybe there's a swimming race."

"They sometimes shoot movies there," Una said, "or scenes for the TV Soaps." *OK, I can go along with this for the time being. He probably thinks this is a diversion. But it won't be the end of it. Not by a long chalk. Need to sort this out one way or another. Soon. That woman hasn't an ounce on her bones … she could see us all out…*

They walked quickly along the narrow stretch of road between the Coal Harbour and the dry dock. A train passed them on the right and a group of kids waved and gestured at them through a carriage window. A blur of pink suggested a mooning, but Peadar couldn't be sure. And Una obviously hadn't seen anything. A gun sounded to indicate that a winning boat had crossed a line somewhere.

They joined the edge of the crowd which had formed around the boat crane. Peadar decided to enlist the help of a tall man next to him. "What's going on?"

"A movie," the man said, "or possibly a scene for 'Fair City'. I don't watch it myself, but do you see your man there?"

"The guy on the crane?"

"Yeah. The wife says she knows him from TV."

They watched the man climb up the jib of the

crane, using the cross struts for footholds.

"He looks vaguely familiar," Una put in, "though he could be a stuntman made up to look like the actor."

"Good point," Peadar enthused. *Just what the doctor ordered. A film shoot ... perfect diversion. None better. Actors, glamour, the lot.*

"You're probably right," the tall man said. "I'd say he's going to jump into the harbour, or hang himself. How much do you bet?"

Gulls fussed and swooped overhead. With people around they probably assumed that trawlers laden with fish would soon appear, though no one fished on Sundays. Men who had been working on their boats in dry dock laid aside power-tools, sandpaper, varnish and antifouling tar, wiped their hands on rags, and joined the crowd of onlookers.

The man on the crane leaned out, caught the chain and brought it towards him. He tugged on the hook to make sure that there was no give in the chain.

"There's gonna be a hangin'," the tall man predicted in a cowboy drawl.

"I think you're right," Peadar said. "A lynching."

The man on the jib produced a length of rope from inside his shirt and looped it over the crane-hook. Everyone could now see that the noose at the other end of the rope was already around his neck.

"Any last requests?" someone called out and was promptly shushed.

"It's a bit unnerving," Una said.

"It's OK," Peadar replied, "He's wearing a harness. He knows what he's doing. These guys have it down to a fine art."

"But still…"

At that moment the man jumped. After the initial wrench he swayed for a while, his head at an angle. The crowd was silent for a few seconds, then broke into a round of applause.

"Well, that's that." The tall man and his wife left and the crowd began to melt away.

As they walked towards the main road Peadar sneaked a look at his watch. *OK for time. Croker was still on. But he was back walking on the old eggshells again. Better say something.* "Gives a kind of perspective, doesn't it?"

"Yes." *So, my concerns are unimportant? And you're so obvious it's pathetic. He really wants to go to the match. And doesn't want to feel guilty. OK, I won't object now. But I won't forget either. Wait for a better opportunity … to make him choose. He's not going to have it every way. He must make a choice…*

They walked on towards the car which they'd parked on the main road just above the National Yacht Club. The Stena Link ferry was in, and had its huge visor down. Trucks and cars drove aboard and disappeared into the ship's cavernous maw. Trade and holidays now, and emigration picking up again. Why could the country never create enough jobs?

The trees along the seafront wore their seasonal colours well; they were festooned with Chinese lanterns and yellow and white bunting. It was only one-thirty but the mist which rolled in from the sea gave the impression of an early dusk.

As they pulled the car away from the kerb an ambulance passed at speed, going in the opposite direction and was followed by a fire brigade. The sound of both sirens was almost deafening.

"Must've been an accident." Peadar made conversation. *When I leave her back to the flat I'll wait five minutes and then take off for Croker. It's a commitment after all. I can't let the lads down. She'll understand.*

Una made no response. She was waiting for him to raise the subject of the match again. *I'll object, then reluctantly let him go to the bloody game. I'll be the bigger person, but insist on ground rules in the future* ... Suddenly she tired of going around in these mean and self-absorbed circles. Her heart turned over. *I didn't see a camera. There was no camera.*

The Crib

SHE KNEW HE'D COME. The prediction was based on three weeks' research – and stalking.

It was late August and dusk was beginning to erase the light which had filtered through the trees. Sheila sat on a bench in a remote corner of the park, the leather hold-all leaning against her thigh. She wore a smart light-grey business suit and high heels.

She hated him for what he had done to her youngest sister, Maria. It was a corrosive hatred that would never diminish over time.

She checked through the bag and the zippered pockets. Everything was there, in order, just as she had planned. She glanced over her shoulder although there was no need. She knew that her friend, Brendan, was there behind her, though well hidden.

Her watch said 6:30, later than she'd expected, a little outside his normal routine. But still, she knew he'd come. With that confident walk, almost a strut, blowing smoke out of his mouth and nostrils. It seemed odd, somehow, that he was a creature of habit as if he were a civil servant or a bank official. Gerry Staunton. She tried to dismiss his name from her mind. A name made him human, but he wasn't.

Anger had sustained her thus far. But now that

the moment had come there was a sense of anxiety lodged in the pit of her stomach. Not that it would throw her off track. But it was a distraction she could do without. Precision would be required – and a steady hand.

She used her phone to give herself a countenance, but the text of the messages danced in front of her eyes. She went back to the bag and started another check of the contents, beginning to obsess. When she looked up she saw him in the distance. Her pulse quickened and spiked.

He was walking along the path towards the bench, just as she had predicted. The same brown suit and shoes, thinning sandy hair combed forward, a half-smoked cigarette between his fingers. Time behaved strangely. It seemed to take ages for him to reach the bench.

"Would you have the time please?" Her voice was surprisingly firm, perhaps a little too loud.

He stopped and sized her up. "Yes." He flicked the cigarette on the grass behind her and consulted his watch. "Six-forty."

"Thank you. I think I've … been stood up."

"Oh, I'm sorry to hear that. Is there anything I might be able to do to help?" Without a moment's hesitation he sat on the bench beside her. "An attractive woman like you shouldn't be treated like that. Some men just don't know how to behave. Do you work in the hospital?" He jerked his head in the direction of St Mark's, which was just across the road on the same side of the park.

She didn't want to answer him, but didn't want

to raise any suspicions either. She pretended she was a representative of a drug company which had business with the hospital.

"There are such wonderful drugs nowadays." He would cue on to anything she said to keep the conversation going.

She didn't want to listen to him or respond to anything he had to say.

His head was suddenly snapped back in the crook of a powerful forearm as Brendan came up behind him and applied the pad of chloroform. Staunton's legs threshed and his body twisted. One of his kicks caught Sheila on the shin and drew blood. But his spasms gradually grew less, and soon he was under.

Sheila looked around nervously, then she told Brendan to go. She didn't want to involve him further. He had a family and needed his job as hospital orderly. He didn't wait to be asked twice and quickly disappeared into the laurel bushes, heading for the exit.

Sheila's hands shook a little as she took the syringe from one of the pockets in the bag and injected Staunton in the arm through the sleeve of his jacket. This would keep him under for a half hour at least. That would give her plenty of time. As she fumbled for the case of surgical instruments she thought about what he had done to her sister, Maria, who was nineteen at the time and had just started nursing in the same hospital as Sheila. He had beaten her to a pulp and then raped her while holding a used syringe to her throat.

Despite counselling, Maria still hadn't recovered from the attack and she refused to go to court. She didn't want to bring more public attention on herself and the family. Her sense of shame was intense, and there had been instances of self-mutilation. One wound had become infected and almost caused the loss of her left arm. She had spent weeks in a mental hospital on suicide watch. Sheila's heart was broken by what had happened to her gentle sister, but gradually her attention began to focus on the man who had brought all this misery into their lives.

Methodically, and just as she had rehearsed it, she placed a plastic bowl on the bench and took hold of a scalpel the way her colleagues in the operating theatre did. She cut through the waistband of Staunton's trousers and then through his underpants. A nick drew a little blood from his stomach; it flowed down in a trickle no bigger than a thread. She folded the fabric down on his lap until his genitals were exposed in their bed of straw-coloured hair. The penis with its milky blue vein was cradled between the testes, and appeared to be sleeping. It was hard to imagine that white, helpless-looking organ causing so much harm to so many lives.

She had grown up on a farm and had seen castration before. Her grandfather sometimes fried the large testes with sage and onion in a big black pan. Her pet Spaniel had been doctored and had lost his aggression. She intended to remove Staunton's penis as well although there was a risk he would bleed out. That didn't bother her unduly but she wanted him to regain consciousness, if only for a while, and see his own testes in the bowl beside him. She took a firmer hold of the scalpel and brought it to the seam of the scrotum...

During Maria's first Christmas on the wards, before the rape occurred, she had tried to cheer up the patients by painting seasonal scenes on the windows. Her favourite was the nativity scene at the centre of which the innocent, helpless baby lay in the manger of straw. The image played over in Sheila's mind; it refused to go away, and she hesitated.

Dead Meat

"MAY I TAKE THESE away?" Catherine gathered up a few dishes and reversed away from the table on mincing little ballet steps. It was Friday night; the bistro was virtually full and the diners seemed to be enjoying themselves, if the excitable chatter was anything to go by.

She and her chef husband, Billy, owned the restaurant and were at pains to make it succeed. They had mortgaged their home to buy the place and Catherine, who ran the business end of things, was acutely aware how tight things were. The premises were too small to make any real profit; seven tables left them shy of the break-even point. But if they could develop a reputation here they could move to a bigger place in the next couple of years. She and Billy had sunk a lot of sweat equity into the bistro and they had to succeed. Had to. She had to pay those psychiatric bills for starters.

Concentrating solely on cooking – and loving it – Billy was not aware of his wife's strategic thinking, but it probably wouldn't have bothered him much one way or another as long as he had a well-equipped kitchen and his beloved copper pots, spices and cast-iron skillets.

Catherine didn't mind clearing a table every so often. It was a personal touch which she felt the clients appreciated. It also enhanced the 'artisan' image they were trying to cultivate.

Her professional smile quickly evaporated as she spotted a particular client who had just come in. She backed through the swing-doors into the kitchen, laid the crockery aside and peered through the clouds of cooking steam.

"Where's Billy?"

"He's in the pantry picking out some asparagus tips," Peter said. With his small fly-away moustache Peter looked more like a chef – the sauce-bottle variety – but he was the head-waiter. At least he insisted on that title even though he only had one other waiter working to him.

"Get him." Catherine's voice shook from a strange blend of excitement and fear. She looked through the sweating porthole of one of the doors.

"What's up? Billy appeared with a saucepan of asparagus. A burly young man, he had amazed his football pals when be revealed his ambition of becoming a chef.

"Do you know who's out there?" Catherine pointed to the porthole.

"The Pope?" Peter shrugged. "Put on some pasta."

"He's from Argentina," Billy said.

Catherine stamped her foot. "Dorothy O'Boyle. That's who!"

That had the desired effect: a moment's silence.

"The food person?" Billy inquired. He had obviously forgotten their previous encounter.

"Yes. She writes for the Sunday Star. She's their top restaurant hack, a real prima donna."

"I thought she looked familiar when I seated her," Peter said.

Catherine looked up to heaven; Peter wasn't professional enough. They would have to leave him behind when they moved on. If they moved ... How had Dorothy O'Boyle found them? Her presence changed everything; this, suddenly, was the big league and they weren't ready for it, not really. Billy had great potential; she knew that, but he still had a lot to learn. His instincts were so good that he didn't have to consult cookery books – which was just as well since he suffered from dyslexia. The rest of the staff didn't amount to a row of beans. If Dorothy O'Boyle gave them a bad review they would be finished; she had caused the demise of other small restaurants.

She had attacked Billy in print twelve years ago when he worked in a hotel kitchen. The head chef had the bright idea of sending Billy out to ask her how she enjoyed her meal of ox-cheek in star anise. She said that it wasn't tender and that in her view not enough cooking liquid or wine had been added to the pot to break down the tough connective tissue of the meat. During the conversation in which Billy had, in confusion, referred to the dish as only a sort of simple stew, he had become agitated and rushed back to the safety of the kitchen. In her next column she lambasted the hotel and the young chef who, according to her, knew nothing about cooking but didn't have any idea of how to deal with patrons. Catherine had managed to keep the review from Billy. But she hadn't forgotten the malice. There was even the suggestion that the young chef was as simple as the stew.

"Why didn't you seat her at a better table?" Catherine asked.

"It was the only one left," Peter said. "She hadn't a reservation. Maybe she's not working tonight," he added helpfully.

"Of course she's working. The woman never sleeps." Catherine peered out again. "She's having the soup. Who served her?"

"The woman asked for soup. She wanted soup." Peter made a modified Italian gesture.

Catherine turned to Billy, who thought for a while. "I've made better but I think it's OK. Do you want me to go out to her?" It was clear that he didn't want to. Maybe he remembered something of the previous encounter.

"No," Catherine said. If he messed up again there would be hell to pay, especially if Dorothy O' Boyle recognised him. She thought of going out herself but knew that she just wouldn't be able to schmooze with that despicable creature. She had a different thought, a crazy fantasy that she quickly dismissed.

Billy gave his infuriating slow grin. He tended to smile when there was no solution. It was his way of disqualifying himself as problem-solver. Catherine had to remind herself that he was really apologizing for being out of his depth and unable to contribute. He was shy and preferred to stay in the kitchen, well out of the limelight. They had established through counselling that he was somewhere on the autism spectrum, fortunately towards the functioning end.

"I'll ask her." It was rare for Peter to volunteer and although he didn't seem to be seized by the gravity of the situation, Catherine agreed to let him do it. She watched as he approached Dorothy O'Boyle and tried to read expressions as well as lips. Peter's smile was phony; he came across as a rat with a gold tooth. O'Boyle didn't smile once, not a flicker. But then she rarely did. As a foodie, she took life very seriously.

"Well?" Catherine demanded when Peter returned.

"She seemed to like the soup OK. The wine too."

Catherine now realised how unsatisfactory this was, how inconclusive. The critic was not going to vent her spleen there and then; she would reserve that for her column. That was her modus operandi. And she could be sharply critical, worse than that, sarcastic.

"Did she say anything else, anything specific."

"Too much turmeric."

"Shit." Catherine knew that Billy was going through a turmeric phase. They had discussed that – and coriander – the other night in bed.

"What main course did she order?"

"The filet mignon."

"Christ!" Catherine knew that O'Boyle often picked the simplest dish so she could go to town on it. She would conclude that if the chef couldn't do a decent steak then he certainly couldn't do anything more elaborate.

Billy overheard and turned to face them; his expression was as grave as she'd ever seen it. "The steak isn't the best. The butcher let me down. "

"Did you recommend it to O'Boyle?" Catherine pinned Peter with a look.

"I didn't," Peter said. "I recommended everything else, including the Chef's Special and the Penna. But no, she wanted the steak. It's as if she suspects something."

"She's trying to catch us out. That's her job. Going for the Achilles' heel..." She'd already caught them out on the turmeric; she knew what she was doing all right, the bitch. How many good reviews had she ever given? Two or three out of hundreds. Putting the boot in was good copy and it sold newspapers. Now she was moving in for the kill. To her they were just so much cannon fodder.

"Did you tenderise it...?"

"Of course," Billy said. "I tried everything short of jumping on it."

"Tell her it's off," Peter suggested with a shrug. He couldn't see what all the nervous energy was about. It was only food. He blamed the TV and all those celebrity chefs for trying to elevate cooking into an art form. They'd all lost the plot. Catherine mulled over his suggestion. Could the solution be that simple? But she'd ordered the steak over ten minutes ago and would obviously wonder why they hadn't told her it was off at that stage. She would smell a rat. The fact that Peter had gone out to inquire about the soup would already have indicated that they knew who she was. The chances were that even if she accepted one of the other entrées she would be prejudiced against it, believing that she was being manipulated.

That raised a troubling question in Catherine's mind. Up until now she had assumed that O'Boyle had just chosen their bistro more or less randomly. But suppose she had found out that Billy was one of the owners and was deliberately tracking him?

Both men waited for a decision.

"No. We … can't tell her it's off. Too risky…" She trembled slightly. The thought she'd locked away earlier kept knocking on the walls of its confinement, demanding to be heard.

Billy came and put his arm around her shoulder, "It's just not our night."

Catherine wouldn't accept that and wriggled out from under his heavy arm. What contribution did O'Boyle make anyway? She was a parasite, feeding off other people, good people trying to make something of their lives.

"Sprinkle ecstasy on the dish," Peter suggested with a sideways grin. "Give her good vibrations."

"Don't be daft," Catherine countered, and then the thought came again, and this time it had shed its fantasy clothing; it stayed, like a barbed hook in her brain, and refused to be dislodged. The dehumidifier hummed quietly in the background and failed to make any impression on the condensation that dripped down the stainless steel surfaces of the kitchen.

"We'll have to do away with her," she said, not

fully aware that she'd uttered those words.

"Oh, come on now." Billy wiped sweat from his forehead. At first he treated it as a joke and then he seemed confused.

How to dispose of the body? Catherine wondered. O'Boyle had arrived late, so she would still be there when the other diners left. At that point they could put her body in the van Billy used for collecting the fruit and vegetables – there was no CCTV around the back – drive her into the hills and dump the body. Just another missing person. If the body was discovered there'd be an inquiry of course. They would admit straight up that she'd been in the restaurant and then left on her own after the meal, a little unsteady on her feet. They could use a turkey baster to pump wine or brandy down her throat after the rat poison had done its work. No! Rat poison would show up in the autopsy. Better to bash her over the head with Billy's heaviest cast-iron pot, the one he had cooked the ox-cheek in. Yes, that would be consistent with a drunken fall in the hills. Perfectly logical and clear-cut.

"So we're all agreed?" She looked from face to face.

Peter shrugged. It was a dilemma, caused by the damn butcher. He felt that Catherine and Billy would go far in the restaurant business, right to the top. He could do worse than hitch his wagon to their star. Truth be told, he couldn't stand any of the fat pigs who lived to eat. He himself liked Chinese take-aways, and fish and chips with plenty of brown vinegar.

Billy was not quite with the programme but that was his way; floundering in awkward situations. He seemed wraith-like in the steam, a big, looming ghost.

Peter picked up the order, the mediocre filet mignon and moved towards the swing door to bring it out to Ms. O'Boyle.

"Wait," Billy said anxiously. "Hold on for a second. A little more parsley and thyme to garnish, I think."

Catherine put a gentle restraining hand on his arm. "No Billy. There's no need." She loved him more than ever at that moment.

Langan's Respect

WITH GOOD REASON Langan hated his boss, Mr. Staunton.

It had taken Staunton years to become office manager and part of his reward was to treat his subordinates with contempt. He reserved special humiliations for Langan and staged them in full view in the open-plan floor of the accounts department.

He might ridicule a set of accounts or a memo by holding the offending document up by a corner and asking in a loud voice what exactly he was supposed to do with such drivel. He was daring them all to respond to the feed, and a smug expression would settle over his broad features when silence greeted his question, and the staff busied themselves in their own tasks, concealing themselves like chameleons behind potted plants.

On one occasion, a kindly lady clerk, Tilly Somebody, suggested to Langan that he did not have to take such abuse, that there were regulations covering bullying in the work-place. In her view, Staunton had a psychiatric problem and would never change his behaviour. Langan knew she was trying to help but he felt demeaned by the implication that he couldn't handle the situation without outside assistance. He thanked her for her concern but had no intention of taking her advice.

In any case, Tilly had not been successful in trying to get rid of Joe, the hawk. For some reason a hawk had decided to take up residence on the roof of their building. From his elevated nest he would launch attacks on smaller birds, especially pigeons, and bring them back to his building to devour at leisure. Often he could be seen dismembering a pigeon on the ledge just outside the accounts department. Many of the ladies were upset by such a spectacle and Tilly, who had felt ill on more than one occasion, asked Mr Staunton to do something about the hawk. Staunton refused. He liked the hawk and thought it symbolised the cut and thrust of the business world. So, Joe the Hawk continued to decimate the surrounding birdlife at will.

When Langan was younger he had prospects as a footballer and probably would have turned professional if not for a trick knee joint that required surgery. Something went wrong with the operation – he never did find out what – and so his athletic career never got off the launching pad. Being a book-keeper in a miserable office was no substitute for what could have been.

To make matters worse for Langan, there was no antidote in his home for the toxicity of the workplace. His still glamorous wife, Eva, expected him to have done better by her and the children. He could sense her reproof even when she held her peace; he knew that she was disappointed in him and in her own life. Twenty-two years ago she thought she was marrying up – becoming a WAG – whereas she was actually marrying down.

Turning the key in the lock of his own front door in the evening, Langan often had the feeling he was walking into an ambush. Everyone was on one side, with him on the other. And he spent many fraught evenings under concentrated fire from the distaff side. He couldn't win for losing, and after withering remarks spread over a decade or so, he gave up trying.

By the time he was forty-three he had grown a large and growling duodenal ulcer which, thanks to advances in medical science, he was able to have treated with drugs. But he felt weary and defeated. Even his lovely daughters looked on him, not with contempt, exactly, but disappointment. He thought they probably did like him – but in the way they might care for a stray cat or a gun-shy dog with mange.

In the autumn of Langan's forty-fifth year, Staunton ramped up the humiliation. It was as if he was developing a tolerance for this particular drug and needed to increase the dosage to reach former highs. He told Langan that the external auditors had discovered serious discrepancies in his book-keeping and that a formal meeting with them would take place the following week.

Langan had a dreadful time. He knew he hadn't engaged in creative accounting or embezzlement of any kind but there was always the possibility of a sin of omission which might be misinterpreted by the auditors, who were trained to suspect the worst. It was almost impossible to keep up with accounting standards which, since the big financial crash, were being changed almost every month.

He was being turned on a slow spit, and to make matters worse, it was Eva's week to host her bridge club. He tried to keep out of the way of her bridge pals but on a couple of occasions he was caught, button-holed and ritually ribbed to the point of evisceration. Eva never defended him but laughed at all the jokes at his expense. By siding with them rather than him she was raising her own stock. He decided that fun-seeking women in groups could be a trial.

On the morning of his meeting with the auditors he spent a long time in the bathroom throwing up. Back at his desk he waited and waited. The auditors never showed. At 11.30 Staunton appeared on the floor and announced that it was all a joke but it did have the advantage of 'keeping Mr. Langan honest'. When Langan went pale and had to swallow some regurgitated bile, Staunton invited the staff to observe how difficult it was for some people to take a joke. They laughed to show that none of them fell into that category.

Langan visited his doctor later in the day; tests had come back and the prognosis wasn't good. He went to bed early that night, slept reasonably well in the circumstances and didn't wake when Eva inserted herself between the sheets. He woke early in the morning and dispensed with his customary shower. He had an errand to run.

Just before lunchtime that day Staunton again emerged from his glass box to make one of his appearances on the floor. He spoke with a few of his subordinates, dropping gems of wisdom and wit as he passed among them. A faint whiff of aniseed breath-sweetener emanated from him. As he approached Langan he inquired if he'd yet seen the humour in yesterday's joke.

"It took me a while…" Langan began.

"Well, you're not the sharpest knife in the drawer," Staunton said with a grin. There was a faint ovation from the *claqueurs* of the department.

"The problem lies elsewhere," Langan said quietly.

"Meaning?"

"Humour is not something one associates with sick pricks like you." The floor went strangely quiet; even the background murmurings faded out.

"What did … you say?" Staunton's eyes bulged.

Langan repeated himself and added, "You're just a pathetic little shit who needs the applause of the crowd." He waved his hand to include the silent sycophants, some of whom were peering through their ferns and rubber-tree plants.

Staunton drew himself up to his full height. He had an instinct that the worm had turned, that this subordinate had nothing left to lose. "You're fired, Langan. Clean out your desk and get out. Now. No references from me. No references. Do you hear?"

"I don't need any."

"You won't work again. And your wife isn't going to hang around. How does that sound…?"

"How would you know that?"

"Oh, I know. Count on it…"

Most of the onlookers said afterwards that it

was at that point or very shortly afterwards that Langan produced the gun and shot Staunton. He didn't hesitate, not for a second. He fired as soon as he produced the weapon. First, he shot him in the leg just above the knee. Then he stood over him for a long time while Staunton begged for his life. The conditioned air of the office was filled with screams and sounds of retching.

"I can't hear you," Langan said. "Louder ... speak up."

"Please ... please ... don't kill me ... I meant no harm ... Please..."

At that moment a young woman who had just started with the company came out of the rest-room and stood frozen in the middle of the floor. Then she began to moan and sway on her feet. The ululation of the on-lookers reached a crescendo when Langan shot Staunton through the head, leaving a neat round hole not much bigger than a cat's anus. From the side of his eye he spotted Joe the Hawk, feeding on a small bird on the outside ledge. He aimed the gun at him but decided not to fire. He put the gun back in the brown paper bag and addressed his colleagues of the accounts department.

"One of you will call the police and say that a thief broke in and did the shooting. If any of you tell what really happened I'll come back and kill you. I'll kill you all if I have to. Do you understand? I'll kill every last one of you. I'll kill your friends and relatives." He pulled a sheet of paper from an inside pocket and showed it to them.

It contained all their names and addresses.

The break-in was the version of events which was reported in the papers and on radio the next day. Langan, however, told Eva what had really happened. She didn't believe him at first. His daughters laughed uproariously, saying he couldn't harm a fly. They skipped out to the movies, leaving a trail of giggles behind like bubbles in a fish tank.

When Eva realised that he'd told her the truth, she threatened to turn him in. He could plead temporary insanity, throw himself on the mercy of the court.

"But what will you tell your friends? What will you live on?"

She fell into a reflective silence. Her husband the murderer. She couldn't live with that. … Maybe he could get away with it. She would have to play the odds for the moment, keep her options open.

"I want you to tell the kids. But neither you nor they are to breathe a word about it to anyone else. Is that understood?"

She looked at him as if for the first time. Diffidently she asked if there were not other witnesses.

"Yes, there are. But they won't talk."

"Why not?"

"I told them not to. I told them if anyone did talk I'd kill them, their families and friends."

"You what…?"

"You heard me. I've nothing to lose." He didn't tell her about his medical prognosis; it was none of her business. Anger was liberating. He felt exalted;

he was the hawk soaring above the city, picking out prey at will.

He spent a lot of time around the house. Eva and his daughters crept around, sneaking bewildered glances in his direction when he wasn't looking. The bridge players didn't come near the house any more. He controlled the TV zapper, and his meals were delivered on time. The quality of the cuisine had improved beyond recognition. He didn't know whether Eva or one of his daughters did the cooking but he had never tasted anything like the pot roast or the imaginative pasta dishes before. The distaff side, knowing his views on long phone calls, kept them to a minimum; even their Skype calls were little more than a brief series of hurried whispers. When his daughters promised to be home before ten at night, they erred on the side of safety.

One night Eva turned to him in bed – for the first time in almost a year – and it was clear that she was hot. There was no longer that awful smell of aniseed on her breath that used to turn him off – for obvious reasons. Her breathing and sighing were infused with a sense of shame and wantonness and she did things that she had never done before – not with him at any rate. He lay back and let her romp.

He went into the office once or twice a week, took over Staunton's glass box and arranged that two of the staff do his former work in their spare time. Thus he collected two pay cheques – one for book-keeping and a much fatter one for his new management duties. He also figured out a way of embezzling a substantial chunk of the pension fund.

The staff treated him with reverential awe and a couple of the younger ladies made it quite obvious that they were keen on him. He let them down gently and this raised his stock further. The tea-lady always brought him a special treat – a rock bun or a fairy cake. Tilly could not have been kinder and thanked him warmly when, one afternoon just after lunch, he shot Joe the Hawk as the latter set about deboning a kittiwake on the ledge. Langan was now the only high-flier in town.

The office was more efficient than ever and the workers were obliging to a fault. There was no longer any need to do those time-wasting appraisal sessions that some management guru had foisted on them a few years before. During the first few weeks of the new regime the police called frequently and Langan gave them *carte blanche* to interview anyone they wanted. They acquired no useful evidence and, as time passed, they stopped calling around. They may even have closed the case.

In autumn when the rusty wet leaves were clogging the gutters, Langan visited the clinic again and told the doctor how fit and well he felt – better than at any other stage of his life – and suggested that the previous prognosis be abandoned. The doctor hesitated for a while, then laid the X-rays aside, and did as he was told.

Hamlet the Nth

THERE WAS THE USUAL BUZZ of excited chatter in the auditorium. You'd think a large part of the audience had been let out of institutions for the evening. Maybe they had. A recorded announcement in Irish told us to 'extinguish our pocket voicers'. Then the curtain went up and the great play began. As a production it was reasonably good. At least the actors didn't carry on the props. The feigned madness of Hamlet was played up even to the extent of his donning a red nose in a couple of scenes. His mother, Gertrude, didn't know whether to laugh or cry. We were sorry to see poor Ophelia go over the edge. Frail girl. It was hard to imagine that fussy old fart, Polonius, fathering such a fine young woman.

My partner, Luna, seemed to be enjoying it, as far as my sidelong glances could establish. I gave her knee the odd squeeze to make my presence felt. For some reason I can't explain to this day, I had a feeling that something was going to happen before the end of the play. And I was right. Let me tell you about it.

It began with the sword fight towards the end of the play. Hamlet and Laertes were fencing in that choreographed theatrical way, you know, where one guy so obviously aims his weapon at the opposing weapon rather than at the man. Anyway,

Hamlet wins a hit, a palpable hit. King Claudius starts passing poisoned chalices around to all and sundry. The protagonists start dropping like flies. Horatio kneels over Hamlet, "Good night sweet Prince, and flights of angels sing thee to thy rest." Then this Norwegian dude, Fortinbras, enters and takes charge of everything even though no one has a clue who he is. There was no sign of him during the previous two hours. There was a reference to his Da, also called Fortinbras, who was apparently killed by Hamlet's Da, also called Hamlet. The play is about fathers and sons. Shakespeare's youngest son was called Hamnet; he died when he was six years old.

Suddenly, there's a shout from the audience. Luna looks at me. We both turn around. The entire audience has turned around. Fortinbras stops in mid-sentence. Then we can see a man standing up in the audience, near the back.

"No No No No! This is no good." The man says loudly.

People shush him but to no avail. Luna starts to laugh and I know why. Everyone on stage is dead or dying and no one knows or cares anything about Fortinbras. Yet the audience want to see the end of the play – as if something else is going to happen, when it's obvious that the play ended when Hamlet hit the deck.

"No, No. This is totally the wrong ending." The man repeats loudly. Even the dead Hamlet opens one eye to see what's going on and his mother Gertrude props herself up on an elbow. The loud man sidles out of his row and walks towards the stage, talking as he goes.

"Is this part of it?" Luna asks me. "Is it deliberate, I mean?"

"Well, we already had a play within a play. This would be overdoing it a tad, don't you think? But your guess is as good as mine."

Then the director of the play comes out on stage and asks the man to resume his seat and let the play conclude.

"No," the man says as he makes his way on to the stage with a vault. He has crossed the moat and breached the castle; somehow there is no longer any divide between the audience and the actors. At this point the audience doesn't want to see the end of the play at all. As I said already it was over when Hamlet went down. They want to see how all this new stuff is going to play out. It's like an encore, a little more value for their hard-earned cash. Curiosity has them in its spell.

From the stage the man faces the audience and introduces himself as Malachy, then he launches into a long argument about how plays have to adapt to the times. Security men come out and try to bundle him into the wings, but a few members of the audience call out that they want to hear his views. Malachy thanks them for their support and says that plays should be more democratic and actors and audience should interact in a more organic way. He thinks he knows how to end the play in a way which they will appreciate more. Appreciation is not the same as liking, he tells us; it goes deeper.

"You're talking about The Bard," the director says. "The Bard."

"I know," Malachy replies. "A great man. In his day. No question about it. But I can finish this play in a better way. Rhyming couplet, get it?"

The actors get involved in the argument and of course there's no point in the traditional ending now because we don't believe that any of these actors have died at all. Disbelief is not suspended any more. Actually it never really had been, the sword fight was so poorly staged, and the poison had worked so suddenly. Theatricality only goes so far. But in addition some of the actors who fell dead are now beginning to stir and gaze at the commotion.

Malachy asks the audience for permission to end the play properly and, to my astonishment, the audience, by loud applause, signals assent.

"Let him do it. Give him a chance," people call out.

Even Luna shouted up, "Yes, thrice yes."

Anyway, between the jigs and reels, the director, a well-known liberal and advocate of demotic theatre, has to let it happen. His reputation as a free spirit is on the line.

They drop the curtain for a 10-minute rehearsal and we all troop out to the bar where the buzz of chatter reaches fever pitch; it's like the chimps tea-party in the zoo. Luna doesn't think Malachy is a plant; in fact nobody does. This is the real deal. Although it's getting late no one leaves, and when the bell sounds we all troop back into the auditorium.

The curtain rises. Hamlet and Laertes are fighting. All the others are present, including Fortinbras. And there at the back of the stage is Malachy in doublet and hose. He notices Claudius poisoning the drinks and he comes forward to Fortinbras and draws his attention to it. Fortinbras draws his sword and stops Claudius in his tracks. Hamlet wounds Laertes who falls. Hamlet stands over him, hesitates, then throws away his foil.

"I cannot kill the brother of Ophelia," he says. "And I deeply regret stabbing Polonius."

Laertes gets up, bows stiffly and exits. King Claudius and Gertrude also leave. On the way out Gertrude puts her hand on Hamlet's shoulder indicating that he has done the right thing.

Hamlet then approaches Fortinbras and offers him a dagger, hilt first.

"Vengeance is not the answer," Fortinbras says.

"Even though my father killed your father?"

"Even so. We are no longer Vikings."

Revenge would go on and on without end, Hamlet says. That was why, despite his own father's bidding, he had been so reluctant to kill Claudius. His experience at Wittenberg had changed him, made him question old tribal customs. Why does any realm wish to be supreme? Wealth from the shipping tolls of Elsinore Sound should, he argues, be distributed among the people and not end up in the pockets of the nobles. The day of kings and courts has passed.

They discuss the politics of the region. Denmark had apparently conquered some land in Norway which Fortinbras doesn't really care about. They make a pact. Peace will reign. They will leave Claudius as a token presence on the throne. He is a spent force, already weakened by age.

Malachy goes to the door of the hall and admits Horatio, who announces the good news that Ophelia's suicide attempt had been foiled, that she spent some time in a convent and has been restored to health. Hamlet falls to his knees and gives thanks.

In the next scene Hamlet and Ophelia meet. He takes her hand and regrets having killed her father. She forgives him. They have a second chance, not given to many, and they resolve to make the most of it. He tells her about his mission of peace, and she too is sickened by war, religion, the mad ideas of kings and nobles while the crops wither in the fields. Change is in the air, he tells her. The influence of Luther was still everywhere in Wittenberg. The reference to Luther didn't go down well with the audience. There was a collective clearing of throats and Hamlet changed the subject from politics back to his love for Ophelia. I can see from Luna's profile that this change of tack appeals to her.

Hamlet and Horatio enlist Malachy to their cause. He is their link to the people of Denmark. It becomes clear that their mission is to cede power to the people, following the example of Pericles in ancient Greece. Laertes hears of this and reports the matter to Claudius who immediately has Hamlet arrested. He must cease his subversive activities to be freed.

Hamlet begins a hunger strike and refuses to stop, despite the entreaties of Ophelia and Horatio. Malachy sets up a people's directory which begins undermine the power of the throne. Revolution can't be ruled out. When Claudius dies it is likely the monarchy will die with him.

Unfortunately, by now Hamlet is in a very weakened condition. Ophelia visits him in the prison. I have to admit this was a very tender scene and I could also see that Luna was moved, more than that, upset. Ophelia talks of their future life together and prays for him to recover his strength. But it is not to be. Hamlet dies in Ophelia's arms. It is she who says, "Good night, sweet Prince, and flights of angels sing thee to thy rest."

I looked sideways to see big tears welling up in Luna's eyes. The ending is very sad, I have to admit, but at least Hamlet has excised the rot in the State of Denmark. His life had meaning. In my opinion this is a much better ending. The re-worked play is now a tragedy that might very well do good. By his death Hamlet has done away with old enmities and tyrants, and given power back to the people.

To my consternation, however, a voice in the audience cries out,

"No, no, no. Not acceptable … Malachy has betrayed our trust."

The voice is very close to me, and I recognise

the lilt. In a state of shock I realise it is Luna. She is on her feet, berating Malachy, whipping up the audience. I try to get her to sit down but she pushes me away.

Malachy comes to the front of the stage and says quite firmly that this is the only ending that makes sense. He is sorry that Hamlet has to die and leave Ophelia a widow. The play is a tragedy and Hollywood endings have no place in the legitimate theatre.

"That's bullshit. You're not so democratic now, are you, Malachy? Look, you had your opportunity and you blew it … You and the Patriarchy" Not only is Luna shouting but she is also shaking her fist. And the audience is behind her; she has won them over.

I tug at her skirt but I don't think she even feels it. Then she shouts out at the top of her lungs, "This ending will not do at all, and you must listen to our call."

I hide my face in my hands; it's only a play after all.

Trove

SOME OF THEM THOUGHT Joe Caulfield had gone a bit mad when he bought himself a metal detector and spent most afternoons treasure-hunting on the strand or in the fields going down to the cliffs. But he had a number of stout defenders too. Mrs. Frizelle, the grocer, argued while trying to wrap cabbages, that Joe Caulfield had worked hard all his life on that stony farm and was entitled to do whatever he wanted in his retirement. He also had to keep himself occupied since his wife passed on, although that was a good few years ago.

"True for you," one of the shoppers concurred." And he could be doing an awful lot worse. Hasn't he a daughter married in America?"

This non-sequitur was deemed to be true by the other people in the shop.

"But isn't that what I'm saying?" Mrs. Frizelle asked querulously. For some reason even when she said something that everyone seemed to agree with, there was always the suspicion at the back of her mind that they might only be trying to humour her. "Well, isn't it?" She directed this question to her husband, Tom, who was busy hauling sacks of potatoes into the storeroom at the back of the shop.

"It is." He agreed with alacrity. "Joe Caulfield is perfectly entitled to do what he likes with his free time."

Mrs. Frizelle confronted her customers. "There. You see now? He's not one bit mad." She could say it with authority because everyone knew how smart her husband was.

"We never said he was." The woman who was buying the cabbages looked at Mrs. Frizelle in some perplexity. "Those rough diamonds in the bookies may have said it but not me."

"Well, there you are then." Mrs. Frizelle folded her arms triumphantly.

That evening over tea she changed her tune, or at least conceded the other possibility.

"I wonder if maybe he has gone a bit … you know … eccentric."

"Who?" Tom Frizelle was chewing a segment of steak and kidney pie and his question dislodged a few crumbs of pastry from his mouth . With one sweeping movement his wife cleaned his mouth with a napkin and then scooped the crumbs from the table into a cupped hand.

"This is hopeless." It wasn't clear whether she was referring to her husband's table manners or Joe Caulfield's new hobby of metal-detection.

"I'd say there's all sorts of stuff under those fields," Tom said after he'd swallowed.

"Especially the ones going down to the cliffs. There's a cromlech in one of them. The ruined monastery isn't far away. And the Vikings came ashore just a little further down the coast."

Mrs. Frizelle went into a reverie; this bore thinking about. It was one thing to sympathise with a man who'd lost his wife but what if he did come across some treasure? How would the town react to that? How would she feel?

"Just suppose he did find something...?" she mused aloud.

"He'd be expected to hand it in to the National Museum," Tom said. "There's a law about that nowadays."

"Oh is there?" This put a different complexion on things. It was only right that the Government prevented individuals from becoming wealthy overnight – an occurrence that could be very disruptive in a small community. The Government was wiser, she told Tom, than she'd given them credit for.

"That's not the purpose of the law," he explained. "It's to protect any treasure that's found, and to let the National Museum show it to the people." But this law, like most others, was rarely implemented; it just made governments look good by having it on the books.

Joe Caulfield enjoyed using the metal detector. All he'd found to date were bottle caps, lids of jam-jars, bits of ploughs and harrows, tinfoil, some coins of recent vintage, one tractor seat which he kept, and several horseshoes which he nailed to the doors of his out-houses for luck. But he enjoyed walking slowly through the long grass and wild flowers of the meadows listening to the faint clicks of the detector and the slightly different clicks of grasshoppers.

It was a good summer and the sea breezes kept him cool. He sensed that people were talking about his stupid hobby and maybe they were right. But he needed something to keep busy since his wife died and since he'd rented out the farm a couple of years after that. What the neighbours didn't know was that three months ago his daughter, Maureen, had been killed in a car crash in Idaho. Her husband had seen to the arrangements. Joe just couldn't bring himself to go to America for the funeral. He was warned that it was a closed coffin. He couldn't bring himself to do much of anything except walk back and forth through the meadow grass and look out to sea, sometimes with tears in his eyes.

When Maureen was young, he and his wife would bring her to that field on a fine Sunday for a picnic, keeping well back from the cliff edge. After they had their tea and sandwiches Maureen would play on her own, knee-deep in grass, cow parsley and thrift. Maybe that's why Joe knew there was treasure there; he only had to find it again. The idea that there was an important object under the soil gave him some sort of consolation. It meant history, continuation; life went on despite everything. In a way it wasn't necessary for him to find anything – searching was enough.

Sometimes he would rest in the shadow of the cromlech, his back against one of the ancient standing stones. He didn't know what purpose this monument had served, but it was a sign that distant forebears had lived and died there. It was enough to know that much.

Occasionally he would walk towards the edge of the cliff and look down at the strand below and the spent waves of the tide moving slowly along the sand. He remembered as a boy playing among the rocks on the eastern side of the cove. The rocks seemed much further out than they used to be; that was because the sea had eroded the cliffs. He wondered if the cromlech might be in danger of falling into the sea – probably in a million years.

When he found the bible box with gold clasps and silver filigree it might have been put down to beginner's luck. On the other hand, it was just possible that Joe Caulfield had unusual instincts like those possessed by water diviners. When he brought the wondrous object back to the cottage and laid it carefully on the table he stayed up all night looking at it from every angle – this object which had been contained by the earth and which, itself, had contained the Word. It was the most beautiful thing he'd ever seen even though there was still a lot of debris on it – he had been afraid to clean it too vigorously in case it fell apart in his hands. The two women who had been the light of his life would have loved it and would have stayed up all night with him, gazing at the awe-inspiring object. It could have been a magic lamp that brought them to life, if only for a while.

A week later he ran into Tom at a cattle mart and when the business was over, he told him about his find. Tom listened carefully and then said, "It could be priceless, Joe. The Museum will only give you a tiny fraction of what it's worth."

"But it's the law, Tom. And people should see it."

"Do you think there's one politician in the country who'd hand it over? They make the law, remember ... or even a bishop for that matter? Perish the thought." Now, listen, this is what you'll do..." Tom outlined a plan which involved a dealer he knew in Dublin who was bound to have contacts in London or possibly further afield. "They'll all want a cut, but you'll be far better off at the end of the day." Tom advised him to hide the bible box in the safest place he could find; one possibility was to wrap it up carefully and bury it somewhere in one of the fields, taking care to mark the spot.

Later that evening Tom relayed the story to his wife whose eyes grew rounder as the significance of the find was brought home to her.

"When you say 'priceless', what do you mean? How much?"

Tom shrugged. "Last year a man found a small gold brooch in Wales. It went for three or four million at auction..."

"God Almighty." Mrs. Frizelle's hand flew to cover her open mouth.

"So you see..."

"He'll have to hand it over."

"What?"

"He'll have to give it to the Museum," she insisted. "It belongs to the Nation ... the people ... It belongs to us."

Tom held his head; he should have known better. She wouldn't tell all the customers, would she? If word got out the whole plan would be scuppered. The Museum would hear about it and the culture vultures would descend on the town and take possession of the box. They mightn't even pay Joe a penny.

"Don't breathe a word…"

"What do you take me for?" She turned aside as if insulted.

He wasn't convinced that she could keep a secret like this to herself, but in that same moment he had an inspiration. "There'll be a huge commission in it for us."

"What?"

"I'm like a broker, making the contacts, bringing the interested parties together, the principals, as we call them. Oh yes, there has to be commission. No doubt about it."

He scanned the headlines of the, evening paper as he sipped his tea.

"A sort of honest broker?" It was as much a prompt as a question.

"Absolutely. You've hit the nail on the head. So you see, discretion is essential. Because if word gets out there won't be a penny in it for anybody."

Mrs. Frizelle put on a wronged expression. "I wasn't going to say anything ."

"I know you weren't." It was only a white lie, he thought, happy now that the fix was in. He was fairly confident there would be no loose talk over the vegetables.

During the next few weeks Tom visited Joe Caulfield as often and as covertly as he could. They talked and made plans. He wouldn't let Joe tell him where he'd hidden the box. But they had photographs of the find which they'd dispatched to the relevant parties.

The Dublin dealer, having come in person one night to examine the box, made contact with two colleagues in London and some very big figures were being discussed. One of the London dealers had a few wealthy Irish-American clients who had expressed an interest.

"You're heading for the big-time, Joe," Tom said on one of his visits.

"Looks like it." Joe gave a wan smile. He didn't seem overjoyed, but then he didn't have much spring in his step these days. In Tom's opinion he probably spent too much time on his own up in the cliff fields. There was one day during those visits when Joe was missing. Tom searched every nook and cranny of the outbuildings but couldn't find him. What added to the mystery was that Joe offered no explanation of his whereabouts when they met the following afternoon.

But some days later the mystery was resolved. Joe had gone to Dublin and had discussions with the Keeper of Antiquities in the National Museum. He accepted the modest fee without negotiation. He wanted only one thing, that when the bible box went on display, there would be a little plaque indicating that it had been given to the museum by his wife and daughter.

He mentioned this to Tom one evening as they sat in the small flag-stoned kitchen. Tom could not conceal his disappointment; also at the back of his mind was the thought that his wife would take it out on him. At the very least she would blame him for raising her expectations. He was put out as well because Joe had not seen fit to confide in him, though he could just about understand Joe's desire to do the deed quickly – before anyone could talk him out of it.

But when Tom discovered that Joe's daughter had died so recently he began to understand, and his irritation faded away. He was sorry that his friend had chosen to cope with that tragedy on his own, and he understood why he had spent so much time alone in the fields overlooking the sea. When they parted later that night their friendship was still intact, closer than it ever had been.

Joe didn't use the metal detector much after that; there was no need to find anything else. Besides, archaeologists came down from Dublin and fenced off the site. There was a small bonus for Mrs. Frizelle – some of them stayed in her house as paying guests.

In December the Frizelles went to Dublin for Christmas shopping. During the afternoon, Tom left his wife to her own devices in Grafton Street and he called in to the National Museum. He couldn't find the bible box donated on behalf of the Caulfield women, and when he inquired, an Assistant Keeper told him that it was in storage, that only the most important objects were put on display.

He hadn't the heart to tell Joe.

It Started with a Club Selection

GROANING OVER A PLUMP midriff, Paul pulls on his golf shoes, and crampons his way over gravel towards the first tee where cameramen are lounging untidily to snap the celebrities playing in this charity golf classic. He smiles easily for the cameras and jokingly bats away questions about whether a political colleague should resign or not.

"Oh now guys, you don't really expect me to comment on that, do you? Come on, we're here today to support a really deserving charity, schizophrenia. As you know, this is a dreadful affliction…"

His wife, Maeve, a former teacher of drama and elocution, has provided him with many useful tips for dealing with the press, and indeed for other forms of social interaction which are necessary for a rapidly rising political star.

Knowing that a duffed drive on the first tee would be an embarrassment, especially with so many colour hacks present, he keeps his swing slow and smooth. The ball starts low and rises in that magical way that most golfers dream about. He could not have asked for a better start. The trajectory of the ball is exactly the path his career is on, rising, rising, straight and true, sun in front, wind behind. A ripple of spontaneous, and grudging, applause sends his four-ball on its way.

The hacks re-assemble to check out the next quartet of celebrities to mount the first tee-box.

There is some light banter between Paul and his golf partners as they walk down the velvet fairway, freshly mowed for them. He knows the others fairly well but has never met the caddy who has been assigned to him. He is of average height with a moustache; he is wearing a green boiler suit and a baseball cap pulled down over his forehead. Paul thinks he may have seen him somewhere before. He could well be from his constituency so he will make it his business to get to know him. Every vote counts and some count more than others.

For his second shot Paul chooses a four-iron. The caddy shakes his head.

"Less?"

The caddy nods. Paul selects a five-iron but the caddy shakes his head again and says, "Pin at the front. Following wind. A lot of run."

With the six-iron Paul leaves the ball three feet from the hole. Unfortunately, there are no hacks there to see it. He looks back wistfully to the first tee where they are fawning over the next group of celebrities.

"Thanks," he says to the caddy as he returns the well-chosen club to him. And that was the moment of recognition that made him question his sanity. The man posing as his caddy had appeared to him in a nightmare the previous week. He feared him then, and he fears him even more now...

Earlier that morning as the toaster popped his one slice of organic wholemeal bread, Maeve, reminded him about the speech he would be making at the party conference. It was indeed an honour to be chosen to introduce the party leader. It was a portent of his career. He wouldn't always be a junior minister but was destined for higher office, maybe even … the top job? This was Maeve's assessment, and who was he to disagree? The friends who once advised him he was overqualified for politics might well have to revise their opinion. He would leave nothing to chance with the speech, especially since the party faithful – and more importantly, the party hierarchy – would be there in droves.

On the way to the charity golf classic he relaxed in the back seat of the Mercedes and rehearsed certain phrases and rhetorical flourishes for the speech. To avoid being late and missing the photo-call on the first tee, he told his driver to use the hard shoulder as a fast lane…

Rhetoric is now far from his mind as he stares at the caddy who has removed the baseball cap. Paul would have dismissed it as a practical joke if he had not had that dream. Even so, he looks around the tree-lined fairway as if he just might see a camera or a zoom lens peeping from the foliage.

"It's not a prank."

Paul's head is full of noise like the pounding of surf. He barely hears the voices of his golf partners urging him to catch up; they are already on the green. His first instinct is to turn and follow his colleagues, hoping the spectre will disappear. But it follows him and keeps up a one-sided conversation.

"I know it's a shock, but there is no other way of doing this. You may ask why I chose you. Well, it came down to a short list of about two hundred and your name came out of the hat, as it were. We have much in common. We both lost brothers, were beaten as kids, tried to compensate by dreaming and planning, especially at night. I hope you will be able to help me."

"Please go away. You're not real. You … Hitler died at the end of the war."

"I am real, though admittedly I exist in a somewhat different plane of being."

"I thought your body was burned outside the bunker in Berlin…"

"Ah, you have read about me. Good. Incineration makes no difference to incorporeal reality…"

"Go away. I don't want to meet you or think about you." Paul breaks into a trot. It is exactly the same sort of escapist manoeuvre used to shrug off a beggar or pan-handler. Except that Hitler manages to keep up. He even stays with him on the green as

Paul sinks his putt, despite a yip-like tremor in his arms. As they walk towards the next tee-box he looks sideways, hoping that the spectral presence might have vanished. But it is still there as large as life, and it is plain to him now that his colleagues cannot see it. He's on his own with the greatest villain of the twentieth century.

"It's not so much that history has been unfair to me. It's rather that by 'balancing the copy' as it were, it will be possible to make atonement. I'm aware that most people see me as the embodiment of evil but no one really knows what evil is. If I can provide some explanation it might help politicians and churchmen the world over to apprehend how terrible deeds occur and how they can be avoided in the future, how not to do as I did."

"What has this got to do with me?"

"Christ, Paul, keep it down. I'm trying to take my shot here." The golfer who has the honour aborts his swing. "Who are you talking to anyway?"

"No one. Sorry. Go ahead."

"You have connections with the media. You belong to a republican party which originally included men like Pearse and Connolly, men who had values and could be trusted. Finally, Ireland was neutral during the war and still has credibility abroad, despite some recent scandals. There were other reasons too why your name made it into the shortlist. You are the best choice."

"With all due respect, being chosen by … you … . is hardly a ringing endorsement." Paul keeps his voice as low as possible. The conversation ceases while he addresses the ball and hits it straight down the second fairway where it runs right up to the angle of the dog-leg and gives him a straight shot to the green. Odd, that on a day like this, he is playing out of his skin.

"You should also know that we never invaded Ireland, and never intended to."

"Thanks a lot. But you bombed Fairview just because Dublin fire brigades went to help the people in Belfast."

"No, that's wrong. The Fairview bombs were a mistake. The Luftwaffe jettisoned them as they were retreating. It wasn't an act of war. And De Valera never thought it was. That's why he signed the book of condolences in the German Embassy. You probably know that the men of 1916, especially Pearse, admired the German people, and would even have accepted the Hohenzollern throne."

"You'd have treated us as an inferior race." Paul said dourly. The other golfers had gone ahead and were waving him on again.

"No. Aryan. We regarded you and the English and Scots as Aryan. You all fought well in the first war. There would have been no problem there."

"Anyway, it's all racist bullshit."

"By today's standards, yes it is. I agree with you now. But back then it was all different. We didn't even understand evolution. I regret most of what we did, what I did. The important thing I want to communicate is how to avoid becoming me. Only I can teach that lesson. And you need to understand it."

Paul raised a hand. "Sorry. I can't take any more. Please leave me alone." He grabbed the golf-bag and rushed forward to catch up with the other players.

"It's a lot to take in. I'll leave you be for now. But remember, only I can teach the world how not to be me."

With relief Paul noticed that the figure had disappeared. He caught up with the others and continued his game. He still played better than he'd ever done before and, fearing some kind of Faustian pact, tried occasionally to slice a drive or duff a chip. But nothing worked; he continued to play like a man possessed.

A couple of days later he was opening a supermarket in a western town and shortly after he'd cut the tape, his *bête noire* appeared at his side, wearing a McGee thorn-proof suit and a flat cap.

"Isn't it amazing what politicians have to do." There was a forced smile on Hitler's face that would frighten children. He didn't seem comfortable with humour. It reminded Paul of that idiotic little dance of triumph he did in the Wolf's Lair, after the fall of Belgium.

"I hope you're not making comparisons…"

The rebuke went unnoticed. "Your national poet, Mr. Yeats, described the motivation behind the rising of 1916 as an 'excess of love'."

"So what? There's no relevance…"

"Paul, who are you talking to?" His wife

extricated herself from the press melée and gave him a stern look.

"No one, Maeve."

"Well, get a move on. The mayor has invited us for lunch." She sometimes treated him as a project, a promising work-in-progress. He often felt like the fly on her coach-wheel.

"I'll come too," Hitler said. "Don't worry, I won't be intrusive. My point is this, Pearse and the other leaders loved their country in a fanatical way. I was in the same mould. Love of country is an outmoded concept today. You would be laughed at, called a romantic fool. But it was very real in the first half of the last century. Every time I saw the Rhine I felt my heart would burst. Ireland was a beautiful young woman; Germany was a father figure. All right, I didn't have the charisma of Pearse, but I was also prepared to lay down my life for my country. I wouldn't have hesitated, not for a minute. I faced death all through the first war, running between the trenches, watching my comrades being blown apart by artillery barrages. I participated in all the major offensives, Ypres, Soissons, and Reims. I should never have survived. The fact that I did survive reinforced the idea that Fate had a destiny for me. Do you doubt my sincerity?"

"I know you were awarded the Iron Cross and promoted in the field. But that is cold comfort. I don't doubt that psychopaths can appear to be brave."

"You may feel that I am insulted by that

remark. But I'm not. In fact you are very close to an important truth … But I see your wife is a little impatient. I will take my leave for now."

Driving back to Dublin after lunch, Paul closed the glass partition between himself and the driver and tried to explain to Maeve why he had seemed 'distracted' during the opening ceremony.

"You don't have to explain to me," she said glacially. "But a lot of the people there were loyal party workers and you dissed them. Look, you just can't leave anything to chance. You already have an aloof image which is not good for you. Don't you get it? This could be your year, a real turning point. Don't forget the party conference speech. That could be the game-changer…"

He listened in silence, feeling like a school-boy being specially groomed by the head teacher to sit for a scholarship exam. She was right of course but how could he explain himself to her without appearing insane? Maybe he was going mad – not just hearing voices but seeing apparitions. For now it seemed better to keep his own counsel. The phrase 'excess of love' played over in his mind. It couldn't possibly be true. If this monster appeared again he would give him a piece of his mind.

He had learnt a bit about Hitler as a young man and had come to the conclusion that, although he read a lot, his thoughts were confused. He hated Marx not just because of his Jewishness but because he predicted the withering away of the State. The Jews were stateless people who, in Hitler's mind, could not understand the idea of patriotism; they had no affiliations beyond themselves and their religion. Their role in international finance – the first form of globalisation – also undermined the idea of the nation state. So, without knowing it, the Jews were on a collision course with Hitler's core values. He couldn't conceive of existence without the Fatherland. In his mind the Jews conspired to destroy it. How could he have believed such idiocy?

And he had this weird theory of the survival of the fittest. He believed in the right of the powerful to take from the weak. He admired Britain in this respect. Those of strong will had the right to govern. Yet he hated the elitism of the Weimar republic and indeed invented his own form of socialism, national socialism rather than the democratic form. Maybe it was some kind of twisted love that drove him. But why did he assume that he was the messiah who would lead Germany to a glorious future? Was it some form of overcompensation? Or emotion – raw, primitive, unstoppable? Emotion came first. His thoughts were mere rationalisations of powerful feelings. Had he learnt that letting emotions rip made other men compliant, either because of embarrassment or for the sake of a quiet life?

"I don't know what's got into you," Maeve said when the Mercedes purred to a stop.

"Oh, just mulling things over."

"About the speech, I hope."

There was a vote in the House the following day and Paul was in his office bright and early. To while away an hour he browsed through 'Mein Kampf' just to see if he could get any insights. When the Party Whip came in to give notice about the vote, he spotted the book.

"That book should be banned," he said. "And I'm a liberal. Burn it now."

Paul wasn't sure if he was being serious or not but he closed the book and put it in a desk drawer. He felt like a teenager with a copy of Playboy. He went into the chamber to vote. Then he went out to the plinth and gave three interviews about the looming referendum on further European integration. Sometimes he felt nauseous about his ability to churn out the bromides when they were called for by the party. Occasionally, he would have liked to slip the leash, but never did so. He toed the party line. If he played ball and eventually got the top job then he could put his own stamp on things. Then he could go on solo runs. That was the theory anyway.

"You mentioned the word 'psychopath'. There was never a diagnosis but my own view is that when I got back from the first war I was very ill. Certainly shell-shocked, possibly worse. What would now be called severe post-traumatic stress disorder. There was no treatment. You were expected to get over it. I don't think I ever did. There was depression and terrible anger, misdirected anger..."

"Misdirected against the Jews?" Paul didn't like being button-holed in the corridor. He pretended to study the portrait of a former Taoiseach.

"Yes. I believed that the Jews and Marx occasioned the revolution in Russia which brought the first war to an end – a war that Germany could, and should, have won. Yes, I blamed the Jews for the destruction of the Germany I loved and wanted to die for. They refused to fight in the war and sabotaged all of us Germans who put our lives on the line. There was no greater act of betrayal. Even if the Jews had crucified Christ, that act would have paled into insignificance by comparison with what I believed they did to the Fatherland. I see now that this belief was wrong, paranoid and delusional…"

"So, you regret the Holocaust?" Paul blurted it out.

"Yes. Absolutely."

"And you condemn it?" Paul took his cue from RTÉ interviewers who, during the Peace Process, kept on putting this question to former members of the IRA.

"Yes. Absolutely. I just wish there had been someone around who could have said, 'Look, Adolf, your thinking is confused. You are suffering from acute depression and stress disorder…' But no one said that. Everyone pretended I was doing the right thing. I wanted an authority figure to guide me but they saw me as the authority figure. For me the only higher power was the Fatherland (and God to some extent) but they, unfortunately, don't give you advice."

"Why are you telling me all this?"

"I hope you might broadcast it in some shape or form."

"More propaganda?"

"No. The truth. It must be told. I can't rest. I committed the worst atrocity on the Jewish people and on other ethnic groups. And I undermined my own country for generations. None of this happened just because I was evil. I was acutely ill without anyone realising it."

"So, mad not bad. Is that what you're getting at?"

"No, both mad and bad."

"It's not going to fly." All of Paul's knowledge of the media and of public perception went into that comment. He felt sure Maeve would agree with him.

"Why do you say that?"

"Because a combination of mad and bad isn't enough. We need evil on its own." At convent school when the nuns asked Paul what the devil was called, he would answer, 'Hitler'. The nuns would say 'Lucifer 'or 'Satan', but they never said he was wrong about Hitler.

"That's very cynical if I may say so."

"It's reality. We need a back-marker. How can we know what white is unless we have black? Anyway, I'm not going to ruin my career for you. You can't even mention your name nowadays without being attacked from all sides." Paul thought of his colleagues who had accused their opponents of nazi behaviour and been severely rebuked for it. He thought of De Valera's famous saying, 'The majority is not always right.' But that was excusable given his religious conviction. God and a minority are always right. Dev, on his own, was always right.

"The thought police. I suppose I invented them in a way. Ironic isn't it…? Still, do what you can for me. I don't have anywhere else to turn."

"Why don't you try one of the Blueshirts?" Paul knew he was being disingenuous. The Blueshirts probably didn't know the first thing about fascism; it was all play-acting.

"I think you're missing the point. I now accept that fascism is a mutation. Please think about my request. I am well placed to explain how evil and insanity can harm the world. You could say I am uniquely qualified."

Paul felt a hand on his shoulder and turned around. It was the Taoiseach, who inquired about how the committee on immigration was progressing. Paul brought him up to date and admitted that the question of social integration was still causing difficulties for some members. No one wanted integration at the cost of destroying ethnic differences.

"Well, I can rely on you to achieve the best balance, Paul," the Taoiseach said. "Politics is all about finding the balance, isn't it? Anyway, you're the right man for the job. Don't forget the speech for conference, and please feel free to use my script-cooks."

"Thanks, Taoiseach. It's coming along nicely." Paul was hoping to write it himself, most of it anyway.

"By the way, you look a little tired, if you don't

mind my saying so. You should take Maeve away on a mid-term break."

"That's good advice, Taoiseach. Thank you." Paul watched the newsmen converge on his leader and swallow him up.

Maeve wanted to know why his sleep was so disturbed. She put it down to bad dreams. He didn't demur even though it was implied that bad dreams were brought on by a guilty conscience. One evening when she left him alone in the sitting room of their neo-Georgian suburban home, Hitler appeared in the armchair opposite, expressing the hope that he wasn't interrupting.

"You didn't want to die for your country after you attained power," Paul said accusingly.

"It was always a possibility though. And there were those bomb attempts which, unfortunately, made me more convinced about the rightness of what I was doing. But you're correct in the sense that I believed I could benefit my country more by being alive."

"It's easy to say that now." Paul brought the teacup to his lips, conscious of the fact that he hadn't offered a drink to his visitor, or visitant.

"If at any stage I believed I was no longer useful to the Fatherland I would have been quite happy to die. I did commit suicide after all."

"When all was lost."

"Yes."

"Anyway, being prepared to give your life doesn't excuse the unbelievable atrocities."

"No it doesn't. It simply goes to the fanatical

element. Pearse believed in blood sacrifice too. We all did. Maybe it is partly a Catholic thing. He wrote poetry. I painted. Both of us had homosexual leanings, latent ones…"

"I don't think you should drag Pearse into this," Paul interrupted sharply.

"You don't like your icons tainted." Again there was an unsuccessful, and rather painful, attempt at humour.

"Pearse would never have murdered millions of helpless people. Never, never. It would have been inconceivable."

"You're right. The Holocaust was my responsibility. I lost control … my madness … it was like hyper-inflation … numbers meant nothing. I was trapped … drowning in innocent blood … How do you control a madman who has absolute power? Checks and balances don't work … It took me years to realise that the Jews were innocent. There was no Zionist conspiracy. Marxism did not mean the withering away of the state. Socialism ultimately failed. It was all paranoia … wrong, wrong, so wrong…" His voice began to break. "I'm sorry. It's hopeless. I had one chance … It's too late now … I shouldn't have presumed to … .I won't bother you again…"

He was as good as his word and Paul was greatly relieved, though the awful experience was not expunged that quickly from his mind. There was no need to bother Maeve with any of it. The sooner he could put it behind him the better.

Working on his speech helped the process of

forgetting. He did get some help from the Taoiseach's own speech-writers, one of whom turned out to be a good phrase-maker. When the day of the party conference dawned he was as ready as he could be. He was more nervous than he could have imagined as he peered through a chink in the curtain and saw the huge hall fill up with delegates and party faithful from all parts of the country. There wasn't so much a buzz of chatter as a low roar of expectancy which grew and grew and would continue to grow. It wasn't going to be that difficult for him to build an atmosphere of welcome for the Taoiseach. The mood was already bullish.

The Taoiseach wished him well from the make-up chair, between applications of a powder puff.

"You too," Paul returned.

"Five minutes to launch," someone said.

The Party Whip led Paul out to the stage. The blast of light and sound rocked him back on his heels. It was an irresistible force-field but once he gave into it and surrendered to the energy, there was nothing to fear.

"Ladies and Gentlemen, Delegates, Party Officials. Friends, it is my great pleasure and honour this morning to introduce you to your party leader and our Taoiseach..." The applause lifted him off his feet, and he'd said nothing yet. This is what was meant by a captive audience. It was going to be a huge success. "As is the custom of this great party, my introduction will touch on some aspects of our shared political values..." A good-humoured groan went around the hall, followed by a cheer of encouragement. They would hear him out regardless of what he said. He was one of them. "The founder of our party, De Valera, established the core values, patriotism, republicanism and strong leadership. These values came seamlessly from the leaders of 1916..." He had to stop for a long time because the applause was so loud. He smiled until it subsided. Then he continued, "These values are, in many ways, similar to those of another strong leader, Adolph Hitler, who was devoted to the Fatherland..." All the jubilation disappeared and was replaced by a shocked silence like the aftermath of an explosion. Paul continued for a while on the theme of excessive love, and noticed several delegates leaving the hall. He was astonished when the Whip appeared at his side and escorted him away from the dais. Backstage he was shoved out a side door by aggressive, grim-faced people, including Maeve.

Some photographers followed him out. Attempts were made to keep them at bay.

"You don't understand..." Paul said. "He admits mistakes ... condemns them..."

"Shut up, and get in the fucking car," Maeve grated. He tried to say something to the nearest journalist. She caught him by the coat collar and shoved him head-first into the back of the Mercedes.

Junk Bonds

IT WAS THAT WARM, huggable moment towards the end of a party when the closest friends, having been given subtle signals earlier in the evening, remained behind for brandy with their hosts. They sat in a square formation in front of a log fire which the butler kept in good heart. These were the few friends who had stood by Roger Grantham and his wife, Sibyl, when they had 'their difficulties'. The fact that they'd stayed behind for this more intimate session helped to restore Roger's faith in human nature; indeed for one awful knife-edge moment he felt like crying.

This was the best welcome home he could have imagined and it reinforced his belief that he had been cruelly victimised. But it wasn't over. He knew that. "It had to do with Glasnost," Roger said, turning to Sibyl who, despite having heard this opening gambit before, gave a very sweet smile. "I was the first casualty of global peace."

There was a grain of truth in that assertion. It could, for example, be argued that in the afterglow of Glasnost the democracies of the West put on their best bib and tuckers and launched an implacable campaign against white-collar crime. The capitalist system was cleaning up its act to impress its new admirers in the Eastern Bloc. Hence the much-vaunted market mechanism was stripped down, gutted, refurbished and put back together again. The sludge and detritus of years was let flow down the gully.

Roger Grantham was a rather large clot in that sludge, though that is not quite how he perceived it himself. They got him for insider trading, cornering the market in tin futures, and various forms of stock-market manipulation, including the rigging of share values of several of his interlocking companies. He was fined two hundred million pounds – not nearly enough according to the financial press since his illicit dealings had netted him almost three times that amount. Thus, the self-righteous press, combined with the Glasnost effect, meant that Roger was not going to be allowed serve his two-year jail sentence in a comfortable open prison. No, it was going to be hard time in a nightmarish Victorian redbrick pile. And it was.

"It must have been a truly awful experience," one of the wives opined, looking to Sibyl as if she would be the better interpreter of Roger's feelings. The three women in the high-ceilinged room gave a collective shudder in the face of such unimaginable horrors and travails.

"It wasn't very pleasant," Roger answered, reaching for the decanter of Armagnac. "But, you know, human beings have an amazing ability to adapt. Homeostasis, I believe the shrinks call it."

Lying on the lower bunk, he ground his teeth between sobs, listening to the complacent snores of his cell-mate, Arthur. About a month had passed and he wasn't sure he could take it much longer, the ignominy and degradation, the insults of other inmates in the showers and exercise yard and during the morning ritual of slopping out when, more than once, he had puked into his own bucket. They exulted in his fall from grace and because, despite his legendary wealth and influence, he hadn't been able to square things. They hated him but not as much as he hated those smug City bastards who had betrayed him, howled for his blood to save their own skins. Maybe hatred could sustain him ... Arthur turned in his sleep in the upper cot and dislodged some dust which fell on to Roger's face. Was he going to masturbate? No, the snoring continued. Small mercies. But three more years of dust, shit and abuse stretched out before him. An endless stretch.

Sibyl asked the butler to bring another pot of coffee then cosied up to Roger on the couch in a proprietorial way.

"How did the other inmates ... cons treat you?" the same woman asked with a slight self-effacing grimace to apologise for yet another faux pas.

Sibyl wondered if these Freudian slips were not designed to show how completely beyond her ken the whole experience was.

"What we really want to know," her husband put in with less delicacy, "is whether they were at their wits' end, to coin a phrase."

Roger laughed and laid his balloon glass on the coffee table. "AIDs put a stop to their gallop.

Anyway, I was lucky. My cell-mate, Arthur, was a fairly harmless old bloke, and his blood-pressure medication put a crimp in his libido. He did manage to masturbate once a week, on Friday night, regular as clockwork. But that was it. There was the usual King Rat thing though … you know, the self-appointed leader of the cons. Frankie was his name. For some reason he saw me as a challenge to his leadership. So there was this confrontation on day one. He had to sort me out in front of all his henchman. Pathetic really. A trial of strength in a jungle clearing. That sort of thing. I'm sure anthropologists would have found it a dreadful cliché. He said I needn't expect any favours, that money didn't count for shit in stir, etc., etc. It kind of upset him when I said I didn't want any favours, least of all from him. It sort of threw him off balance, I think."

Frankie drew back his arm and slapped Roger across the face. It all happened so slowly Roger could easily have feinted but somehow he knew that would be the wrong thing to do. So he stood and took it. There was a calculated humiliation in the slap; it reduced him in the eyes of the spectators and symbolised his pampered existence. It was clear that he didn't rate a punch. Frankie waited. A slim man sculpted into his denims, his hair greased back in the modern style, there was no hostility in his expression but his narrow eyes calmly weighed up the effect and possible reaction. It was pure ritual. Having made sure that Roger would not even attempt to retaliate, Frankie signaled to his followers and they moved off down the metal cat-walk. Roger went back to his cell. It was almost lock-up anyway, and Arthur, who had witnessed the incident, said he had got off lightly, though there might be more to come. Roger wondered about his cell-mate. Although he looked beaten and was in poor health, there was something about him that suggested a residual capacity for playing both ends against the middle. His eyes were an older, more jaundiced version of Frankie's.

"The point is," Roger announced to his comfortably captive audience, "that Frankie had to establish his street cred. Natural really. We do it every day in boardrooms, don't we? I let him away with it of course. It was his world, not mine. I didn't have to impress any of those mouth-breathers. He was doing ten years for armed robbery and I believe his stash came to less than thirty grand. Imagine! And that impressed the hell out of his hangers-on. No, I wasn't a contender in that league. There was no point. I was more than happy to leave the field clear for him..." He stopped abruptly, conscious of becoming too defensive, of conferring too much importance on Frankie, a man he wouldn't even hire as a motorcycle courier. But deep-down he knew that Arthur was right. It wasn't over.

"I'll never forget my first visit," Sibyl said. "It really is an appalling place. And all the other wives kept looking at me. In this room painted in institutional green..."

"Well you were rather over-dressed, darling," Roger directed his smile towards her and then to the guests. He stood with his back to the fire and turned to place his glass on the Adam's mantelpiece.

She was tearful and yet somehow distant with the detachment of a volunteer prison-visitor doing her duty. He had to keep from looking at her cleavage. Did she have to dress like that? A Dior suit in ultra suede. The other wives were staring at her and several of the prisoners too. Roger didn't appreciate the attention she was getting, not out of jealousy but because it would reflect back on him later on. After the encounter with Frankie he wanted to retreat into the anonymity of the pack. Reminders of wealth and lifestyle were the last things he needed.

"Oh Roger ... seeing you here..." She dabbed her eyes with a corner of lace. "It's so unfair. You've so much more to lose than..." She looked helplessly around.

"You look good, Sibyl," he said quickly to change the subject. He wished she'd go.

"Thank you." She had acquired the habit of acknowledging compliments. In other circumstances he found it funny and fetching. "You look..." She hesitated.

"I'm O.K." He saved her further embarrassment.

"Sure?"

"Yes."

246

"Is there anything you want?"

"No." It was the most stupid question he'd ever been asked. He wanted out. He wanted to take her in the back seat of the Limo that waited outside. And he wanted revenge on his former colleagues, especially those who'd given evidence at the trial. Was there anything he wanted? Jesus Christ.

Finally he gave her some instructions for the CEOs of his companies if only to let them know he was still in charge.

"There is one other thing," he said at length. "Ask Roberts if there's any way he can get me a mobile phone."

She left shortly afterwards. The sound of her high heels tapered away just as the conversation had. He watched her until the warden closed the door behind her.

He imagined the elegant way she had, of sitting into the car, butt first, knees soldered together.

Routine and hatred kept him going and some quickly developed sense of keeping out of harm's way. He crawled into a rut and stayed there. He lost almost thirty pounds in weight mainly because he just couldn't eat the prison food and had to share out his own parcels. At night he would lie on his bunk trying to keep the bile down; he was sure there was an ulcer forming all over his stomach. The overcrowding, lack of facilities and disproportionate number or sadistic wardens demoralised even the most hardened inmates.

Half way through his first year the thought began to form in his mind that some protest was being planned. He couldn't put his finger on it, but something was afoot. Sudden silences and hastily extinguished cigarettes indicated a sullen excitement. The mood in the yard had changed from resignation to a sense of thinly repressed hope. There were nights when he felt Arthur wanted to tell him something but Roger didn't encourage him. Whatever the hell was brewing, he hoped it wouldn't involve him. He was wrong.

As if on cue, one of the guests, well-fortified with good liquor, asked, "So, come on, Rog, did anything really dramatic happen? Like a break-out or something?"

"There was going to be a protest, about the conditions," Roger answered slowly. "A violent affair with hostages and so on. The plan was well advanced … But it didn't happen…"

"Roger defused it," Sibyl put in with immaculate timing. "In fact he stopped it dead in its tracks."

In the impressed hush that followed Roger made a self-disparaging moue. What could he say?

Sibyl nodded to the butler, who began to re-charge the glasses.

"I don't want to hear about it." Roger covered his ears when Arthur finally began to unveil the plan.

"We're going up on the roof," Arthur persisted. "And you're in. Frankie said so. Something about PR."

Roger went to the farthest corner of the cell. "I'm in nothing. Nothing, you hear me?" He had visions of cons stripping slates and tiles, cameramen swarming around, Swat-teams and prison wardens bellowing through loud-hailers. He didn't want his sentence extended. And, above all, he couldn't afford to be seen demonstrating on a prison roof. Whatever credibility he had left in the City would be shot to hell.

As things stood his companies were ticking over, just about, but this would be ruinous; he would become a laughing stock from Fenchurch to Threadneedle Street. Somewhere at the back of his mind was the thought that Arthur was closer to Frankie than he'd realised.

This was partly borne out during the next exercise period when Frankie approached him, flanked by his henchmen, and said without preamble, "You're the star attraction. Grantham, the ace in the hole. The tabloids will really go for you. Rich City gent leading the protest!" Behind the patter there was real menace. It wasn't negotiable ... Or was it?

"Look, could we have a word ... in private?" Roger's legs were trembling but he somehow managed to keep his voice steady.

"You can't buy me, you bastard." Frankie read his mind. "You're going up on the roof and bare your arse to the news cameras. You're going to be the spokesman too."

To Roger's consternation, he handed him a list of grievances. "Study that."

"I ... can't..." That was as much as he got out when the short powerful jab caught him under the heart. He slumped to his knees in the dusty yard and began to retch. That was when, out of desperation, the idea came to him.

"I liked the product so I bought the company," Roger said. The reaction of his guests was not unlike that of the inmates, when Roger dragged himself to his feet and made his final, desperate proposition.

"It's true." Sibyl laughed in a way that rebutted the disbelieving honks of her guests. "Remember that privatisation was very much the thing then and even the prisons were on Thatcher's list. It was even rumoured that she and her advisors were considering selling off the police force as well."

"I became the beneficial owner all right," Roger nodded with a smile. "Never thought I'd own a prison, but there you are. I used several different companies to cover my tracks. Soon things began to improve. We sacked the more cretinous screws, improved the food, provided a proper gym and started construction work on a new wing and sick bay." He glanced around the rapt faces of his audience. This was his moment of triumph, the story of how he'd surmounted impossible odds. The faces of his listeners beamed in postural echo against the backdrop of dancing firelight and Laura Ashley upholstery. To them he was a champion, a master of the universe. Their smiles said so. In their minds he had won hands down and had the not inconsiderable satisfaction of getting his own back on the Labour government that had sent him up river in the first place. Almost.

To his amazement, Arthur cautioned him one night in the cell just before lights out. "You may own the joint, mate. But you don't run it."

"I don't follow," Roger said.

"Wait and see."

It didn't take long for Arthur's prediction to be borne out. Frankie increased the demands.

At first it was just a matter of flush-toilets and pool tables. But the more Roger delivered the more Frankie's demands grew. Ownership became a technical matter of little consequence, and Roger was fast becoming a gopher, delivering on the promises Frankie made. But he still posed a threat to Frankie's leadership and had to be shown up at every turn as the junior partner. Roger had never expected to curry favour with the prisoners (least of all male bonding, the very thought of which made him cringe) but he had expected a reasonable modus vivendi from the deal, and not even that was going to materialise. Frankie lost no opportunity to flaunt his new-found leverage, vicarious as it was powerful, and Roger's brilliant coup blew up in his face. Ownership had bought him very little.

When Roger heard from the Governor that he was up for release in a fortnight's time – his sentence was commuted by six months – his first instinct was to keep the news to himself. Despite everything he'd done for the inmates he was still an outsider. Nothing would change that.

"What an amazing coup, Roger," the most sober of the guests remarked, "It was a stroke of genius to buy the damn place. I imagine it made the rest of your sent ... stay far more comfortable."

"It didn't hurt ... Not my most profitable venture, however," Roger demurred with a smile.

"No, I reckon not," one of the husbands opined. "You probably had to spend a fortune on improvements to the prison. You would have to sell a lot of mail-bags to break even! What now? I presume you're going to sell the prison. It's served its purpose. Actually, in this property market, the land value alone would be considerable. I'd asset strip the damn thing if I were you."

"We'll see," Roger said. That had been his intention too. He owed them nothing.

Perhaps he'd spoken in his sleep or else Arthur had a contact in the Governor's office. In any event the news of Roger's imminent release reached Frankie, who paid him a visit on the landing one night before lock-up.

"Let's keep in touch," Frankie said, nodding to Arthur who passed him the mobile phone which he'd somehow ferreted out from its hiding place. "It wouldn't do to dissolve such a good partnership."

"I thought we could part on good terms," Roger said uneasily. He wanted to get out of the prison business in every sense.

"I'm not a fool. You're not one of us. Don't

even think of selling up. We'll be in touch." Frankie let his jacket fall open, revealing a shiv in his waistband.

"We have contacts on the outside too. You're in the prison business for the long haul. Get it? We can get in touch with you and your family whenever we like." He put the phone inside his jacket and turned away.

Roger had difficulty breathing. This was not the freedom he'd dreamt of. Even as he was being released the trap was sprung tighter than ever. Despite his puny stash of money, Frankie's writ ran further because he was prepared to deal in ultimate things, use force that went way beyond that of the free market. By comparison, Roger's assets and contacts were junk, paper claims and useless scrip.

Roger's guests were in no doubt as to what his next move should be. Buying the prison had served his purpose; now he should sell it off, lock, stock and barrel.

So Roger, with a false smile, faced his friends in his comfortable home. Not one of them would be capable of understanding how wealth and financial power could be so easily neutralised.

"We'll see." There was nothing else he could say.

The Brexit Research Team

THERE WAS A STATIONERY press near Alfie Toner's desk. The press catered to all his stationery needs, jotters, foolscap, notepaper, pens and pencils, staplers, paperclips, Scotch tape. Whenever he opened the door of the press he got the smell of freshly sharpened pencils; the smell brought him winging back over the decades to his school days, and he was fearful all over again.

Ms Johnson sat some distance away – her desk an oasis, surrounded by carefully tended plants. Her hobby was indoor gardening; the plants also gave her the privacy she needed and screened her from the impertinent window-cleaner who sometimes gestured at her through the glass. Ms Johnson was responsible for keeping the stationery press stocked. She bought the supplies in bulk and made sure they never ran out of any particular item. She often wore a pencil in her bun and it intrigued Alfie because he never knew for sure whether the pencil was merely an ornament or whether it had some structural function in maintaining the integrity of the hair-do.

Alfie thought that on the whole she did a reasonable job. Whenever he went to the press he invariably got what he wanted, a spiral-bound notebook or a paper punch or some Treasury tags. There was, however, one problem and it had bothered him for at least thirty years: the brown business envelopes were sub-standard, possibly rejects. The flaps did not stick. Some canny supplier had been ripping them off for the last thirty years and Ms Johnson obviously had not been aware of the fact. He did not suspect for one moment that she was in league with the suppliers; she was an honest woman but unfortunately not a very efficient officer, despite what others thought of her. Maybe she spent too much time on her indoor plants which, he couldn't help noticing, had colonised a large part of the open-plan office space.

He had spent a not inconsiderable part of his working life licking the gummy side of envelope flaps, closing them over and applying pressure so as to form a seal. On every single occasion he would watch with sinking heart the flap begin to crinkle as air pockets formed, slowly delaminate, then spring back to the unstuck position. The gum or mucilage was clearly defective, probably dried out. Scotch tape was always required to seal the envelopes properly. Over his working life he had used miles of Scotch tape and had probably spent up to six months applying the damn stuff.

The size of the envelope didn't matter, nor did it matter which part of the stationery press he drew from. The flaps did not stick. Ever. Not once in three decades. Every time he watched a flap slowly open after he removed his thumb, he took it personally and, shameful though it undoubtedly was, he harboured a little ill-will towards Ms Johnson. Why was she so stupid that she allowed herself to be conned by the suppliers of such shoddy merchandise? Did she really think she was providing a good service? Every time a rising flap snapped at his senses he criticised the prim Ms Johnson under his breath. It was intolerable, especially now when they'd been assigned to a major new task, one of national importance.

Over three decades he hadn't mentioned anything in case it might upset her; it was not his job in any case. But she should have figured it out herself. Had she never used an envelope? Of course she had. Therefore, it followed that she had to know about the problem, yet during all those years during which his and her hair had grown white, she had done absolutely nothing about it.

He was always polite when he passed her in the office but he refused to socialise or make small talk. Apart from his normal reserve, it was very difficult to make the effort for a person who had been providing non-stick envelopes for one third of a century.

As he approached retirement, however, he decided to tell her for once and all. He owed her that much. His successor might not be as tolerant as he was. The night before the day he was going to tell her, he didn't sleep very well and he spent hours rehearsing different opening gambits. When morning came the bedclothes were as bedraggled as he felt.

Shortly after the eleven o' clock tea break he decided to take the plunge. The window-cleaner had waved through the glass at him and he took that as a good omen; in seventeen years he had never acknowledged his presence before. He padded towards Ms Johnson's desk. She was half hidden by an aspidistra but he could see that she was on the phone. He would have to wait until she hung up, and he did so by pretending to read the document he had taken with him to give himself a countenance. His pulse started to beat faster the closer he got to her desk. In his peripheral vision he detected signs of movement and assumed that they were being made by the window-cleaner.

"Ms Johnson, I often intended to mention … something … but it slipped my mind…" Maybe something like that would do the trick, but, God, suppose she threw a wobbly? Suppose she cried? Some degree of circumlocution was required.

"Em, you know the stationery press … I've often thought…" No. That wouldn't do at all. The stationery press was her life; if he mentioned that up front she might become very emotional indeed.

"Ms Johnson, you and I have known each other for a long time … We have soldiered here together all those years and I think the time has come…" Christ, what was he thinking of? She might take that as a proposal of marriage. Just be natural. "Look, Ms Johnson, those envelopes won't do. Don't misunderstand me. I don't mind … but other people … you know…" Yes, that was more promising.

He peered through the aspidistra. She'd hung up the phone but was doing something else. What? She had just folded a sheet of paper, a letter, and slipped it into one of her brown envelopes. This should be interesting, he thought, moving closer to get a better view of the sealing procedure. He watched as she turned over the flap and ran her thumb along it, applying a certain degree of pressure. He wondered what her reaction would be when the flap sprang up again. But to his amazement that did not happen. When she removed her thumb the flap stayed down. It stayed down. He couldn't believe it. She had achieved an immediate seal.

His mind raced, skipped across several possibilities like a stone skimming the sea. Had she singled him out for the dud envelopes? Did everyone else get the good ones? Maybe he was being paranoid but how else could it be explained? He waited and watched as she slipped another letter into another envelope. Again, to his consternation, the flap stayed down. The seal was effected immediately and with minimal pressure.

As he rushed back to his own desk he thought the top of his head would lift with the pain. Beginning to doubt the evidence of a lifetime, he picked out envelopes of different shapes and sizes and experimented furiously, vaguely conscious of the window-cleaner who grinned in at him. None of the flaps stayed down. Not one. They sprang up again cheekily, regardless of the amount of pressure he had applied. At least he wasn't losing his mind, but that was cold comfort.

For the rest of the day he was in a torment and couldn't do his work. He worried over the conundrum all the way home on the bus that evening. Surely he wasn't being discriminated against? Was it possible that there were two stationery presses and that he had been using the one with the old stock? If that was the case why had nobody told him, why had Ms Johnson not told him? Was it because, close to retirement, he was regarded as yesterday's man? These and other questions dogged him all evening as he pushed away his pre-packaged meal and switched off the TV. Later, he fell into a fitful sleep and dreamt of hinged planes that refused to lie flat.

The next morning he left his desk and began the voyage towards Ms Johnson's oasis, stalking her behind a tangle of fig, rubber tree and aspidistra. He had no choice now; his peace of mind depended on confronting her and finding out the truth of the matter, even if it reflected badly on him. A sudden movement caught his attention. It wasn't the normal circular arm movement of the window-cleaner but a series of sharp, jerky gestures. Alfie paused in mid-prowl. The window-cleaner who was there again that day, was also mouthing words which could not be heard through the glass. He was beckoning Alfie closer. Then he mimed at him to release the catch on the window. Maybe he was in trouble on the ledge. Alfie undid the latch and the cleaner stepped through the window into the office. It didn't seem as if he had been in danger on the ledge outside.

"Well," Alfie demanded, "What is it? We're

very busy here in this office."

"Oh yeah?" The window-cleaner said with a grin.

"We're engaged on work of National, indeed global, importance. So yes, I'm a very busy man."

"And I'm Bill Gates."

"Who?"

"Never mind. Look, it's about those bloody envelopes. Enough is enough. I can't take any more."

Alfie went on tilt, pulled himself up to his full height, straightening out his scholar's stoop. "What on earth do you mean?"

The window-cleaner told him that he'd been observing the charade on and off for fifteen years and he had had it up to a point at roughly the same level as his forehead. Nor could he figure out why Alfie had never asked Ms Johnson about the damn envelopes.

Alfie bridled and pointed out that this was an 'internal office' matter that would be dealt with in the fullness of time. He was offended by the intrusion from outside, but also astounded by the window-cleaner's powers of observation.

"Is there a second press?" Alfie bit his tongue. He shouldn't have let himself down by asking that.

"No, I don't think so," the window-cleaner said. "That's not the problem." He waited and grinned, waving his chamois back and forth.

Alfie didn't want to concede that there was a problem; it was none of the other man's business. But, damn it all, he had to know. He threw back his narrow shoulders and asked for help. "So, what is the problem?"

"Your problem is spit…"

"I beg your pardon."

"Spit." The window-cleaner mimed a few dry hawks in the direction of his cloth and went on to explain at some length that the technology of mucilage had changed radically years ago. It was no longer necessary to lick envelopes; in fact moisture made matters worse. When Alfie watched Ms Johnson through the aspidistra had he not noticed that she refrained from licking the flaps?

"Nowadays," the cleaner said, "it's a dry seal. Everyone knows that."

"A dry seal," Alfie repeated numbly. His face was burning. No one had told him about that break-through in gum technology, nor had any memo been posted on the bulletin board to that effect. He grabbed an envelope from the nearest desk and was astounded by the efficiency of the unwet mucilage. Maybe it was a fluke, but he grudgingly thanked the window-cleaner who, before going back to his ledge, advised that the codology with the envelopes be stopped forthwith and that no more Scotch tape be used.

Alfie rushed back to his desk and pulled out an envelope at random to double-check the experiment. Without licking it, he pressed down the flap. It stuck on the first attempt. It stuck. With minimal pressure it stayed down. The dry seal had been effected in one slick movement. He was conscious of the window-cleaner's thumbs-up sign outside the glass but chose to ignore it.

He opened a drawer and pulled out a sheet of notepaper. Although the prospect of retirement was not very appealing he knew that the time had come.

Fadings

AFTER HER SECOND CUP of tea Cynthia O'Reilly gave her husband a peck on the cheek and went out to her car. To her amazement the car was covered in thick reddish-brown stains like small over-cooked pancakes. She stood for a long time trying to figure out what might have happened. Tentatively, using an index finger, she was relieved to find that the splodges came off and that her lunar green metallic paint-work would not be damaged. She held the finger to her nose but there was no discernible smell.

She noticed the same rash of stains on the concrete driveway and – across the hedge – on her neighbour's car. What on earth had happened? God forbid it was airborne waste from Sellafield? The sense of puzzlement contained more than a seed of anxiety. She looked up at the sky which seemed perfectly normal for a spring morning; indeed she heard skylarks singing.

On the way to work she observed that most of the traffic was mottled with the same sort of red-brown lichens. Other drivers seemed equally puzzled. At a set of traffic lights on the Merrion Road she wound down the window and asked her neighbouring road-user if she had any explanation.

"I've no idea." she said with an apologetic shrug. "It's extraordinary … Maybe it's something to do with aliens?" she added unhelpfully before revving up when the lights changed.

When Cynthia was young, a morbilliform rash had appeared on her body one morning. The doctor put it down to teenage angst and didn't prescribe anything; a few days later the tiny lesions had all disappeared. Could an entire city or country develop a rash? What the hell was going on?

When she got to the lobby of her office building the receptionist greeted her with a smile which seemed a little more restrained than usual. Cynthia was on the point of asking her about the extraordinary epidemic of liver spots when she cut in,

"Isn't it awful about Jack?" With barely a pause she went on "He died in his sleep on Saturday morning. His remains have gone to the church already."

"Jack," Cynthia repeated.

"And he seemed fine on Friday. Worked his full shift on the shop floor. Was in great form apparently. It's a terrible shock for all of us."

"It certainly is," Cynthia mumbled. "Awful." She stepped into the elevator. She knew most of the staff who worked on the floor, at least to see, but she wasn't good with names. Which one was Jack? Which one had been Jack?

On the fifth floor a woman from Personnel got in.

"Sad news." She looked dolefully down at her shoes.

"Terrible."

"He was so full of life … always smiling…"

Cynthia nodded.

"And he loved practical jokes."

"Yes." She decided to take a risk. "And at such a … young age…"

"Well, he wasn't all that young." The woman looked curiously at her.

"No. But nowadays … you know. The floor won't be the same."

"No. It certainly won't."

When she got to her desk she took the newspaper from her briefcase and turned to the obituary page. But she realised immediately that she didn't have the surname. Then it occurred to her that the surname might not mean anything to her either.

She tried to get on with her work but the matter kept niggling at her. Faces of colleagues swam into her consciousness. Which one was Jack's face? She must have known him to see. Several faces came to her, but she was almost certain that Jack's face wasn't among them.

She was relieved when the production manager stuck his head around the door.

"Come in, Tom. Pull up a pew."

After a sympathetic exchange about Jack they turned to business. "One of the lines is down," Tom said.

"Maintenance…?"

"Yeah, they're looking at it. They reckon we won't be back to full production until tomorrow afternoon." Tom wore a long-suffering expression.

"They just love to milk these situations."

"Well, inventories aren't too bad at the moment," Cynthia said. "But don't tell them that. Maybe we could fit in an extra shift later in the week to catch up."

"It's possible, I suppose."

She changed tack. "Listen … about Jack…"

"We're all devastated…?"

She decided to come clean. She could confide in Tom. "I'm drawing a blank. I'm sure I knew him … but right now for some reason … I just can't place him…" She leant forward across the desk, aware of the fact that her voice had dropped to a lower, almost conspiratorial, register.

"Jack Cremmins. You know … the live wire. Reddish hair, average height … He nearly always wore those faded jeans…"

"Oh, and a moustache?"

"No. Clean-shaven. He had a sort of ruddy complexion. "

"A bit overweight? Cynthia raised her eyebrows in hopeful anticipation.

"Thin as a lath."

"Jesus, I just can't place him, Tom. Don't tell anyone for God's sake."

Tom told her not to worry about it. As he was leaving the office, he said he'd probably see her later at the funeral.

"Oh … yes. The funeral…" Cynthia quickly scanned her diary. She would have to attend. After Tom left she looked up the Cremmin's funeral notice. Mass at eleven, then the cemetery. The usual drill. But there wasn't much time.

She rang Personnel, then went down to the shop floor, ostensibly to have a word with the foreman who said that if a line had to go down, now was as good a time as any. Because of Jack's death no one was at the top of their form. Cynthia noticed several workers standing around chatting, not even making a pretence of work despite the presence of the foreman and herself.

"Remind me where Jack worked," Cynthia said.

The foreman pointed towards the end of the line, just in front of the packaging section.

"Oh yes, quality control," Cynthia dissembled, feeling such a fraud. A young girl in white overalls stood there now, just in front of the framed colour print of a model pizza, against which the pizzas that travelled along the conveyor belt were to be judged. Cynthia couldn't help noticing that she junked about one in eight. She wondered if Jack had been so meticulous or whether the new girl was overdoing it. For the life of her she could not summon up a picture of the man who had stood in that spot for fifteen odd years, junking sub-standard pizzas. She had a sudden vision of a face which might have been the one, but it evaporated as quickly as it had come, and, try as she might, she could not call it back. Why was it so important to her? If she couldn't recall the face, then she couldn't remember the person, and then she couldn't grieve properly. Was that it? Or maybe she would be haunted for years and then wake up one morning and be confronted by the face of the ghost, when she least expected it. Was that it, some loss of power or of closure? Or maybe it was simply a question of respect.

She let her eyes wander all over the floor, looking at the men and women in their white overalls and caps. She hoped that, by some process of elimination, she might be able to establish Jack's identity. She knew almost all of the faces, but which one was missing? She began to realise how difficult it was to perceive absence. She felt bad. A man had stood at that spot for fifteen years doing a menial job, had somehow managed to keep his spirits up, as well as those of his co-workers, and she, Cynthia, could not recall who he was. And she had always prided herself on being a good people-person.

Jack's personal file was on her desk when she got back. It contained a brief CV, a couple of references from previous employers, and an attendance record. There was also a copy of a memo reprimanding him for a practical joke which had backfired, resulting in the loss of an hour's production. A fake rat had apparently so shocked one of the ladies in the pie-crust section that she had to be sent home in a taxi. Cynthia closed the file. There was no photograph.

At the funeral mass, she went to the front of the church. The coffin was closed. She knelt in the pew behind the family members. She had certainly never met the widow, not even at Christmas parties. There were two middle-aged men with reddish hair, probably Jack's brothers. Both of them did readings from the altar. She studied their faces minutely as they read, but they didn't put her in mind of anyone in particular. She found herself staring at the coffin, wondering who exactly lay inside the highly polished oak.

She tried to put his face together, feature by feature, nose, eyes, mouth. But no combination fused into a recognisable whole. Maybe there were no distinguishing features as such. She tried a gestalt, top-down approach, an overall impression of the facial expression, but that didn't work either.

In the funeral procession to the cemetery she noticed how most of the cars were marked by that strange brown substance. The hearse was an obvious exception; it had probably been washed earlier that morning.

At they stood around the open grave Cynthia felt a stirring of memory. A blurred face began to rise up before her. When the mourners threw fistfuls of clay into the grave, they landed on the coffin lid like the red-brown marks she had seen that morning. The strange similarity banished the facial image from her mind.

Afterwards, Cynthia offered her condolences to the widow and explained who she was.

"Jack mentioned you often," The widow said. Although her face was tear-stained she was quite controlled, even to the point of putting other people at their ease. "He liked you."

"Me too," Cynthia said miserably. "We were all very fond of Jack." She felt such a hypocrite. She hoped she would invite her back to the house. There would be family photographs, other memorabilia … But she didn't get an invitation, and she couldn't very well just turn up on the doorstep.

That evening, stuck in traffic, she noticed that the cars and trucks were cleaner than they had been that morning. Many had obviously been washed during the day or the stains had just faded away. Others, including her own, had had the benefit of an April shower at about 5:30 p.m. The rain had at least blurred the splodges which, she learned from the car radio, had been caused by a combination of freak winds and a sandstorm in the Sahara. The other mystery was likely to haunt her forever.

Lifelines

IT WAS ALMOST two years after his mother's death before Sam could bring himself to go through her personal papers. He'd had a few drinks after the Saturday match and sat in the kitchen, an autumn rain trickling down the window. His wife was at the shops and had brought the kids with her, so he had the house to himself. With some trepidation he opened the biscuit tin and rummaged through the yellowing papers, mostly letters, old school reports, birth certificates, even a few locks of hair and baby teeth in brown envelopes. He did a quick inventory first to get an overview and flicked out a small surprised spider. Among the dusty memorabilia a newspaper cutting caught his eye, a letter to the Evening Press. He started to read:

'Dear Sir,

Last Sunday night a boy fell into the canal at Leeson Street Bridge. A young man passing by gave assistance...'

Sam's breath quickened: it had been all of twenty years ago and she'd kept the cutting all that time. Details crowded in on him.

It had been a filthy night after a leaden day that

never let up. He'd been walking down Leeson Street to meet his friends in the local, the hood of his duffel coat pulled tightly over his head. The street was black and deserted, and a north wind drove the rain through the dying elms along the canal. The sodium street lights could barely penetrate the blackness and served only to confirm the relentless downpour. He thought he heard a cry, faintly through the wind.

"… Mister, help…"

Sam walked on faster, over the hump of the bridge. It was probably nothing, just a trick of the wind, distorted by the damp hood of his coat. But why had his pulse begun to race? Already he could see the welcoming lights of the pub at the end of the street. Five more minutes at most. Then he could disremember in peace…

"Please … Mister…"

He couldn't have heard anything. Who would be out on a night like that? Certainly not children … Wait, how did he know it was a child's voice? He slowed, stood in a doorway. Why him? He'd never learnt to swim because he was scared of the water. So he also knew there was water involved. Two minutes earlier he'd have been safely over the bridge, well out of earshot and now, because of a few words on the wind, he was caught. He looked up and down the street but there was no one else in sight, not a sinner to share the responsibility with. It was his call, his alone.

He made a sudden effort to walk on. Then stopped. He imagined reading about a tragedy in the next day's papers … No one else would know of course, but he would know. He turned and went slowly back to the bridge, his mind and heart racing.

Through the darkness he saw the scared white face of a child on the towpath.

"…Me brother, mister…" A shaking finger pointed into the black water of the lock. Sam crept towards the granite edge and peered down to see a struggling figure trying to find a hand-hold on the slimy surface of the lock gate. The face looked up terrified and ashen in the driving rain.

"I'm … slipping…"

"Hold on" Sam's voice choked on his own fear. The water was black and deep and was surrounded on all sides by sheer slimy walls. It was a rat-trap perfectly engineered for drowning; even if he could swim there would be no way out.

Trembling, and not knowing what he could do or where he was being led, Sam crawled along the wooden beams of the lock gate, inching his way across the splintered timbers. Out of the corner of his eye he saw a mongrel dog swimming in circles in the lock. The kid had probably gone in to save the damn dog which was paddling away to its heart's content.

When he reached the middle of the gate he stretched down as far as he dared. It was no use. There was at least seven feet between him and the boy who, just at that moment, made a sudden panicky movement.

"Don't reach up! Hold on tight." Sam was

afraid that if the boy let go of the slimy timbers and fell back in, it would be all over. He straddled the top beam and struggled to take off the duffel coat which was heavy and sodden with rain. He lowered it down but it didn't reach.

"I'm ... slipping." Another desperate plea from the small pinched face.

"Hang on. I'm coming down." Sam had to sound confident but he wasn't sure how much lower he could get. He studied the iron locking mechanism of the gates and began a slow descent using the rusted treads of the vertical bolts as toe-holds. His hands were wet and almost frozen and he couldn't control the trembling in his legs. He moved an inch at a time, not knowing where the next second would lead, or what the outcome would be. He got as far as he could but it wasn't far enough. Holding on with one hand, he lowered the coat with the other; it didn't quite reach. He was about to pull it up again when, out of desperation, the boy jumped. He managed to grab the hem of the coat.

Sam wasn't sure if he had the strength to pull him up. And if he tried there was the terrifying prospect that the boy might fall back in. The best he could do was hold the coat and keep the boy's head above water. Sam was now well and truly caught, the only link in a pitifully weak chain. How long could he sustain this life-line? He called out to the boy's brother on the bank.

"Call the fire brigade. Hurry!" Why hadn't he thought of that before?

"Don't know how to…"

"The house behind the towpath. Tell them to dial 999. Hurry!"

The boy ran off while Sam stayed pinioned on the gate. By now the rain had soaked him right through to the skin but that was the least of his worries. How long would it take the fire brigade to arrive? At least fifteen minutes, maybe more. Already his strength was ebbing. He tried to tighten his grip on the metal strut and felt sharp fragments of rust eating into his fingers. Should he tell the boy to climb up the coat? Too dangerous. If he slipped back … He had a vision of the black water closing over the frightened face. He heard whimpering from below. It sounded like the dog but wasn't; the dog was still having fun, trying to bite the floating end of his leash.

"It won't be long now," Sam called out in a strained voice. "You're OK … Just keep holding on to the coat…" If only he could believe it himself. Maybe he'd made matters worse. Somehow he would have to ignore the pain that was spreading to his shoulders, put it out of his mind. Substitute something else, anything.

A few moments earlier his only concern in the world was how he'd slip into the house after closing time without his mother noticing drink on him. She still tried to keep him on a tight rein. She had given him money to buy himself a good winter overcoat and he'd got this cheap army-surplus duffel coat instead. More money for pints. How firmly was the hood stitched to the collar? Don't think about that

… His adult life beginning, after years of reluctant study. And a few job interviews. One chapter closing, another about to begin, not sure of the link between them. As he straddled some kind of threshold like the lock gates … Christ, the pain, flaring now … Driving out all other thoughts and senses.

The woman from the nearby house appeared on the towpath.

"The fire brigade's on its way," she called out. The welcome news oddly made him even more aware of the pain.

"I can't hold on … much longer…" He had to make this confession, but what could she do about it?

"What about the life-belt?"

"The what?" He doubted his ears. Maybe the wind again …

"There's a life-belt on the bridge. The other side of the street."

"Get it. Fast. Please!" It hadn't dawned on him. How many times had he passed over that bridge without noticing? He got a last spurt of strength and prayed that the life-belt hadn't been stolen or vandalised. This was the very last chance. The time that passed before the woman returned was immeasurable. Then, suddenly, there she was, life-belt in hand, to his undying relief. But now there was a new set of calculations to be done.

Sam didn't have a free hand to catch the rope, even if the woman could be trusted to throw it accurately.

"Tie the end of the rope to the bollard behind you." He watched as she went about the task.

"Another knot," he called out. He wasn't going to leave anything to chance, not now. "OK. Now throw the belt as close to him as you can." This too was risky but then so was everything. He saw the splash; the belt had not gone out far enough.

"Throw it past him. Then pull it towards him." By now he could see that she was quite elderly; would she be able to throw it that far?

The woman walked as close to the edge as she dared but she was standing on the rope when she released the belt and it went nowhere.

"Try again."

This time it went better. The boy made a sudden movement to grab it. Sam almost lost his hold on the coat.

"No, not yet," he yelled down. To the woman, "Now pull it gently towards him." Sam's heart leapt in his chest. They were on the home stretch; it was going to work. The boy relinquished his hold on the coat and grabbed the life-belt.

"Put your arms through it." Sam waited until that was done. His breath was easier or at least he was conscious of being able to breathe. He was also aware that it was his own sweat rather than the rain that soaked his body. He yanked up the redundant coat and flung it over the lock gate, using his free hand to double his hold on the iron strut. The woman kept a tension on the rope while he crawled towards the bank, dragging the sodden coat behind him. The sensation of solid ground beneath his feet was a gift from God. Taking the rope from the woman's hands he began to pull the boy towards the wall.

"No … wait." Was this the same voice that verged on hysteria just moments ago?

"What?"

"I have to get the dog."

"Fuck the dog." Sam couldn't believe his ears.

"No." With renewed confidence, the boy splashed his way towards the mongrel.

Sam had no option but to pay out the rope. The boy caught the floating leash and pulled the dog towards him. Sam then pulled them both towards the wall. With his two hands free he felt sure he had the strength to hoist them both up. His only worry was whether the rope would hold; he hadn't been able to see how the belt was tied to the rope or how sound the connection was.

He started the vertical pull gingerly, bracing himself against the bollard. So far so good; the rope held. After every two feet or so, he looped the same length of rope around the bollard. Having got this far he wasn't going to allow any slippage. As his confidence grew he didn't have to tie off the rope so frequently and sometime later the boy and the mongrel were shivering beside him on the bank.

"Thanks, mister."

"OK. I suppose you went in after the dog," Sam said as evenly as he could manage though his heart quivered with relief. And gratitude for having been saved from a guilt-ridden future.

"Yeah."

The woman came forward and fussed over them. "Come into the house for a cup of tea. You're all soaking." She gathered up the two boys and the dog.

"I'll just put this back first." Sam indicated the life-belt. He crossed the bridge and replaced the belt in its wooden shrine, coiling the rope properly. His legs were still trembling. He thought of the fire brigade that would arrive at any moment. It would be idiotic now to hang around for that, embarrassing even. He decided to forgo the offer of tea and bent forward into the gale towards the pub. He had never needed a drink so badly.

His eyes went back to the letter the woman had sent to the paper and which his mother had kept all those years.

'... The young man disappeared before the fire brigade arrived. I am writing this letter because I am sure the parents of the boy would like to thank the unknown young man who helped save their son.

Yours, etc.

(Mrs.) Molly Frizell.'

As Sam put the cutting back in the biscuit tin, a quirky thought occurred to him for the first time. Even if the parents of the boy had read that letter in the paper it probably meant nothing to them because it was more than likely that when the two young scamps went home that night with their dog – having been dried and fed by the kindly woman – they said nothing about the incident. So who was the letter for? Yet there it was, a record of sorts.

It was, he supposed, as close to a heroic act as he was ever likely to get. Despite his fear he had somehow managed to do the right thing. He hadn't dined out on the story exactly; his recall of fear was too acute for that. He had given his mother a slightly diluted version, so as not to worry her – he had simply gone for the life-belt and thrown it in. What really impressed her was that he hadn't given his name to anyone, but then he hadn't mentioned the fire brigade or the potential embarrassment. Had it arrived at all?

To his pals he was off-hand and cool – "Fished this kid out of the canal. Big deal…"

Much later when he had children of his own he told them of his fear, how his first instinct was to walk away and pretend he hadn't heard the cry for help. He didn't want his suggestible kids to ape any imagined heroics. They were a bit disappointed in him of course; so his reward finally was as modest as his achievement.

One thing he could never get out of his mind was the image of himself spread-eagled on the lock gates for what seemed like an eternity as he held the metal strut with one hand and the coat with the other, not knowing what the next second would bring. He could not express what the image meant to him but it stayed with him over the years.

He rummaged some more in the biscuit tin and found a letter from his Aunt Rita to his mother:

"... you must be so proud of Sam, saving that boy's life ... and not even giving his name. He reflects well on you ... You raised him well..."

So his mother had her version too, bless her heart, and she had certainly done her best to raise him. That much was certain, but there were other areas and other issues which were more complex, subject to different versions and interpretations. The contents of the biscuit tin were unlikely to give firm answers. The pieces of faded paper were no more than belated clues to what remained awkward and private, beyond the scope of language. He replaced the papers and closed the tin. He put on the kettle, switched on the TV and waited for his family to return from the shops.

Final Fling

LIKE HIS HOME in suburbia, Larry has settled in his foundations. At forty-seven his ambitions have descended gently to the level of his abilities. He is a good actuary who can quickly calculate the life span of the average client. Averages are his stock-in-trade; extremes make him uncomfortable. His last attempt at promotion won him praise for reliability, a resounding silence on the question of initiative, and considerable harrumphing with regard to decision-making. He has now resolved not to throw his hat in the ring again; it is much too unsettling. He has an index-linked pension to look forward to and a further 24.3 years with his family.

"'Bye, Dad." His oldest boy, Lawrence, leaves the breakfast table to go to school.

"Work hard," Larry mumbles, his liberal mouth full of toast. He looks at his son. It's a surprise to see him almost filling the doorway.

His wife, Sue, sees Lawrence to the porch, her hand on his shoulder. "I'll pick you up at four. Have you got your gym stuff? And don't overdo it. If you feel a wheeze coming on use your inhaler."

Larry heaves himself from the table and collects his briefcase which contains only sandwiches; the upwardly immobile don't bring work home any more. But he doesn't escape that easily.

"Don't forget your mother is coming for

dinner," Sue says. "Could you pick up some coleslaw in the deli near your office?"

"Sure thing." Larry has a pang of conscience. He will really have to persuade his mother to come live with them. At seventy-nine she can't be left rattling around on her own in that flat in Queens. But she's so stubborn, so keen to parade her independence, that it will not be an easy task to convince her of the error (and dangers) of her ways.

"And Larry, please do something about that tree at the front of the house. It'll fall on the roof one of these nights. We'll be killed in our beds this winter, I'm sure of it. Call someone today to cut it down." Sue tends to dramatize. Because he's so slow to act she has to invent alarms and excursions in the hope of lighting a fuse under him. And since he has grown more ponderous over the years and has become such an inert force, she has had to react by becoming more excitable.

"I'll see to it." He pulls his hat low over his rubbled face and kisses her briefly.

Outside, he looks at the offending elm tree in the garden. The rot has spread up the trunk and into the branches. It is almost dead and certainly dangerous. But how, he wonders as he sits into his car, can you pronounce a tree dead? For some reason he's reluctant to cut it down. Lawrence's tire used to hang from it and they used to dress it with lights at Thanksgiving and Christmas. He remembers too the time they hung a bird house from one of the lower branches and discovered that squirrels were raiding the birdseed. Lawrence, who was only five or six then, asked why the squirrels had to be chased away. He couldn't grasp the difference between vermin and animals. Neither could his father.

Larry grins as he remembers the squirrels. But there's something noble about that old tree and it sort of lends substance to the house with its painted plastic siding. Still, it will have to be felled sooner or later, though his actuarial mind can't quite predict the right moment. What is the precise probability of an unhealthy tree falling through the roof of a house and when is it likely to happen?

Refusing to be collected for dinner that evening, his mother makes her own way to the subway at Queens. A stranger puts a hand under her elbow as she edges towards the escalator. She shrugs it off, then forces a smile to soften the rebuke. A billowing draught precedes the train which comes like a huge plunger down the tunnel. She boards a graffiti-covered carriage.

A small neat woman, her hair is grey and fluffy; she used to put a blue tint in it but doesn't bother any more. Her glasses dangle down the front of her overcoat on a silver chain Larry gave her two, or was it three, birthdays ago. She notices how the young women in the carriage wear their handbags like Sam Brown belts secured around their necks.

She refuses to carry her purse like that, reckoning that at her age she is mug-proof. Against her doctor's advice, she's left her walking stick at home – and her pepper spray.

The train moves off in a wheezing surge, the walls of the tunnel beginning to stream and flow as the speed increases. A man strap-hanging by the door glances at her and looks away. There was a time men used to bother her in crowded carriages, but not anymore. She feels more relief than regret. The subway seems less noisy than usual; maybe her hearing has slipped another notch. That too has its own compensations; there's a lot she doesn't particularly want to hear these days.

Although she's visited Larry and Sue almost every Wednesday since God knows when, for some reason this particular evening doesn't seem to be part of her normal routine. There is something different about this Wednesday evening but she can't put her finger on it. In the surrounding silence her mind is restless, raking the past for memories, the important ones, those that may make some sense of the happenstance of over half a century. She is operating on nervous energy like that surge of adrenaline when her first child, Frank, was born. She'd gone through thirty hours of drug-free labour and had no intention of sleeping once she saw the wrinkled face like a raw frankfurter.

Drawing on that same reserve now, she sits and doesn't bother much with the passing stations or the people getting on and off. She looks forward to dinner and walking in on Frank, surprising him.

That silly grin as if he'd been caught out ... Wait now ... Not Frank. It's Larry she's going to visit. Larry. His hair is almost as white as hers. Mistaken once as her husband, he wasn't amused at all. Although Frank is the oldest, he looks younger than Larry despite his misspent youth. He never worried as much as poor Larry. What a rascal Frank was, impulsive to a fault. Set his mattress on fire once in a fit of temper, then hid in the laundry chute and got stuck. It took the fire service to cut him free and then her husband, Jack, had laid into him. But after it was all over, Jack and she had laughed in private. For some reason they always got a kick out of Frank, though they tried not to let him know how much he brightened up their lives. Maybe now was the time to set the record straight. Where was he now? Billings, Montana, probably selling snake oil. He was always on the move. It would be so good to see Frank again.

As she moves through the underground, the idea takes root and puts out tendrils in all directions. Without realising it, her fingers grope for the credit cards in her purse. She hardly ever uses them for her small amount of grocery shopping, but for something big like this... She knows the idea is crazy but it just won't go away and, besides, at her age she's entitled to go off the deep end. By comparison, dinner in Brooklyn suddenly loses its appeal. Sue would be fussing and clucking and making Larry do the dishes as if she had a point to prove, and talking about that old tree that needed to be cut down.

Jack was impulsive like Frank and he never stopped to think either. That winter he got his first stroke it didn't cost him a thought and he died quick and clean when it was his time. Frank is so like him it's uncanny, even the way he cranes his head forward as if walking into a gale, not looking right or left. She must tell Frank this, all of it. The reason he didn't get on with his father was because they were so alike. It's all so simple and yet she never fully realised it before. Now in her eightieth year it's as if she can look down on the family from a height and see all the interrelationships at a glance.

She could call Larry from the airport. He would say she was mad and try to talk her out of it; so she would have to be firm. She mustn't let his worry and calculations of risk rub off on her.

At the next stop she gets to her feet a little unsteadily. It must be the excitement. She doesn't fully realise that she's made up her mind until she finds herself outside the station trying to hail a cab. A policeman with a night-stick tips his cap to her and helps her flag down a taxi.

She hasn't been in a cab since Jack died and the walls of her life closed in, confining her to the local store where she gets milk and eggs, and the library where she scans the papers and borrows Agatha Christies – in big print versions. She can read these again and again because she forgets the plots – another compensation of sorts. But she can't knit anymore because her hands are too stiff now. Those hanks of wool Larry keeps bringing her are just piling up in a closet.

"You okay there, lady?" the cabbie asks.

"Yes, Frank."

"Joe. The name's Joe. Meeting someone at Kennedy?"

"No. I'm going on a trip. To see my oldest boy in Montana." She tries to keep her voice matter of fact. The driver shrugs. Some old broads never quit.

The city slips by. She's forgotten how big and bright it is. Snow begins to fall, the flakes drawn to the headlights like fleeting memories scoured away by the wipers which work to the rhythm of heartbeats. It's warm in the cab and she opens her coat and angora cardigan. When Frank was small he used to be fascinated by her fox fur, the lacquered claws on one end, the glass-eyed head on the other. He borrowed it once for a school play and lost it. Jack must have been away on business because she had to take care of the punishment. She stood in front of Frank, who was already a head taller than her, and swished the cane. He looked down at her and said, "You must be kidding, Ma." She walked away trying to keep a straight face.

Approaching the airport, excitement stirred in her. She felt young again. It was good to cut loose from her old friends, many of whom had gone funny and mean. Marge had become a miser, squirreling everything away like a bag lady. Lillian spent her days rocking in a chair in a home; it was painful to visit her. Men were luckier; they died quickly, at the right time, while they still had dignity. They went without a thought, like Frank jumping off a diving board before he could even swim.

"Your change, lady," the cabbie said.

"You may keep it." Frank and Jack used to tip big. They also liked gambling. Once when heavy-set men came to the door she had to pay off a debt for Frank. Larry recouped her afterwards, which was strange since he was always careful about money. But he lectured her and she suspected that he also lectured Frank.

A skycap gives her directions to the reservations desk. She pays for her ticket with a credit card, feeling that she's defrauding someone with that bit of plastic.

"Where's the plane?"

"You have to check in first, Ma'am. They'll tell you which gate."

She'd been on a plane only once before when Jack had used his winnings to take them to Glacier Park. Frank got lost looking for bears and a kindly Indian handed him over to the Park Rangers. It will be only a few hours before she sees him again. Life can be a miracle at times.

The stewardess helps her fasten the seat belt. "Enjoy your flight, Ma'am."

"Thank you, dear." She is tempted to add, "Don't fuss. I may be old but I can still get around."

Her spirit soars as the plane takes to the sky; she should have done this years ago. It feels like Thanksgiving with the whole family around her. Frank will be so pleased to see her and hear what she has to tell him. She looks out at the peaceful sky, the vast space above the clouds. God is old too.

She could have met Him at the Senior Citizens Centre and played a hand of pinochle. She closes her eyes and dreams. Frank is waiting at the end of the line and in a way Jack is too. She smiles in her sleep.

———————————

"Frank never came to the funeral," Larry said after the last mourner had left the house.

"Well, he was away on business," Sue answered without much conviction.

"Why was Mom going to see him anyway? What came over her … buying an airline ticket without telling anyone?" Larry held his face in his hands, feeling lost, beyond tears.

Sue put her hand on his shoulder. She knew the old lady had gone on a blast, probably even knowing it would be her last; she had that sort of impetuous kink in her character. Frank had always been her favourite; she doted on him. But Sue couldn't tell Larry − after all he had done for his mother over the years.

Larry had the standard three days compassionate leave from the company. He tried to keep busy; that was always the best remedy against moping. On the third day he asked Lawrence to help him cut down the tree. He lopped off the top branches first; the bracelet of the chain saw just slid through the rotten timber. Then he bent to the trunk, cutting out a wedge from the side furthest from the house. The gentlest push brought the bole down with a muffled crash. The sky looked brighter but less interesting and the house was exposed, as he feared, in all its modest plainness.

Gathering up the dead wood, Lawrence asked, "What are those, Dad?"

Larry knelt on the ground, "I'll be damned." He counted five little elm shoots springing up through the new grass. It was much too early in the year and, he would have thought, much too late for the tree which was as good as dead for a long time. He was glad he hadn't taken Sue's advice last week about cutting down the tree. Maybe there was something to be said for not acting on impulse.

The Lungs of Margaret Daly

MARGARET DALY WORKED for a firm of solicitors in Dame Street. A widow, close to sixty, she organised the office with quiet efficiency and kept her little station outside Mr. Jameson's door as clean as a pin. She sprayed and wiped the leaves of her rubber plant every day because of the soot and grime that floated in from the polluted street.

She organised Mr. Jameson too and would sometimes straighten his tie as he rushed to a conference or a meeting with clients. He was about the same age, and though she'd been straightening his tie for almost thirty years, he was still embarrassed by the gesture and would strain at the leash to get away saying brusquely, "I'm grand … I'm grand."

In the evening she would wait for her bus outside Trinity Gates. College Green was so filthy she wanted to scrub it with a huge Brillo pad. When buses came and went she was left standing in a dense fog of exhaust fumes, trying to hold her breath. It was worse in summer because the polluted air was warm and acrid and carried the faint whiff of stale urine as well as diesel.

One day towards the end of July an American tourist stood next to her in the queue and coughed with some distress when the 7A bus left them enveloped in a warm black smog that never fully dispersed.

"Why do you put up with this?" the American woman asked.

"I don't know," Margaret replied. "It's always been like this." She had no better answer and felt embarrassed because of that.

"Is there no Green movement over here in this Emerald Isle?" the American woman inquired.

"Well, we do have Green politicians. They campaign against global warming and that sort of thing," Margaret said.

"They should start with the buses. I bet they're run by a State monopoly. Imagine what this must do to your lungs," the woman added.

"Well, I must confess … I smoke a little…"

"That's your choice. You shouldn't have to put up with this." She waved a hand as if trying to dispel the fumes that still swirled around them.

Margaret boarded the number 8 bus when it came belching to a halt, and thought no more about it until later that evening when she'd fed the cat and settled down with the latest Maeve Binchy and a glass of white wine – the latter to celebrate her 60th birthday. The American woman was perfectly right, but what could any one individual do about the situation? There was so much talk of 'empowerment' these days but what did it mean in practice? Because of legal fees no one individual could go to court, and class actions were disallowed. There was no pressure on the Establishment to alter the lazy complacent habits of a lifetime.

Later, as she was writing a letter to her daughter in Australia, in the yellow glow of a tall standard lamp, a thought occurred to her. When she finished the letter she went out to the garage of the semi-detached house and rummaged around until she found what she was looking for. Before falling asleep that night she wondered if she would have the neck to put the idea into practice.

Mr. Jameson met her on the way into work the next morning. After a double-take he asked, "Margaret, what's all this about?" His face wore a curious, amused look.

"It helps." She removed the gauze mask that covered her nose and mouth and noticed how discoloured the filter had become during the short walk up Dame Street.

"What got into you?" He ushered her through the door, rather peremptorily, she thought.

"The atmosphere is filthy. I'm just taking precautions, that's all." She tried to sound nonchalant but she was still a little shaken by the strange surreptitious glances she'd attracted during the walk to the office. Still, she'd done it and there was a hint of elation in her mood.

"It's not Tokyo," Mr. Jameson said, "or Beijing."

"No. It's worse. And I don't want to be poisoned."

During the weeks that followed, her confidence grew even though she was conscious that passers-by regarded her as an oddity. Men could get away with being 'characters' but women who behaved in unusual ways tended to be perceived as dotty or menopausal, which was harder to bear. She had never been aware before of how different smiles could be. Some were patronising and rude if not downright hostile; others appeared to be sympathetic but actually belonged to that category which expressed tolerance for the afflicted; some were encouraging; the strangest were those which betrayed a hidden fear. There were scowls and leers, giggles and sneers. And, of course, outright laughs. On one occasion a yob nudged his companion and said,

"Lookah, Darth Vader for fook's sake."

"Maybe she thinks she's a bleedin' courier," the other replied.

One morning, she was intrigued and heartened to see a man wearing a mask. He gave her a conspiratorial wink. A week or so later she saw a young woman with a mask that was colour coordinated with her fashionable clothes. Margaret smiled behind her mask. She thought the other woman did too; her eyes seemed to crinkle slightly in the manner of veiled Arab women greeting each other with letter-box eyes.

In early autumn a young reporter stopped her on the street. They chatted for a few minutes and this led to a couple of column inches in the Evening Herald. That would probably have been the end of her fame had the item not caught the quirky eye of a radio chat-show host who invited her onto his programme. After the usual banal preliminaries he asked her why she wore the mask.

"Because I don't want to be poisoned," she said.

There was some discussion about whether the air quality in Dame Street was higher or lower than that permitted by the mandarins in Brussels.

"All I know," Margaret said, "is that I don't want to be poisoned."

"That seems reasonable," the DJ chirped and then took a break to play some 'mega-tastic' techno music.

Shortly after that, Margaret began wearing goggles as well as the mask. Her tolerance of adverse public reaction had increased dramatically. She paid no heed to a Goth who called her a 'bleedin' Biggles'. She found that the goggles prevented her eyes from smarting when she got home in the evening. At this stage she had become a minor celebrity, a familiar of the College Green area, and was rapidly becoming a Dublin 'character'. That in itself was a sort of empowerment, and several other commuters had begun to follow her example.

"Is all this really necessary?" Mr. Jameson asked in a weary tone of voice. Comments were being made in the office and the senior partner, Mr. Worth, had raised an eyebrow. "We're a rather … conservative establishment," he finished lamely.

"I'm trying to conserve myself," Margaret replied. "I don't want to be poisoned."

"But you're a smoker."

"That's my choice."

"I see." But he didn't really see. She had always been stubborn – it seemed to him that meticulous

people often tended to be stubborn – but this was downright ornery. "I'm grand … grand…," he said as she adjusted what was supposed to be a Windsor knot. He watched as she carefully hung her mask and goggles on the coat-rack and sat at her neat desk.

He met the senior partner, Mr. Worth, for a drink that evening in the Horseshoe Bar. They reviewed some of the cases the firm was handling and discussed the desirability of concentrating on the more lucrative end of the business, namely corporate clients. The firm should move in that direction and lessen its involvement in family law. Mr. Worth then referred to the bizarre behaviour of Margaret Daly.

"I had a word with her," Mr. Jameson said. "But she feels quite strongly about it. She lives alone, of course."

Mr. Worth sucked his teeth. "Women of that age can go a bit odd. I've seen it before. But it won't do, you know. It's bad for the image of the firm." He waved vaguely around the well-accoutred bar. "Tongues are beginning to wag."

"I'm not sure what I can do."

"She's a widow, isn't she?" Mr. Worth popped some cashew nuts into his mouth and chased them with a liberal drink of pink gin, rinsing his jowls.

"Yes, with a daughter in Australia."

"Mmm. So, we're dealing with an empty-nest situation too. She probably wants attention. Difficult … very difficult. We may have to think about early retirement if she keeps up this silly behaviour…"

"She'd be lost without her job." This hadn't really occurred to Mr. Jameson before, but he felt it to be true. He also felt that Worth was firmly putting the ball in his court.

In the meantime, Margaret had progressed to a higher grade of mask – a disposable toxic dust respirator EN149 which coped with gases, vapours, solvents and organic fumes. They cost €2.50 each and she went through three a week. She even had the temerity to buy them out of petty cash. To make matters worse, some of the other secretaries in the office were following her example. Indeed, some of her followers in the street had also traded-up to the EN149.

Mr. Jameson had several chats with her but all to no avail. He couldn't quite bring himself to mention Mr. Worth's threat of early retirement. That would have been disproportionate. But he had to admit a strange thing: after thirty odd years of friendship he now disliked Margaret for her intransigence, her one-sentence replies ("I don't want to be poisoned") and for the fact that she smoked away at her desk and blew the smoke upwards into an air extractor which she had requisitioned. It also irritated him in an irrational way that she never dropped ash or a flake of tobacco on the carpet.

After another fraught session in the Horseshoe Bar, during which Mr. Worth made it clear that the tongues which now wagged were very influential (corporate) ones, Mr. Jameson hit on a plan of sorts.

He converted the office into an environmental-friendly zone which meant, of course, that smoking was banned.

"The building has gone clean," he announced.

Margaret remonstrated, "What's the point? With all the fumes and grime coming through the windows from the street? You'll have to install triple-glazing and air-conditioning. That's the only way this building will ever be clean. We're being poisoned at our desks."

He stood his ground but she ran rings around him. She made frequent visits to the Ladies. He knew she was smoking in there but what he could do about it? He could hardly follow her in to catch her red-handed. If the stalls were occupied she would walk out on to the fire escape at the back of the building and light up to her heart's content. The efficiency of the office suffered. There was only one compensation and it was a small one; she didn't straighten his tie any more.

Mr. Worth was becoming more and more irate by the comments that were reaching him. A Senior Counsel who did some work for the Tourist Board and Dublin Bus told him that corporate Ireland was beginning to champ at the bit. The green image of the country was at stake with all these masked crusaders and loony Greens running around. A bit of dust never did anyone any harm.

"You'd better let her go," he said.

"Whaa…t?" Mr. Jameson wasn't quite ready for this but he rallied quickly. "A risky option … unfair dismissals…"

"There are ways around that." Mr. Worth tapped a finger against the side of his nose. "She could be … aam … de-hired."

"You mean, make life so difficult for her that she resigns voluntarily?" Mr. Jameson was shocked. That sort of thing only happened in America, where companies would engage specialist de-hirers.

"You don't realise how much damage that damn woman is causing. There's a lot at stake."

It didn't occur to either man that something should be done to clean the air.

Even if Mr. Jameson had known the art of de-hiring he wouldn't have had the stomach to put it into practice. So he rode shotgun for Margaret Daly over the next few years. He did his best to screen her from Mr. Worth, occasionally sending her home early in a taxi.

He also had a little partition erected around her desk, and he replaced the air extractor with a more powerful model. She interpreted this as giving her special permission to smoke (which she did) rather than as a means of making her invisible to the senior partner. These little ploys probably helped save Margaret's bacon, but the fact of the matter was that so many commuters now wore masks that the spotlight was no longer on Margaret or the firm. Indeed, the Green Party had taken up the running and were selling masks at every street corner. As one politician put it, "People were going about like extras in Star Trek."

When she reached sixty-five she had no option but to retire. She had been on pre-retirement courses and felt reasonably sure she could cope with it. Knowing that she would not wish to have a grand farewell party, Mr. Jameson kept it fairly low-key – a short speech, a plasma high-definition TV, and a bouquet of flowers. Both promised to keep in touch and each knew that they would not.

Margaret retired to the suburbs of Dún Laoghaire and attended classes in watercolour painting and garden design. Mr. Jameson retired shortly afterwards and spent a lot of time at the golf club, playing bridge in the clubhouse when he wasn't out on the links poking the ball in front of him.

Margaret died just short of her sixty-eighth birthday from a respiratory illness related to emphysema. Mr. Jameson was not altogether surprised that – in a sealed letter – she asked him to be her executor. But he was astonished at two other pieces of information contained in the letter.

The first was that he would be the main beneficiary, since the daughter in Australia had been a figment of her imagination, invented no doubt on foot of some kind of wish-fulfilment.

The second was a request which he could hardly refuse.

After the funeral he drove into the sleeping city centre at about two in the morning. He parked in

Nassau Street and walked towards College Green. When he reached the Number 8 bus stop he opened the urn and scattered the ashes into the air. A gentle breeze helped to spread them over a wide area. Mr. Jameson found himself smiling, as he breathed in some of the clean dust of Margaret Daly.

Eileen and the True Hunger

THE APPLE HAD GIVEN Eileen a lot of trouble. At first she'd tried a sap green but it was too lemony somehow. She added a tad of alizarin crimson but that muddied the mixture. She tried to lighten the tone with titanium white but that gave an unwanted beige hue, more like the colour of a pear.

"You've forgotten all your colour theory," the teacher said in a high-pitched, irritated tone. A young pup, her mother would have called him, with his striped grandfather shirt, designer stubble and hiking boots. Her mother had not been enamoured of men in general and was hard on any man Eileen had brought home. Strange how, back then, she wanted to be free of her mother's controlling influence. It was all so different now that her mother had passed away. Hardly a day went by when she didn't think of her creased, pleasant face, their chats at the kitchen table, and her guiding hand. She could certainly use her mother's gumption now to deal with this supercilious young teacher.

"Green and red are complementary colours, so if you mix them you'll get a dirty grey." This guy knew his stuff; she had to give him that.

"I remember…"

"And this … what's this…?" He pointed at, and resiled from, the easel at the same time, wearing an expression of pained incredulity.

"It's a highlight," she said uncertainly, conscious of the fact that the other students, though painting away, were listening keenly. Her voice seemed to soar above the soft sounds of brushing and breathing.

"It's not a highlight. It's a splodge of mixing white stuck on like a stamp. It doesn't belong to the apple; it's not organic. Look at the light on the apple. Look …" He almost pushed her towards the still life. "What do you see?"

"Well … the light reflected on the skin of…"

"Is it warm or cold, Eileen?"

"Cold." Light had to be cold, she thought, especially neon light. That curious woman, Helen-somebody from a neighbouring easel, came over to inspect and to earwig. And no doubt to earn brownie points by being a contrast-gainer. She was poured into designer jeans which she had carefully distressed with well-placed daubs of paint.

"You're assuming it's cold, Eileen," he said. "You're working from prior beliefs inside your head…"

"But it's neon light…" Her protest was weak and ineffectual, almost a whisper.

"It's halogen actually," Helen-somebody corrected her.

"The point is," he went on, "you must look. Learn to look. The light is warm. Can't you see the glow? Temperature is very important in painting, Eileen. We've been over this before."

"Very important," Helen concurred.

Eileen stood back, squinted, then nodded slowly. Damn it, the highlight was warm … well, warmish.

"And the front part of the apple. What colour do you see?

"Green." What else could it be?

"Another assumption, Eileen. Can't you see the tint reflected from the orange?"

"No…" She narrowed her eyes again. "Oh wait … Now that you mention it …"

"OK. And remember, reflections also have temperatures." He seemed satisfied by her contrite tone and moved on to the next easel, leaving her to her own devices.

She just could not get it right. The apple remained like a flat green disk; it had no rotundity or substance. And the indentation for the stalk seemed like a bruise or a stain. The acrylics didn't blend well together and her hog-hair brush was moulting. God, she was blaming the tools now. She abandoned the apple for a while and worked on the orange. The pineapple was too challenging by far in her present state.

With retirement from her civil service job less than seven years away, she hoped she might have a talent for painting; a small talent would do. Her flat was at ground level and she had images of herself painting away in the relative privacy of the small garden during the lonely years that lay ahead. The other tenants would probably stop and stare but she wouldn't be too intimidated by that, not if she had some ability. She didn't aspire to exhibit or sell, but it would be nice to give small paintings as presents to her nieces and nephews at Christmas or on their birthdays.

The orange, unfortunately, did not go well either. She didn't know how to capture the pitted surface of the skin and the thousand pin-pricks of light that gave the impression of sweat oozing through pores. Moreover, the apple returned the favour of reflection – casting some of its green onto the orange. The different fruits were contaminating each other; they weren't individual objects at all but some sort of collective whole.

She began to panic. The teacher was already half way around the circle of easels and would be back to her soon. It was ridiculous. An adult class and she was acting like a schoolgirl. She heard him say to that interfering Helen-person, "Good work. You're got the mid-tones right. Remember, painting is about tone, not colour." He went on in vaguer terms about painting the volumes of the objects from the inside out.

Eileen returned to the apple but couldn't master it. She now knew what she wanted to do but seemed to lack the skill, or possibly confidence, to do it. She concentrated on the shaded side of the fruit, using raw umber.

Christ, he was at her elbow again. Already.

"That shaded area is not the darkest. You have at least three other areas which are darker. Have you forgotten the chiaroscuro exercise we did three weeks ago?"

"No … I remember it." She tapped the handle

of the brush against her teeth.

"And look, the pigment is wrong. What are you using? Umber?"

"Yes … Maybe I should try a darker green?

"No, no, no. We discussed this earlier. What is the complementary colour of green?"

"Red." Helen called out from across the room.

"Red," Eileen said.

"Exactly."

"But I can hardly use red … for the shaded area of a green apple." She would have to be more assertive towards this young mansplainer. "It's a Granny Smith…"

He held his head for a moment. "Not a primary red, of course not, but a hint of red. Try mixing cadmium into the umber." He peered more closely at the canvas. Her morale was so low she half expected him to ignore her work completely as if it was too inferior to bother with. He pointed again towards the triangle of dark shadow between apple and table. "Yes, that's your deepest tone. Use it as a marker. And, remember, everything is relative."

Helen who had sauntered over again, concurred, "The other tones should relate to that one." She leant back on her heels to appraise Eileen's efforts. "It's a brave attempt all the same."

Eileen's teeth ached, and she suddenly understood what her teenage nephew meant when he told his brother to 'get out of his face'.

The teacher had been looking at her palette and now dipped a forefinger into a blob of paint. With a few deft strokes of his finger he did more for the apple than she had done with her sable and bristle brushes over two three-hour sessions. In fact the finger-painted apple seemed to come forward from the background; it almost bulged.

"My goodness. That's miraculous," Helen said in a gush of breath. "Mark-making at its best."

"It's just a question of confidence," he said, batting away the compliment.

Confidence was everything, Eileen thought, but how could it be acquired if the talent wasn't there in the first place? She had a sudden sense of déjà vu – something her mother might have done or said in a kitchen smelling of freshly baked bread?

Despite her feeling of shame, Eileen could not disagree. The teacher had talent, even in his damned finger-tips.

"Now," he said, stepping back, "that's your base. Build on that. Get the tones right before even thinking about highlights. You're not at that stage yet."

"Thank you," she grated through compressed lips as he moved on to the next easel. She was afraid to touch the apple now in case she ruined what he had done. Hoping the class would end before he circled back, she consulted her watch. She could work hard on it at home and maybe earn some approbation next week. To her dismay, Helen appeared yet again at her elbow.

"What about perspective, Eileen? You have at least two vanishing points there ... Can't you see?" Helen's voice was just loud enough for the teacher to hear. How she managed to pitch it at that precise level clearly took long and diligent practice – or else it was a miracle.

Eileen smiled grimly. "Oh, I can sort that out fairly easily. It's a quick fix," she added bravely.

"Hmmmm. It seems structural to me," Helen demurred. "But good luck with it anyway."

At the end of the class they followed the usual drill of turning their easels around and congregating in the centre of the circle so as to view the work of all the students. The teacher gave a brief critique of each canvas to the whole class, and Eileen dreaded the moment he would come to hers. She didn't have to worry, however, because he ignored her canvas, and that was even worse.

A couple of days later when she got home from the office she set up the fruit on the kitchen table in her flat, and arranged a lamp to simulate the light and shade. She resolved to work really hard to earn the teacher's approval and to get Helen off her back for once and for all. There was something different about the apple, a sort of shiny meniscus floating on the skin. She started to mix paint on the disposable grease-proof palette and kept correcting and over-correcting until she had a whole mound of paint – far more than she needed.

The sense of déjà vu she'd experienced during the recent class now slowly resolved itself into a less fuzzy memory: Her Mom and herself baking together in the Aga-heated kitchen, both wearing aprons, already liberally sprinkled with flour. Eileen was no more than twelve and was keen to learn from, and impress, her Mom. There was a warm feeling between them. Her mother gave such good advice: "Look at what you're doing … See what's in front of you… When in doubt, consult the recipe book." Her mother, of course, never had to do that; she could wing it.

"I haven't got your ability, Mom," Eileen said. As she tried to get her ingredients to blend in the smaller mixing bowl, she felt inadequate. When, at last, they took the finished cakes out of the oven she noticed how her Mom's double-layered flan was so perfect compared to her own miserable cup-cake which, despite its small size, had collapsed in on itself…

This memory now shocked her for one reason. Her mother had never done or said anything to cheer her up or rebuild her confidence. She didn't know why, but it was a fact.

She was just about ready to apply the paint to the canvas when she noticed something. The apple was becoming over-ripe. There was a faint ochre tinge in the skin that hadn't been there before. This was the last straw. Just as she got the colour right the damn fruit changed its appearance.

She looked from the object to the large clot of useless paint on the palette that now reminded her of that collapsed cup-cake. It was too much. With barely a thought, and with tears welling in her eyes, she reached over, grabbed the unbiddable apple and took a vicious bite out of it. Then, aggressively, she began to eat the rest of the still life, including the pineapple which she cut into chunks.

Banning the Eulogy

THE TWO ELDERLY LADIES, Molly and Bernadette, were waylaid by journalists as their taxi came to a halt outside the hotel.

Bernadette did most of the talking. Yes, they were the last two surviving employees of Dillon's Cheese. Yes, they had attended every one of the Work's Christmas dinners in that hotel. Of course they would miss the other ladies who had died over the years. And, yes, they − Molly and she − would continue the tradition of the Christmas outing for as long as God spared them the health.

"Enjoy your dinner," one of the journalists said, switching off her tape recorder. It was a slow news day; this was better than nothing − a colour piece, about three or four column inches would do. The Dillon's dinner had been covered as a puff piece in the press on and off over the years. This would probably be the last reference to it, since only two of the former staff were still living.

"I thought we'd never get away from them," Molly said as they walked into the lobby along a small stretch of red carpet the management had laid out for them − and the press. "I'm blinded by flash bulbs."

"You'd think we were celebrities, arriving for the Oscars." Bernadette turned and smiled at the manager who came to greet them. She pulled her rather loud sequined wrap higher on her shoulders. He'd welcomed them last year too; of course it was good publicity for the hotel but, still, it was nice of him to make the gesture.

As he led them towards the function room, which Dillon's staff had always used, he commiserated with them over the death, during the year, of Jacinta Browne, a former colleague.

"We miss her too." Molly wondered how she would get on with Bernadette on her own. Somehow Jacinta built a bridge between them. It was going to be strange and maybe a little strained without her. She had no business dying at seventy-eight. Dillon's girls, all told, had done much better than that. Molly, herself, was still a couple of years shy of the average age.

"Sure, we're dropping like flies," Bernadette said. "You probably won't see me here next year." She gave a raucous cough as if to demonstrate the state of her lungs.

While the manager demurred, Molly wondered if she would go on her own next year, or whenever Bernadette turned her toes up. No, dinner on her own in a hotel would be stupid, and pathetic. Of course, it could be the other way round; that thought did not appeal to her.

The function room seemed huge with only the two of them in it. The waiter, Phelim, remembered them or at least pretended to. They remembered him well and noted that his rate of hair loss had accelerated over the last year. Molly noticed that he had dandruff even though he had so little hair; it seemed unfair somehow.

"Happy Christmas, Phelim. You'll soon be as bald as a coot." Bernadette sat on the chair he'd pulled out for her.

"And you ladies are looking younger than ever." Phelim handed them the menus and gave them some pointers to help them choose. In keeping with tradition both women opted for the main course of turkey and ham but, for starters, Molly went for the melon and Bernadette for the smoked salmon.

When Phelim left for the kitchen there was a moment of silence during which Bernadette did a proper inspection of the room, noticing the hunting-scene prints on the walls, the heavy embossed Newbridge cutlery, the banked fire in the grate. She sat opposite Molly, conscious of the empty chairs on both sides of the oval table.

"Only two Dillon girls left." Molly read her thoughts and broke the awkward silence.

"Yeah. Imagine when the whole nine of us used to sit around this table. I thought Jacinta would see us all out." Bernadette picked a bread roll from the basket which she then pushed across to Molly.

"Seventy-eight isn't that old nowadays." Molly said.

"No, but she really missed her walks. Once the osteoporosis gets in on you, it can do a lot of damage, especially if you fall down. I think she lost heart when she couldn't get out and about. She loved to walk."

"Remember how she used to talk back to

Dillon…?"

"And get away with it," Bernadette smiled. "She could build a nest in his ear and rob it. And she never worried about anything. I thought she'd go on forever."

"Sometimes, the worriers take better care of themselves," Molly said, thinking that she probably fell into that category. There would be something to be said for outliving Bernadette and being the last of the Dillon girls. A minor achievement.

With a smile that Molly interpreted as an oily professional one bordering on a sneer, the waiter served the starters and poured the wine.

"He makes me feel like a waste of space," Molly said after he'd left.

"I suppose he's used to a bigger crowd in this room. More tips. It's all money nowadays." Bernadette continued to talk even while she ate, and Molly found it off-putting. She had to force herself not to gaze at Bernadette's mouth which, between words, revealed fragments of smoked salmon and lettuce in different stages of mastication. She hadn't been aware of this mannerism when the crowd was larger, when Jacinta was alive.

To make matters worse Bernadette started to talk about her family, how her son was doing in Boston, how her youngest daughter still helped her out in the house and refused to leave her on her own since the day her husband passed on. *She knows I've no family. Why does she go on like this? Jacinta never let her away with it. She, and the other girls knew how to cut her off at the pass. I never knew she was so selfish. Loud, yes, and brash, we all sussed that; couldn't help but notice. But she's cute enough behind it all. It's crystal clear now when she hasn't an audience to impress and there's no banter and laughing.*

"Ah, that's great, Phelim. Just the job." Bernadette clapped her hands as he laid the plates of turkey and ham in front of them.

"Oh, I couldn't eat all that much." Molly's hand flew to her throat.

"Give it a lash." Phelim plonked down a dish of vegetables and left in a hurry.

"Not very well presented," Molly said. "And judging by the rush he was in, he must be working another room, if not two."

"Ah well, dig in." Bernadette took her own advice. *That wan is going a bit weird, the things she notices. Must have thorns in her pants. Never copped it before. She was always a Holy Mary, sucking up to Old Dillon. Telling him if any foreign body fell into a vat in case it might curdle the bloody cheese. I wonder if she fancied him? Kept herself pure – I wonder? She saved herself too long. I gave him a good seeing to on New Year's '78. Or was it '79? Christ, if she only knew?*

"I suppose the turkey isn't too bad," Molly conceded. "The breast anyway. But it needs a little gravy." *God, she's chewing again with her mouth half open. It's putting me right off my dinner. Sorry I came. Had to I suppose for old times ... Never really knew Bernadette. Always in a group, of course ... Who is she really? Without an audience?*

Hard to figure out. Certainly there's a sneaky angle which she got away with before, because Jacinta could take the harm out of anyone.

"I still do a bit of gardening," Bernadette was saying. "Although it was poor Danny who had the green thumb. You don't…? No, you've no garden in that flat."

"I wouldn't have time for it anyway," Molly replied.

"What, because of television…?"

"No. I read a lot."

"I see." *That Molly is a snob as well as everything else. Reading my arse. 'Coronation Street' more like. And 'Fair City'. And look at her with the make-up. Mascara at her age. Who's she trying to impress with that? Still, good luck to her.* "You always had the brains."

"I wouldn't say that."

"And you were always popular with the boys." *Until they found out you were frigid. With scapulars in your drawers.*

"Oh, now…"

"Certainly," Bernadette insisted. "Even baldy Phelim is giving you the eye." *Let's see if she falls for that.*

"The man is half my age." *Bernadette was always on about sex. Obsessed by it. Doesn't realise I know she cheated on her husband. With Dillon of all people.*

"It's a wonder you never married Molly. Sorry, I don't mean to pry." *Who'd've had her? Prim and proper in her pearls and twin-set like the Queen.*

Poor old cow.

"It's no great mystery. I never fell in love. It's just one of those things. And I wouldn't have married without love." *Unlike some I could name.*

"Aaah." Bernadette gave her kindest and most mawkish smile. "In a way you were probably better off. Because when my Danny died I had terrible grief. His funeral was one of the biggest in the parish. And my oldest lad gave a wonderful eulogy for his Dad. Too much really. I hope no one gives me a eulogy like that when my time comes."

"You needn't worry."

"I beg your…"

"I mean the bishops have stopped that practice now." Molly pushed her plate from her. She wasn't sure why the bishops had banned eulogies but they had. Someone told her it was because drug bosses used eulogies to swear vengeance on their enemies. She wondered if that could be true. "I couldn't eat another bit."

Bernadette did a quick perusal of the plate. *Almost licked clean. Never realised before how full of old notions and balderdash this woman is.* "Do you remember the time the hair-net fell in the rennet? 1973 was it, the spring?"

"I do." Molly nodded. "A whole batch of cheese could have been destroyed."

"And you told Dillon about it and saved the day."

"Did I?"

"Yeah. It was Jacinta's hair-net. She was acting the maggot and the damn thing slipped from her fingers into the small vat. She nearly got the sack over it."

"Did she? I don't remember that." *What's she driving at now?*

Bernadette stared over the rim of the wine glass at the other woman. "Wasn't it just after that when you became a supervisor?"

"Do you know, I can't remember. 1973 you say? A very long time ago." Molly dabbed her mouth with a starched napkin and replaced it on her lap.

"I'm pretty sure that's when you got promoted."

"Maybe so."

"Strange isn't it? Jacinta was nearly sacked and a week or two later you got promoted."

"These things happen." Molly said with a wave of her hand. *Why not spit it out?*

"I don't go much on coincidences myself." *Get the picture now, sister. I know you snitched on Jacinta. And you know I know.* "Some people put too much emphasis on their jobs. And then they regret it later on." Bernadette used the end of a roll to mop up the last of the gravy which had crumbs of stuffing in it.

"I suppose there are some people like that," Molly replied. *And to think I regarded that bitch as a friend once. She's all right in company but when you get her on her own the claws come out. There's an evil streak in her. I wonder if she goes to mass.* "Is that nice priest, Father Delahunty, still in your parish?"

"Father Delahunty? I don't know." Bernadette

speared the last half Brussels sprout with her fork and used it to gather up the remains of the cranberry saucy. *What's she on about now. She's hopping around from one thing to the next.*

"He always said the 10 o'clock mass." *I knew it. She doesn't go any more. Maybe never did for all I knew. No sense of right or wrong; that's her problem.*

"Good luck to him." Bernadette saw the shiny-headed Phelim open the door with his foot and carry in two big dishes of plum pudding. "Ah the plum duff. Put it down there Phelim, old son. Give Molly an extra helping before she goes anorexic on us."

"What did you mean by that?" Molly asked after Phelim had withdrawn.

"What?"

"Anorexic?"

Bernadette looked directly at her, hesitated for a second and then said, "I meant tight-arsed."

"What?"

"Ah come on, Molly. Sure, we all go queer in our old age. There's women in Our Lady's Home who keep shit in their handbags. Don't let it bother you. I'm probably gone daft too."

"Yes, you are." Having spat that out, Molly's mouth formed itself into a stern line, except for slight puckers at the corners.

"Ta. It's nice to have it confirmed." Bernadette passed the brandy butter across the table. "Have some. It's good."

"What exactly is tight-arsed?" Molly could

hardly open her lips and was conscious of her racing pulse.

"Worrying over nothing, taking offence easily, being pernickety. All of the above. What of it? I'm probably worse…"

"Anything else?" *This bitch thinks she knows it all.*

"Now that you mention it. You snitched on Jacinta over the hair-net in the vat. That's how you sucked up to Dillon and got promoted."

"At least I didn't fuck him behind my husband's back." *Christ, did I say that? Mistake coming here without the others. Big mistake … Never again. Never, never, never. Feel sick now, exposed. Leave, leave now.*

Bernadette got quickly to her feet, flushed with anger. Something fell off the table and hit the carpet with a muffled thud. She stared hard at Molly who tried to return the stare.

Phelim stuck his head around the door and quickly withdrew. The tension gradually seeped out of Bernadette's body and suddenly she was laughing. The laughter started slowly but gathered momentum until tears came to her eyes. She wheezed and rocked on her heels. "Look … look … at the two … of us … oh God…" With a spoon she flicked a dollop of brandy butter in Molly's direction.

"Don't do that!"

"Don't be such a tight-arse," Bernadette wheezed. "You couldn't get a Visa Card between the cheeks of your buttocks."

"Better than being a hoor."

"Stop it. I gave old Dillon the best ride of his life." Bernadette used the napkin to wipe her eyes. "Look at us!"

Molly had started to laugh before she realised it. It was like a dam bursting; she'd never felt such release. She took a fistful of the chestnut stuffing and threw it at Bernadette who had fallen back into her chair. She tried to reciprocate with some left-over mashed potato, but was too weak with laughter.

Phelim returned. "Ladies … ladies … please…"

"We're no ladies," Bernadette sang out.

"Get lost." Molly also turned on him. *This was good. It was like old times … Well, nearly like old times … But what would happen when they stopped laughing and silence reigned again?*

The Clinging Smell of Incense

THEY WERE WAITING for his decision, or at least his endorsement. The hall was filled with a high-pitched buzz of excited debate. He was conscious of eyes being turned towards him, eliciting his seal of approval. But moral questions were never easy. An elderly Monsignor not in good health, time had somehow caught up on him, outpaced his achievements. This was his chance to leave something behind; a new church roof might not be a monument more lasting than bronze but it would be a tangible contribution nevertheless. He would wait for a while and let them debate it further, wait for the *vox populi* to chime…

Earlier that evening the congregation found it hard to concentrate on Benediction. When the Monsignor turned round to bless them with the monstrance they bowed their heads by rote but were thinking of the draw that would take place afterwards in the pipe-band hall. The selling of raffle tickets had gone on for almost two years and the first prize – a brand new Mercedes – was the best that had ever been offered in the town.

The Monsignor replaced the monstrance,

wishing the altar boy – Jimmy – would go easy on the thurible; the heavy wafts of incense were choking him. He also thought about the raffle. Despite the efforts of all concerned it hadn't been an entire success; he was still about £1,500 short of the estimate for the church roof. With the country in the grip of a recession it could take another year or two to raise that kind of money. At his age … well … He forced his thoughts back to the liturgy.

Jimmy swung the thurible back and forth with conscientious gusto, delivering up great clouds of sweet-smelling vapour. He was fascinated by the monstrance; the gold rays, jagged as icicles, that surrounded the lunula. It was the holiest object he had ever seen. Being on the marble altar, inside the communion rail, gave him a special feeling. Maybe this was an early sign of a vocation to the priesthood.

At the back of the church Mosey Keane knelt on his cap. He had come in from the coal yard just an hour earlier to have a wash. But so deeply engrained in his pores were the accumulated years of coal dust that scrubbing wasn't enough; his collar was already developing a grimy ring and his face a blue-visaged piratical look that was at odds with his mild manner. He was going to the hall too, but since he had bought only one ticket he didn't fancy his chances. With his luck he might even be called out to a fire. His boss, TJ Bowers, had volunteered him for fire-brigade duty last year and he dreaded those high ladders, but couldn't of course admit it. He listened to the water dripping into the buckets placed under the leaking roof; the rain seemed to be easing off.

After Benediction, most of the congregation trooped down the hill towards the pipe-band hall. The rain had stopped by now and the sky, hoarse with crows, looked as if it had been scoured by a dirty mop. The Monsignor and TJ Bowers led the scattered procession with Jimmy and the altar ladies bringing up the rear.

"Well, we nearly made it, TJ," the Monsignor said, trying to inject a hearty note into his voice.

"I thought we would have sold more tickets," TJ answered defensively. The Mercedes had been his idea; he thought it would have drummed up huge interest. He hoped he wouldn't be accused of over-reaching himself.

"Times are hard," the Monsignor said and added, "For most people."

"For everybody," TJ insisted. He didn't want to be singled out even if his own businesses – two bakeries, coal distribution and Guinness bottling – were doing well despite the recession. As a member of the Town Council he was at the centre of things, had a high profile, and, all going well, had a good chance of being nominated by the Party for the national elections in 1976. He would poll well, he felt sure; he had done a lot for the town. He wasn't quite sure where he stood with the Monsignor, however; there was something inscrutable about the elderly priest. It was a pity the raffle hadn't been more successful but at least it was well known that he (TJ) had worked hard at it, making speeches and giving time off to his employees to sell tickets.

The bagpipes and drums had been put away when they arrived at the hall. The rafters supporting the corrugated-iron roof still seemed to have the skirl of bag-pipes echoing around them. The hall was also used for plays and melodramas, whist drives, Legion of Mary and Patrician meetings.

Sergeant Fitzpatrick's bulk filled the entrance; he acted as doorman now but would later supervise the draw.

"Everything in order, Sergeant?" TJ inquired as he brushed past him.

"Yes, sir." The sergeant tipped an index finger to the peak of his cap and stepped back a pace to let TJ and the monsignor pass.

"Remind me to send up the baps and turnovers to the barracks for the weekend," TJ threw back in a stage whisper.

"I will. Thanks."

The monsignor sniffed the air. He didn't much care for the way TJ reminded people of favours. Still, no one was perfect … better not to make the best the enemy of the good. The town needed TJ's drive; emigration was high enough already and was beginning to affect the congregation – and the church dues. For TJ there was always a way. Should he suggest that to him as a political slogan. "TJ will find a way."

The altar ladies set about tea while the drum of tickets was manhandled onto a simple wooden stage. The children, including Jimmy, naturally 'gravitated' to the loft which served as 'the gods' whenever a play was being put on. On the way up the stairs Sergeant Fitzpatrick's daughter handed him a rubber ball which he put in his pocket.

"Thanks, Sarah," he said. "Does your Daddy know?" Sarah could always be relied on to recycle balls confiscated by the Sergeant from kids playing in the streets.

"I don't know." She shrugged. It didn't bother her one way or the other.

Jimmy looked down from the balcony; the stage was the altar now and he was outside it.

Most people crowded into the body of the hall, including the local reporter who brought his good camera. Corballed pyramids of sandwiches appeared on trestle tables and vats of freshly brewed tea. TJ bit into a sandwich and gave a grunt of acknowledgment. Yes, it was his bread all right. He had introduced the sliced pan to the town and was glad to see it catching on. He kept a large tray under the slicing machine to collect crumbs and dislodged crusts; these were gathered up to make Chester cake, which also sold well.

TJ asked for silence, using flat hands to tamp down the chatter. He introduced the monsignor, who wished to say a few words.

The monsignor crossed the stage to a makeshift dais. "My Dear Brethren, this is a very happy and special occasion. It shows what great community action this town is capable of. I want to thank all those who organised the raffle, ticket sellers, the drama group, the altar ladies, TJ Bowers and the Council ... and not forgetting the pipe band for providing the hall. I also want to thank those who bought tickets, mainly your good selves. You'll be glad to hear that your efforts resulted in a net figure of £8,655, almost enough to re-roof the church," He put it as positively as he could. "I now call on TJ Bowers to make the draw. Sergeant Fitzpatrick will ensure fair play."

Trying to quell the laughter with a grave demeanour, the sergeant shifted his bulk closer to the drum and stood, legs spread like a soldier guarding a catafalque.

As TJ made his way to the drum the local bookie whispered to his pals, "That Mercedes is mine. I bought ten tickets." He pounded a fist into an open palm to impress the gods of chance.

A piper still dressed in saffron kilt nudged him in the ribs. "That's more than you give for the Easter dues."

"I only bought one ticket," Mosey admitted. "I haven't a prayer." But his eyes looked bright and hopeful through the patina of coal dust. If by any chance he did win the car he'd have to sell it; he'd be ridiculed by all and sundry if he drove a Mercedes around the town.

At a given signal, one of the altar ladies spun the drum. TJ pulled out a ticket and passed it to the monsignor who announced, "The third prize of a week for two in London goes to our own … Tommy Sinnot of Lady Lane. Is he in the hall?"

He wasn't, but a cheer went up from his friends and neighbours, many of whom wondered how Tommy, who was a bit simple, would manage in

London. The second prize – a week for two in Lourdes – went to Pat Kinsella, who grinned from ear to ear as the monsignor handed him the certificate. Another popular winner, Pat had seven children, one of whom had a deformed foot. Lourdes might just be the job. The reporter scribbled in his notebook, then took a photograph of Pat standing beside the monsignor and TJ with the drum in the background.

"And now for the grand prize…" The monsignor didn't have to ask for silence. The crowd pressed forward around the foot of the stage. "…the Mercedes motor car with a three-litre engine, leather upholstery and a walnut dashboard is valued at almost £4,000 and worth every penny of it." The sleek, powerful car, draped in yellow ribbons and assorted bunting, had been on show in every town and village of the county for the last eighteen months, and now it stood in gleaming splendour just outside the pipe-band hall waiting to be driven away by the lucky winner.

As the drum was spun, the crowd went quiet, storming heaven with silent prayerful hopes. With slow deliberate movements bordering on the funereal, TJ picked out a ticket and handed it carefully to the monsignor. Sergeant Fitzpatrick craned forward to fulfil his supervisory duty.

"And the winner of this magnificent automobile is…" the monsignor paused with a dramatist's instinct. The reporter's pencil hovered over his note-book. The rattling of teacups ceased; even the kids in the loft were quiet.

"…Michael Staunton of Wellington Road…"

"Who?" Someone asked. People exchanged glances of startled curiosity.

"Wellington Road … Dublin." The monsignor looked up from under his glasses to see the collective grimace of his flock.

"But who is he?" the bookie asked in a pained voice.

TJ furrowed his long face, raking the corners of memory. "He left the town several years ago. He's a doctor – a surgeon – up in Dublin."

Despite the presence of the monsignor, various forms of the Lord's name were murmured in different parts of the hall. The earlier excitement had suddenly seeped away and was replaced by a fatalistic sense of disappointment. They couldn't win for losing; that was their lot. It was foolish to get their hopes up. Ever.

"I … I sold him the ticket," Mosey Keane volunteered, as if he were making a public confession. "He bought a whole book…" Conscious of inquisitive glances, he added, "We were in the same class in primary school." He fell silent and withdrew into his shell. Maybe he'd said too much already.

"Isn't it just typical," one of the altar ladies sighed. "Money gets money. Surgeons up in Dublin charge a fortune. Mrs. Moloney had to pay £250 for her veins. Two hundred and fifty pounds!" This was greeted by gasps followed by a murmur of resigned assent.

"Maybe…" TJ began, and stopped as if to

gather strength for what had suddenly occurred to him. "Maybe he wouldn't accept the car ... or maybe he'd make a large donation ... What do you think, Mosey?" TJ moved to the front of the stage and craned forward, cupping a hand to his ear.

Mosey shrugged helplessly; he didn't know. But the bookie, who also remembered Michael Staunton, was less reticent. "Oh a mean so-and-so, if you ask me, and a snob as well ... Still, the louser's won. So that's that." He knew about luck and chance, or enough to realise there was no logic to it – or justice.

Outside the front windows they could see the Mercedes occupying half the street, a powerful and exotic genie waiting to serve its new master. From the balcony Jimmy looked down on the stage where, although there was no play in progress, some kind of plot was nevertheless beginning to unfold. He placed the rubber ball Sarah had given him between his chin and the balustrade.

"I wonder if..." TJ began again, diffidently for him, and with a covert glance towards the monsignor, "...if we shouldn't ... make another draw...?" He waited. The monsignor was impassive, the bushy eyebrows like tendrils growing on the inside of his glasses. "Or better still..." TJ's voice dropped to a lower register, "we just sell the car and give you the proceeds ... Then you'd have enough for the roof..." He gently stroked his chin, senses so alert he could hear the faint rasp of stubble.

"Oh, now..." The monsignor went into a sort of

reverie that people had witnessed before when he stood in the pulpit, mustering his thoughts for the sermon to come. In a way the crowd had been transformed into a congregation again and they waited in respectful silence, until the bookie could restrain himself no longer, "Look, the gouger's won it. Fair's fair. It doesn't matter if he's got bags of money or..."

TJ interrupted quickly, "What do you think, Sergeant?"

A doleful perplexed expression clawed at the sergeant's face; instinctively, he looked to the monsignor, who still seemed a million miles away.

"I ... dunno," he began lamely then, on inspiration, added, "The drum wasn't spun very hard..."

"That's right," TJ concurred heartily. "It was hardly spun at all. We should declare the last draw null and void." More confident now, he went on, "What it comes down to is this. We give away the car to a man who's got everything, or we put a new roof on the church. What did Staunton ever do for the town? He got a good free education from the Christian Brothers and then took off for the big smoke..." From the corner of his eye he saw the reporter making notes. "This is off the record."

Having formed a mental picture of the regular half-page advertisement for 'TJ Bower's Bread and Coal', the reporter put the notebook in his pocket. The trouble with a small newspaper was that it made any principled stand seem faintly ridiculous. He would really have to apply for a job on one of the Dublin papers.

"What about Mosey Keane?" the bookie asked. "He's supposed to get £20 commission for selling the winning ticket."

"That can easily be fixed," TJ answered, realising that by shifting his ground the bookie had weakened his argument. "I'm sure the monsignor will see Mosey all right." He waited for confirmation, then wondered if the priest had heard him at all. He was about to repeat the suggestion when the monsignor suddenly spoke out.

"Ah, but you see the dilemma that now confronts us. If we give Mosey the commission for selling the winning ticket then how can we at the same time say that the draw was null and void? Do you see the inconsistency?" He opened his hands, turning over to the people this logical conundrum which, to TJ's less cluttered mind, was neither here nor there. In fact, he smiled inwardly because the answer had already come to him.

"What I propose is this," he said with all the gravitas he employed at Council meetings. "We declare the draw null and void. So, there was no winning ticket. But as a gesture of goodwill the monsignor could make an ex gratia payment of £20 to Mosey Keane who, as we all know, worked very hard during the campaign." He stepped back from the dais; it was his last and best word on the subject. The bit of Latin never hurt. Case closed.

The bookie pursed his lips and looked around, reading the hall; no one was rushing to his standard. Whatever support he might have had earlier on had now evaporated…

———————————

The monsignor had at last heard the voice of the people. He simply said, "Well…" in the same tone as he might have said, "Amen." Christ had supported pragmatism when he praised the steward who was wiser in his generation than the children of light. One word, "Well…" was the endorsement that finally cleared the air. Before stepping down from the stage the monsignor's eye caught a steady face in the balcony and for a brief moment he sensed again the over-powering smell of incense.

Dies Irae

WHEN PEADAR REACHED the top of the hill he stopped and looked back to see his own footprints in the snow, just one track of prints, for no one else was up yet on this Sunday morning in early December. From his vantage point he could see some of the chimneys begin to release curls of smoke into the frosty air; the town was just beginning to stir. He felt sort of special, a trail-blazer. Slinging the black draw-string bag over his shoulder, he turned into the churchyard and passed the cross on his way to the sacristy. The cross, which held a life-size figure of Jesus, was fringed with snow but not the face of Christ, which was slumped under the crown of thorns.

Peadar liked serving first mass; it felt good to be up early even in winter. The other altar boys were glad to leave it to him. Indeed, they thought he was mad to volunteer for it every Sunday, but he regarded it as a privilege. Some of the adults in the town were sure he would develop a vocation and often said he had the makings of a priest. He wasn't sure yet; time would tell.

Although it was still only twenty minutes to seven he quickly donned his soutane and surplice and put on his black canvas shoes. The Sacristan arrived in a little while and started to fire up the boiler. His name was Matt and he was tall, stooped and completely bald except for an isolated sprig of grey hair between the temples.

"It's old Father Nolan this morning," Matt grumbled. "He'll freeze to death if I don't get this boiler going."

"Can I do the bell?" Peadar asked, knowing that Matt would be more than happy to delegate that task.

"All right," Matt said grudgingly. "You'd better go now. It's almost ten to."

Peadar slipped out, went round to the front of the church and entered the side door leading to the belfry. He caught hold of the great knotted rope that drilled its way down through several wooden floors, and pulled until he got the huge cast-iron bell to swing. The first peal came down to him like the voice of God. Instead of letting the rope slip back through his hands he held on tightly and was carried up some fifteen feet as the bell swung back. He rode the rope for all nine peals then rushed back to the sacristy, his face flushed despite the icy conditions. His breath turned white in the air and the hem of the soutane flapped against his thin calves.

Father Nolan was robing in the vestry, struggling to get the chasuble over his old sagging head. Matt stood at a discreet distance, knowing better than to offer assistance. Peadar, who was in awe of him, gathered up the silver tray bearing the lavabo bowl and the cruets and, without a word, carried them out to the altar and placed them on the credence table. Already the church held some early arrivals, the 'Holy Marys' and the altar women who, the day before, had arranged the flowers and linens. Peadar had schooled himself not to look out at the congregation; it didn't seem right somehow. A certain decorum was called for, though sometimes he couldn't resist an occasional peep, especially if he thought Sheila Hennessey might be out there. The smell of the wine reminded him of Christmas, which was only three weeks away.

Back in the sacristy Father Nolan was awkwardly putting the altar breads into the ciborium. "*Forti et fideli nihil difficile,*" he said in a hoarse whisper.

Peadar wondered what it meant; it wasn't mass Latin, he felt sure. He also noticed a tremor in the priest's hand as he lit the taper for him. From a distance Matt looked on, touched a finger to his temple, twirled it and grinned. Peadar often wondered how Matt could be so off-hand and disrespectful, as if his job was only a job and nothing more than that; in Peadar's mind anything to do with the altar was special, sacred.

"Thanks Father," he said when the taper was finally lit. The priest gave him a strange look as if he didn't recognise him; the whites of his eyes were yellowing like old enamel, and his vacant face seemed to be collapsing into its lifelines.

Bearing the taper in front of him, Peadar went out again to the chancel, this time going behind the altar where there was a simple wooden structure almost like a gallows.

He went up the ladder, holding the taper in one

hand, and walked carefully along the wooden platform that ran the whole length of the altar. He picked his steps delicately so as not to trip on the hem of the soutane which was a little too long for him – he had not 'grown into it' yet, as his mother had predicted when she'd run it up for him on her Singer sewing machine.

Peadar had to stretch as far as he could to reach the wick of the first candle and was relieved that it took light almost immediately. But he had five more to do and there was always one that caused difficulty – where the wick had become embedded in the wax. So far so good, he thought moving cautiously along the narrow platform to the sixth candle. To reach it he had to go perilously close to the edge of the platform which was at least twenty feet up – higher even than the reredos. He touched the top of the candle with the lit taper. Nothing happened. This was the one. There was always one. He bent the taper a little to improve the angle and tried again.

Nothing.

Without meaning to, he glanced out towards the body of the church, which was surprisingly full, and couldn't help noticing Sheila Hennessey kneeling at the front of the organ gallery. In the early morning light those green eyes seemed to be directed at him. Not wanting to look foolish in front of her, he tried a different angle with the taper. His hand began to tremble and through the thin canvas soles his toes could feel the edge of the gradine. Keep cool, he thought, and don't overbalance.

There had to be six candles lighting; five would be no good. The mass wouldn't be right with five. This was his responsibility. Oh God, let it light, he thought or prayed, and not just to save his face in front of Hennessey. The wax was now running down the candle and still there was no sign of the wick. He bent the taper again, almost breaking it in desperation. Then to his immense relief it took; the little flame spurted up, flickered for a while and steadied itself.

Like the plate-spinner in a circus, he did a quick inventory of all six candles. Satisfied, he extinguished the taper and climbed down the ladder. Passing the side altar, he noticed a woman kneeling at the rail. She beckoned to him and whispered, "C'mere, sonny."

It was Mrs. Sheehan from up the town. For some reason the poorer people lived up the town whereas the merchants and shopkeepers lived lower down, near the river.

"Tell the priest I have to be churched," she said.

He nodded and went inside.

Father Nolan didn't react well. "What ... now? No. Can't do it now." His grave, lined face was more confused than angry.

Peadar looked for help to Matt, who said in a soft, knowing voice, "He's forgotten the drill."

"Can't you get him the book?" Peadar suggested. He knew most of the Latin but not exactly what it meant. Something to do with cleansing and child-birth.

"I don't know where it is. Or the aspergillum

for that matter," Matt said indifferently. "Anyway that's not my job. They're going to retire me at sixty-five. He's already," he jerked his thumb at the priest, "in his late eighties."

"What'll I do?"

"Oh, go out and tell her something." Matt went back to the boiler.

Rehearsing a number of excuses, none of them satisfactory, Peadar approached the woman. "Mrs. Sheehan," he said apologetically, "Father Nolan can't do it just now…"

"Well, what am I supposed to do? Young Father Doyle who did the baptism said I was to come here this morning to be churched." Her face showed vexation but also a fear that she might be derelict in her religious duty.

"Don't worry," Peadar said as if he had power to bend the rules; in a way his presence on the altar did give him status. Continuing to improvise, he added. "If you call at the presbytery after mass the housekeeper will give you an appointment." It worked. Mrs. Sheehan got to her feet, genuflected and went back to her pew.

What was it about the altar, the surplice and soutane that gave him such authority, that turned him from a schoolboy of little account into a figure of leadership, a priest in the making though not, he hoped, a priesteen? He knew he shouldn't get carried away by these borrowed plumes. Had Hennessey witnessed the incident from the gallery? That too was an unworthy thought.

"Introibo ad altare Dei." They were off. Peadar

responded in his loud voice that was just beginning to break, leading the congregation who mumbled the Latin as best they could. Of course, no one understood what it meant except for him and the priest. He had to stay alert though, especially with Father Nolan, and carry the hand-bell with him when he changed from one side of the steps to the other, making sure that the bell didn't emit as much as a tinkle, since that would throw the congregation into confusion. So he had to move smoothly and carefully as if walking on eggs, trying also to prevent his slippers from squeaking on the marble surface.

The chancel area between the rails and the altar was his domain; he was possessive about it and in turn it gave him a sense of inclusion. He was the bridge between the priest and the people. From time to time he couldn't help musing on the green eyes in the gallery and the possibility that they might be aimed in his direction. It was a pity his soutane was a little too long and that, thanks to his mother, the surplice put forth an excessive froth of Carrickmacross lace. He felt it was cissyish.

"*Spera in Deo...*" His voice rang out, answering the priest, as promptly as an echo.

He knelt on the third step, directly opposite the missal, keeping his back straight, the hand-bell within easy reach.

He bowed during the Confiteor, turning towards Father Nolan at the words: 'Tibi Pater'. Apart from the seasonal sniffles and coughing of the congregation, it was going like clock-work. The

Kyrie and the Gloria came and went and then the priest read the Epistle, after which Peadar transferred the missal to the Gospel side of the altar, taking care to genuflect as he passed the Tabernacle.

At the end of the Gospel he sang out, "*Laus tibi, Christe,*" and shortly afterwards went to serve the cruets even though no cue had been given. Father Nolan washed his fingers in the lavabo bowl and then a strange thing happened. He looked down at Peadar without any recognition in his eyes and said hoarsely, "*Fiat experimentum in corpore…*"

Peadar had never heard this before and wasn't sure if he was meant to respond or not. So he simply said, "Amen."

Replacing the cruets on the credence table, he went back to his place and, before turning to kneel, had a brief glance out into the body of the church but was unable to locate Hennessey. Instead he saw Miss Corcoran, the principal of the girls' school in the front row. He would recognise those glasses and that mantilla anywhere. He lowered his eyes immediately and put on his most devout expression while at the same time holding his right hand to his breast like a Roman centurion. He looked forward to serving communion, holding the gold-plated paten under all the chins of different heights, seeing the assortment of tongues in all their weird shapes, the fluttering eyelids He hoped Hennessey would be up to receive. There wouldn't be eye contact of course, but he might just touch her slender throat with the edge of the paten and see if she acknowledged it.

With any luck he might see her again later that afternoon at the matinée in the Ritz cinema. He would be going because his mother had no reason to prevent him when the weather was bad – and there was a scary picture playing, 'Psycho'. That meant that all the girls would be rushing with muffled shrieks in and out to the Ladies. He could stand at the back and maybe bump into Hennessey in the darkness…

He snapped to in time to ring the bell three times during the Sanctus. Father Nolan made the sign of the cross once over the host and once over the chalice, then bent low for the Consecration. The church fell silent for this most sacred moment and Peadar crept up the steps, bringing the hand-bell with him. He knelt near the predella and, at the elevation of the host, he raised the hem of the chasuble with one hand and rang the bell with the other. Alert, he waited to repeat the procedure during the elevation of the chalice.

But, to his consternation, the moment never came, and Father Nolan went straight into the Pater Noster. This was wrong, terribly wrong; the sacrament of the Eucharist had not been performed properly. Peadar didn't know what to do. On an impulse he rang the bell a second time to remind the priest but Father Nolan had gone on to the Agnus Dei. He didn't seem to hear the bell and carried on in a world of his own. Gone, suddenly gone was Peadar's self-assurance; a feeling of dread crawled over him. Was the mass no good now? An arch without a keystone? He himself could avoid mortal sin by going to a later mass but what of the congregation? Responsibility for their souls now rested on his shoulders. What should he do? What could he do? The enormity of the mistake made him feel faint. And to think that just twenty minutes earlier his only concern was lighting the sixth candle.

But wait, surely God would understand. Father Nolan had gone by the book for fifty years. God wasn't going to blame him now for one little slip. He tried to put it out of his mind and concentrate on the job in hand just like Matt would do. He also tried to pretend he didn't hear the harsh whisper coming from behind him but he could feel the bespectacled eyes boring a hole through his back.

"Come here at once:" Again, inevitable, even harsher.

Reluctantly and with heart racing, he went to the altar rail where Miss Corcoran was kneeling in such a crouch that little more than the black mantilla appeared above the rail. "Father Nolan omitted to consecrate the wine. Go and tell him." The bifocals carried authority but the misplaced eyes behind them were tight with worry.

Peadar knew that this was beyond him. An acolyte had never dared to instruct the celebrant. It was unthinkable. Besides, Father Nolan might well give him a clip on the ear right then and there in full view of the congregation – and Hennessey.

"I ... don't think so," he stammered. And then, with a silent prayer for forgiveness, he lied, "He said the words over the wine … softly."

"Well I didn't hear. Go and check with him immediately. Go now before it's too late." It was clear that she would have done it herself except that women weren't allowed on the altar. A teacher out-ranked an altar boy, even one with the makings of a priest. Miserably, Peadar dragged himself up the steps and stood hang-dog until the priest became aware of his presence, and gave him a brief sideways glance.

"The wine, Father … Did you … consecrate the wine?" There were times in the past when Peadar had to wait longer for an answer, but this moment of silence was the most fraught by far, as he looked up fearfully into the face of the priest which held in every confused line and wrinkle the revelation that there were no answers even after half a century of prayer and sacrifice. It came suddenly to Peadar that you make your own certainty – and then surround it with ritual.

"*Nitor in adversum*," Father Nolan mumbled. "*Frangas, non flectes.*" He made a slight dismissive movement with his hand.

Whatever had been said, had said it all. So be it, Peadar thought, returning to the altar rail.

"It's all right."

"What did he say?" Miss Corcoran demanded.

Drawing on some reserve of articulacy, Peadar replied, "Transubstantiation has been accomplished. *Dignum et justum est*," he added for good measure. He braved Miss Corcoran's stare until she eventually prised herself away from the altar rail and returned to her seat. Peadar had his chancel back to himself, and his sanctuary.

However, despite the coldness of the church – thanks to the ineffectual sacristan – he felt sweat in his arm-pits and he now had a personal dilemma. Should he receive Communion or not? If he didn't, it would be noticed by the owlish and ever-vigilant Miss Corcoran. If he did, he wouldn't be able to receive at a later mass. But that assumed that transubstantiation had in fact occurred at this one. There was also the question of the lie he told; could he receive the sacrament at all without first confessing the sin and making a firm purpose of amendment – or could he put it down to a 'mental reservation'? It was dreadfully complicated with so many 'ifs' and 'buts', and he had precious little time to decide.

He rang the bell at each *'Domine non sum dignus'* and watched Father Nolan administer Communion to himself. God forgive me, he thought. In for a penny, in for a pound. He fetched the paten and went to receive. He thought the host might burn his tongue but it didn't. He accompanied the priest to the altar rail where part of the congregation already knelt. There was no sign of Miss Corcoran, who was normally one of the first up; she had obviously made a different decision. He couldn't help noticing how slow and ponderous were Father Nolan's movements, how difficult it was for him to pick the hosts from the ciborium with his arthritic fingers. Who could not forgive him for his one fall from grace? He felt an onrush of pity for the old priest and was also ashamed, for who was he to pity this most respected of men? So absorbed was he that he missed his opportunity to touch the paten to the elegant throat of Hennessey, but he did notice her trim figure gliding down the nave.

Ita missa est … Go, the mass is ended.

Then there were the prayers for the conversion of Russia and suddenly it was all over. He watched Father Nolan disrobe in the vestry, then sought out Matt to tell him what had happened at the Eucharist.

"I told you he was gone gaga," Matt observed. "'Twas bound to happen sooner or later."

"We'll have to tell someone," Peadar said, nervously. "What if he slips up again next Sunday? Maybe you could have a word with the monsignor or one of the younger priests." His attempt to delegate the unpleasant task was thrown back in his face.

"Me?" Matt queried with a leer that made his ears move. "It's not my job to tell anyone anything. They don't even let me count the collection."

Peadar put his shoes and altar clothes in the draw-string bag and left the sacristy. There was sleet falling; it looked as if it might soon turn into ordinary, disappointing rain. He saw the last few stragglers – no longer a congregation – leaving the churchyard. What had he done to them and what was he going to do? He would have to decide before next Sunday. This was a different kind of responsibility which had nothing to do with tasks, rites, rubrics, candles and Latin responses; it went right to the heart.

Passing by the big cross in the churchyard, he looked at the slumped face of Christ.

Help me out of this, he said under his breath.

He walked down the hill. His footprints were no longer visible in the snow, which had been churned up by the other mass-goers.

That afternoon he did meet Hennessey at the matinée and it was she who started the conversation, "What was all that about this morning?"

"Oh, just a technical problem. We sorted it out," he said lightly.

"What did you say to Miss Corcoran?" she asked, peering at him in the darkness. There was a smell of liquorice on her breath; she had been to the shop during the cinema ads.

"Miss Corcoran?" Her teacher. Of course. She wasn't particularly interested in Father Nolan. "I told her not to worry. There was no need for her to interfere," he added, leaving it a little vague as to whether those were his exact words.

"You said that?" She let out a sigh of appreciation that sang in his ears.

He was on his way. Any day now he would be bringing her to the matinée, instead of lurking in the back waiting for a chance encounter. He would buy her a bag of Liquorice Allsorts if he had the money.

By the middle of the week he began to worry again about having to tell the monsignor. Maybe he could get his Dad to do it. As it happened, no action was needed.

On Thursday evening, at tea-time, his Dad announced that Father Nolan had passed on.

"A good man," he said. "And a great age. Gone to his eternal reward."

Peadar sat transfixed. When he passed the cross and asked for help he hadn't meant … No, steady on, it was just a coincidence. Father Nolan must have known he was going to die soon. Despite his brusqueness at times, he had remained a humble man. Peadar knew now that he didn't have the makings of a priest – not one like Father Nolan anyway – and that he would never set foot on the altar again, even as an acolyte.

There was too much protection inside the altar rails, for him at any rate. Sanctuary might keep enemies at bay, but what else would be excluded? He would have to make his own way through life. Maybe his younger brother would grow into the soutane.

And so began the questioning and self-doubt that would last until he had children and learnt from their innocence how to see things as they are, without the distorting lens of ritual.

Bedrock

IT WAS THE THIRD or fourth time Father Tim hadn't mentioned 'Heaven', the Sacristan reflected as he put away the tall candlesticks and coffin table in the crypt of the church. John Canavan had been Sacristan at Christ the Redeemer's for almost thirty years and he was concerned about the changes the new curate, Father Tim, was introducing into the liturgy.

Maybe it even went further than the liturgy. Just after the funeral mass John had approached the new curate and mentioned that the monsignor – now unfortunately retired – always announced that the dear departed had gone straight to Heaven. The Mons, as he was called, felt that the mourners appreciated the mention of Heaven; the word itself had a comforting ring to it.

"Well, John, Heaven is a difficult concept for people nowadays, post-Vatican Two." As he spoke Father Tim was rapidly changing out of his altar clothes in the sacristy. He left them for John to hang up. "Have to be on the first tee in twelve minutes." He rushed out in a flurry of regretful gestures about his own mismanagement of time.

John was coming to the conclusion that this new priest was a little too easy-going about his duties and about doctrine. He had only just arrived at the parish when John decided to apply his usual test of going to confession with a selection of sins which included a few which were really mortal sins but which were now called grave moral disorders. Father Tim was far too easy. There was no penance at all, only an act of contrition. Liberalism, they called it. It wouldn't do.

John sat for a while in the crypt. It was one of his favourite places, cool and quiet, and he liked to examine the massive foundations of the church, the huge blocks of granite that carried the walls and buttresses. Peter was the original rock, imperishable, unchanging... When he finally left the crypt he carefully bolted the door behind him. Altar boys had been known to get in there to play scary games and desecrate whatever few bones they might find lying around.

He walked around the churchyard jangling his keys, which were attached to a large metal loop almost as big as a Chinese magic ring. He passed the cross with the life-size figure of Jesus yielding up his spirit. Figures at the foot of the cross included Mary, to whom John was especially devoted, due to his mother's influence before her recent death. The figure of the centurion piercing Christ's body with a lance always upset him. It was partly because of the deed itself but also because of the superior sneer on the face of the soldier. He was often tempted to smash in that haughty pagan face.

Sometime later, having carefully cross-checked his watch with the clock in the vestry, he went to the belfry to ring the Angelus. He climbed the steeple steps to the first floor and unhooked the bell rope. Of all his many and varied tasks this was his favourite. And he was good at it. Once when he was off sick an altar boy had to stand in for him, and the bell-ringing was so badly done that several people complained to the old Mons, including Miss Mooney, a local teacher and devout Catholic. John took that as a compliment – one of the few he ever received.

By dextrous pulling of the rope he got the big bell, Ned, swinging but not so much that the clapper made contact. Each time the bell swung back the rope rose like lightening through his hands which he automatically loosened to avoid burns. When he was younger he sometimes rode up on the rope but he was too old for that now. Of course the altar boys always wanted to ride the rope and he had to keep a sharp eye on them. The altar girls had no interest in it whatever; that was something to be grateful for, he supposed.

Having put cotton wool in his left ear he waited for a while, then, at the right moment he gave a hefty pull that brought the clapper fully into play. The first peal rang out. The mighty affirming sound seemed to be confined inside the belfry but he knew it could be heard all over the town and beyond. He visualised the long powerful echo as a comet's tail. Before it died away he tolled again. And then again. The first three peals were followed by a pause. He knew that people had stopped what they were doing; men would be removing hats and caps, women would be crossing themselves. He was calling people to prayer. What higher calling was there?

Then he tolled the second set of three, and then the third set. Pause. And the final nine in fairly quick succession, each new peal silencing the echo of the preceding one, except for the very last which resounded for what seemed like infinity. He loved the pattern of threes; it was a holy sequence that chimed with the mystery of the Trinity. Tolling bells were part of the colour and fabric of life in the town.

Oddly, it never occurred to him to say the Angelus. He assumed implicitly that ringing the bell was a prayer in itself; he made it speak to Mary in a private language. Tongues; it was a form of tongues.

Afterwards, he climbed further up the steeple, using the ladders that joined the trapdoors on each floor. He kept a sharp eye out for woodworm, termites or any form of infestation. As he went higher he could see more and more of the town through the narrow Gothic windows of the spire.

When he eventually reached the belfry proper he examined the big bell, which had been cast in Pennsylvania, the clapper like a bull's scrotum. The bronze was wearing well, all seven tons of it. He had read about hundred-ton bells in Moscow, but Ned was big enough for him, and the sound was sweet and clear. As he examined the huge timbers on which it swung, cold lamenting winds came through the louvred shutters. He felt at home there even though his first experience in the belfry had not been a good one. His predecessor, hating the prospect of imminent retirement, had instructed John to remain in the belfry while the noon-day Angelus was being rung from five floors down. It had been a frightening experience and John had lost almost half the hearing in his left ear. He never complained but he did take precautions to protect his hearing from further damage. The experience had taught him to respect the power and majesty of the bells.

He fetched the binoculars from the niche in the stone wall and looked down at the town. He could see Mrs. Farrelly taking a cauliflower out of the window of her grocery shop but couldn't quite make out who the customer was. Other shops and businesses were closing for the evening, the workers walking or cycling home for their tea. The district nurse had just dismounted her bike and was knocking on the door of Frizelles, where the oldest daughter had some sort of strange, wasting illness. It wasn't all that long ago since the nurse visited his house to check on his mother… He could see across the river to the jetties where a couple of Dutch ships were moored. It was too early for the prostitutes but they would be out later, picking up sailors and bringing them to that infamous lane where the hedges were flattened and only recovered in the weeks following the annual mission.

He next focused on the presbytery, which was behind the church on slightly higher ground. Through the branches of the orchard he could see Father Tim put his golf clubs in the Rover and drive out through the wrought iron gates. Judging by the spray of gravel from the rear wheels of the car, he was very late indeed. The housekeeper was on her knees picking up windfall apples – the June drop. John looked at some of the upstairs windows but couldn't penetrate them. In thirty-five years he had never been inside the presbytery.

He liked to observe. He was invisible to most people and had come to accept that; with the exception of Ms Mooney, they probably didn't even realise it was he who rang the bells. But that didn't mean the townspeople were invisible to him, quite the reverse. He knew more about them than they would ever realise, for example, that the daughter of the chemist gave birth to an illegitimate child right down there in the churchyard, behind the cross. In the light of the waxing moon John had watched the birth throes; he had seen the girl cut the cord with her teeth, bury the afterbirth, wrap the baby in her cardigan and creep out of the churchyard. What became of the baby he never knew. He presumed it was sent for fostering somewhere else in the country, though of course there were other possibilities. The chemist and his even more snobbish wife still behaved as if nothing had happened but John knew the truth. His vantage point was as close to perfect as made no difference.

Before replacing the binoculars he had a final look at the crucifixion tableau in the churchyard; the centurion's lance still pierced the body of Christ. He gave Ned a farewell ping with the nail of his index finger and began the long climb down through the series of trap-doors. It was like going back to 'go' in a game of snakes and ladders.

"Heaven is a difficult concept for people nowadays." He could hardly believe Father Tim had said that. He knew that the Pope had abolished Limbo and that some theologians had doubts about Hell but was it possible that Heaven was on the way out as well? No, they couldn't do that; they couldn't take away people's only reason for hope.

In the nave of the church he can hear his footsteps echoing. He climbs the marble steps to the altar and, once inside the brass gates, basks in that special sense of belonging. He checks the sanctuary lamp, which must never be allowed to go out as long as Christ resides in the tabernacle. As he examines the flowers and altar linens he makes a mental note to have a word with the Ladies' Altar Committee. Having checked the six large candles he prises up a couple of buried wicks from the candle grease; this will make them a lot easier to light. He looks down the body of the church and his gaze rises to the organ loft. God be with the days of proper choirs and himself working the bellows of the organ. It is hard to accept the pop hymns of today and the tinny, trendy guitars. The abolition of the Latin Mass was the thin end of the wedge. There's no ceremony any more, nothing uplifting. Father Tim doesn't seem to understand how important the fundamentals really are. He puts out the banners for the Ladies' Sodality, then locks up and goes home to the cottage he shared with his mother until her death four months ago.

He sits in a chair opposite the one she used to sit in, a plate of ham-and-tongue-paste sandwiches on his knee. His mother's statue of the Infant of Prague is on a shelf of the dresser. There is no head on the statue. He remembers the time the head was accidentally knocked off and his mother's superstitious belief that it was a good omen.

There is no one to confide in. On the stroke of ten he kneels and starts a rosary, offering it up for a strengthening of Father Tim's faith. He would of course continue to keep an eye on the misguided man and drop hints every so often to the effect that currying favour with the liberal element would do him no good in the end, no good at all.

The Mons was a lover of tradition, a great old defender of the faith. It was he who told women not to wear lipstick if they were going to receive Holy Communion. Cosmetics tainted the priest's anointed hands. John's mother was delighted with that rule; it would put a stop to the gallop of the hussies. Her son could only agree. It was a matter of respect, decorum.

Of course his mother always wanted John to become a priest. In her view he had the makings of a great priest, so devout was he by nature. Everyone agreed and when he was fifteen he was sure he got the call. But he couldn't study; his mind was always flitting around from one topic to the next, refusing to settle on anything in particular. And some people said he was too full of scruples. Priests could not afford to suffer from scruples or feelings of unworthiness. No problem there for Father Tim. Anyway, becoming a sacristan wasn't a bad compromise in the end. He couldn't administer the sacraments but he could keep the church in good order – and perhaps some of the trendy priests as well.

A few days later the altar girls failed to turn up for first mass and John prepared to serve it himself, donning surplice and soutane. The collectors were in place – two men who were up early because they were going shooting in the wetlands immediately after mass. John rang the ten-to-seven bell and observed the congregation filing in through the main door. Many stayed smoking on the top step until the very last moment and some of them walked across the mosaic of the Madonna and Child which was set into the concrete. One man actually dropped a cigarette on the mosaic and ground it out with his foot. John winced and turned away.

Some twenty minutes later the same man presented himself at the altar rails to receive Holy Communion and, as John held the paten under his chin, he wondered if this man was in a state of grace at all. At least Miss Mooney, the teacher, set a good example by not wearing any lipstick and by being very devout when she received the host. Father Tim lived up to his reputation as a speed merchant and the mass was over in twenty minutes flat.

Aping the Protestant ministers, Father Tim stood at the church door chatting with the congregation as they left. John stood behind him, noting the people who walked across the mosaic. A light breeze ruffled the lace of his surplice. He couldn't help overhearing Miss Mooney talking to Father Tim, "...two species next Sunday? Wonderful, Father ... very *avant garde...*"

"We have to keep up with the times, Miss Mooney. The symbolic effect of both species is very powerful." The young priest looked into the middle distance as if reflecting further on his pronouncement.

John was trying to cope with this worrying snippet of conversation when, to his astonishment, he saw Miss Mooney walk towards him.

"How are you, John?" Her eyebrows arched, waiting for his response.

"Fine, thank you..."

"I mean since your poor mother died." She tilted her head and gave him a studied though not unsympathetic, look.

"I'm all right, thanks." Nosey biddy, he thought, what's she getting at anyway? To be fair though, she always gave handsomely to the church, fifty euros at least for the Easter dues.

Later, when he was helping the curate disrobe he tried to hold his tongue – know his place, as his mother used to advise – but he just could not and eventually he broached the question of the two species. Next Sunday, Father Tim told him, the communicants would receive both bread and wine.

"Body and blood," John corrected him without thinking.

"Well … yes. Symbolically speaking…" Father Tim brushed his hair, checked his shoulders for dandruff and quickly donned his coat.

John felt a headache coming on; his temples began to throb. God in Heaven more symbols. What about reality? Transubstantiation? The fundamental change that occurred?

"No…" he began. "Not symbols…"

"We must accept modern thinking…"

"But, Father, it's real … It has to be…"

"Must rush now, John. I'll try to explain later on." Father Tim left the vestry in a flurry.

Partly because he needed air, John walked for a while in the churchyard, grim-faced, praying under his breath, praying hard. He couldn't sleep at all that night and in the morning could only face a slice of toast for breakfast. Conscious of the fact that his mother would have rebuked him for that, he forced himself to have another slice – with the chunky marmalade she preferred. As he was leaving the pot of marmalade back in the cupboard he noticed another jar. He spooned some of the contents into a plastic bag which he put in the pocket of his coat.

As he walked through the church yard he was stopped in his tracks by a strange sight near the cross. The figure of the centurion was completely smashed and the lance had been removed from the wound in Christ's side and broken in several places. Vandals or drunks? John thought it unlikely. Father Tim might have hit it coming back from the golf club in his Rover. He gathered up the plaster pieces of the centurion and left them in a pile. They could certainly not be glued back together again; perhaps it would be better not to replace the figure of the cruel Centurion at all.

John had more serious concerns. The time had come to prove Father Tim wrong. He phoned the altar girls and told them there was no need to turn up. He would serve. He spent some time on his own praying in the church, this special hallowed place with its huge pillars, pulpit like the prow of a ship, flaring candlelight, the sanctuary lamp that he would keep lit forever, and the tabernacle which lay at the heart of all belief and was so mystical and awe-inspiring he could hardly bring himself to look at it. Could Father Tim not see the beauty of his own church, the richness and truth?

Father Tim was in the vestry when John arrived and he broached the subject of the smashed statue. "The centurion is a hate figure," the priest said, "so the damage could have been done by a fundamentalist." His tone of voice suggested that there was something very wrong about fundamentals in general. What about the Redemptorists? John thought. Great men. After a one-week mission the town would be flooded with grace. Even the prostitutes would stay at home. He had proved as much with his binoculars on several occasions in the past.

"You said yesterday, Father, that … you would explain…" John hesitated but eventually finished the point.

"Well, John," Father Tim began in a rather offhand way, "there are different views nowadays about transubstantiation. Theologians are allowing more liberal interpretations…" He continued at some length and John felt his scalp lift with pain. There was also an element of fear. When he was a child his mother used to threaten him with the coming of the Anti-Christ when all belief would be lost. Even the priests would turn their backs on the faith; the foundations would crumble … He would have to prove Father Tim wrong. In God's eyes, of course, proof was not as virtuous as blind faith, but where the latter was so obviously lacking, what alternative was there? It had to be proof, proof positive…

Father Tim reminded him about the two species and told him that two extra bottles of wine would be needed as well as a linen cloth to wipe the chalice after each communicant had drunk from it. John said he would see to it and went to put on his surplice and soutane.

Miss Mooney was one of the first to arrive and she knelt in the first pew with a worried expression on her face. Yesterday as she took a short-cut from the school through the church yard she had seen John kneeling at the foot of the cross. He was praying and tears were rolling down his face. Half concealed behind a holly bush she watched as John blessed himself, picked up an iron bar and set about destroying the statue of the Centurion. She had never witnessed such anger, even though it was directed against an inanimate object.

Now as she knelt facing the altar she wondered how she might be able to help him. He was a man who kept himself to himself and would not appreciate interference of any kind. Maybe he was still grieving for his mother. In any case something would have to be done. Perhaps she should enlist the help of Father Tim.

In the sacristy just after the ten-minute bell rang, John uncorked the bottles of red wine. He could prove it. The wine did change into the blood of Christ after the miracle of the Eucharist. It was no longer wine. Why could Father Tim not understand that? Well, he would understand it today because the substance John was about to put into the wine would no longer be present after transubstantiation. *Suscipe Domine sacrificium de manibus*... These were the beloved Latin words that went through his head as he sprinkled rat poison into the wine bottles which he then carried out to the altar and left on the side table with the cruets, chalice and ciborium. He genuflected and returned to the sacristy. All was prepared. Real faith would soon be tested. The poison would not exist after the miracle of transubstantiation – any more than the wine would exist. It would be a red-letter day. His mother would be proud.

Father Tim put the finishing touches to his

vestments. "Ready, John?" He started to walk towards the altar.

"Yes, Father." John fell in behind him, carrying the open mass-book in his spread hands. Both men processed to the altar in single file. The congregation rose as a sign of respect. John had an expectant, devout smile on his normally stern face. Miss Mooney, who stood at the front of the congregation, was glad that he seemed to be in better form.

Grey and Brown Unrelieved

COLD BREEZES THAT SWEPT down from the hills indicated that summer was drawing to a close; there would be few good days left and those would have to be carefully husbanded. Dermot had let the farm go after the tragedy and still hadn't recovered lost ground. He looked up when he recognised the sounds of a tractor as it laboured up the lane and turned into his farmyard. Jim Doorly was returning the buck-rake he'd borrowed to bring in his own hay before the weather turned.

They greeted each other and set about unhooking the apparatus from the back of the tractor. Dermot knew his brother-in-law well enough to sense that his silence was denser than usual – almost to the point of rebuke. Maybe he was still grieving for his sister, Dermot's late wife. Her death had hit them both hard.

"What's up, Jim?"

Jim laid down the spanner and ratcheted up his complaining back. He seemed to be more annoyed than sad. "That yoke below in the field … What … what got into you? I still can't believe … especially now."

"Well, it's done." Dermot doubted himself for a while but he didn't really regret his decision, and he thought Betty would have approved. Of course if she hadn't died, the idea would probably never have occurred to him. It was hard to explain his motives to Jim, even to himself.

"You know what people are like around here." There was a trace of accusation in Jim's tone, and a hint of offended pride. And there was an injunction to toe the line, obey the conventions of the townland, and do nothing that might draw attention to himself. People who sought the limelight were looking for trouble.

They carried the buck-rake to the back of the hayshed and propped it up against the wall. From a nearby stable they could hear the calves head-butting the milk buckets. One of the many cats passed Dermot by with a disdainful glance, going towards the stables on the scent of fresh warm milk.

"It's only eight months since Betty … passed on."

"I know that, Jim."

"Well … I mean … that gazebo down there in the field … for all to see…"

Dermot was beginning to understand. His odd behaviour was probably interpreted by some as showing disrespect for Betty's memory. The rules of grieving were the strictest of all; no errant behaviour of any kind was permitted. It was ironic because Betty had great style about her and shone wherever she went. She didn't worry much about convention. From the moment Dermot met her six years earlier, everything was brighter, more colourful. Even the grey, misty rain had a touch of slate-blue if you looked closely enough. What he had done was not disrespectful, just the opposite.

He was trying to preserve her brightness.

In the weeks following Betty's death, it seemed as if a grey fog descended and settled all over the valley. Dermot let the farm work get on top of him, and mud and slurry spread over the yard, right up to the door of the house. Even the greenest field turned mud-brown when the rain swept over the hills in squalls or, more usually, in an endless drizzle that could drive people quietly mad. The cattle, once his pride and joy, seemed lumpish and dumb.

He began to use the computer that Betty had installed in the spare room. He discovered the internet and spent hours going from site to site, distracting himself with the news and facts of the world. He buried himself in trivia, and allowed himself to be led from one site to another for no reason, other than the existence of links. It was numbing and it passed the time when he couldn't sleep.

Maybe it was some website that triggered the notion. And he sensed, even when he rang the zoo, that he might have been embarking on a mad venture. Wheels were put in motion and carried him along. The appropriate EU passport was arranged and eventually, almost to his surprise – as if someone else had made the decision – the zebra arrived.

She walked with dignity down the ramp from the back of a truck and drank delicately from the trough in the farmyard. He stood watching, unable to take his eyes away. Her stripes dazzled him at first; his eyes didn't know whether to follow the black or the white and went from one to the other until he felt dizzy. The black made the white look even brighter. He gradually learned how to look at her amazing coat. He took in the gentle eyes and thick mane. His heart felt lighter and he couldn't deny the ridiculous feeling that Betty was standing beside him again in the yard.

"You've gone on a bit of a solo run there, Dermot," the vet said as she got out of her car and walked towards the zebra. She wore green wellingtons and blue overalls and carried the stethoscope around her neck. "I know a couple of farmers who've gone in for ostriches but this is a first."

Dermot didn't mind the ribbing. Maureen had been a good friend of Betty's and indeed of his. They used to kid her about her dungarees and boots but Maureen had little interest in clothes. Dermot didn't interrupt while Maureen examined the zebra. She eventually pronounced her to be in good fettle.

"She's also in foal."

"In foal? I didn't know that." Another gift, Dermot thought. He would care for the foal. He

Didn't have a name for him or her yet but the mother would be called Zoe. It had to be an exotic name and it had to have a 'z' in it – for zebra and for the stripes. If the foal was a male he might call it Zorro.

"Isn't she amazing?" He noticed that Maureen was still patting the zebra's neck.

"Yes, she is." Maureen paused for an instant. "I

think I understand why…"

"Why what?"

"Why you got the zebra…" She produced a handkerchief and blew her nose. Then she consulted her watch in an impatient gesture, turned and walked quickly towards her car.

Zoe didn't exactly blend in, in fact she stood out a mile but the cattle didn't seem to mind her. In fact one old Friesian cow followed her wherever she went in the field like a faithful chaperone. Whenever Dermot looked into the field his eyes would be immediately drawn to the startling vertiginous coat of the zebra. It was like a powerful spotlight and it brought the proper colour flooding back – to the rolling pasture with clumps of purple clover, the furze-rich hedges, and the trees and hills that formed more distant boundaries.

In the past there wasn't much traffic up and down the lane but after Zoe's arrival it increased five-fold. People came out from the town on Sundays to look over the hedge. Dermot often knew the people well but whenever he went to greet them, they would invariably hurry off, pretending they hadn't seen him. Were they embarrassed for themselves or for him? Did they think he had gone mad with grief, or worse still, had become a loud and fancy man indulging a superficial whim?

Whenever he did manage to encounter someone looking over the hedge they would try, rather sheepishly, to make light of it. "Just passing," was a common response. There were also some comments about the zebra and though these were complimentary for the most part, they seemed to be either a little forced or to leave a lot unsaid.

Once when Dermot was standing in the field, admiring Zoe – who was drinking from a galvanised trough – Jim came up behind him.

"Special, isn't she?" Dermot hadn't even heard the tractor chugging up the lane.

"Just another animal." Jim gave him an odd look. "I'll leave the fodder in the yard." He walked back to the tractor, swinging a stick through the long grass, knocking the heads off the taller shoots of cow parsley and thistle. The indifferent and absent-minded way he walked and swung the stick suggested he was at a loss.

Dermot realised that he would have to explain himself more fully to Jim, how he still loved Betty and would never look at another woman, how some of the radiance had returned. He owed him that much.

A couple of days later he received a letter from Maureen which merely wished him well and referred him to an enclosed poem. The poem read:

PATTERNS
Chess-piece horses, recognisable
at a glance by their foals;
finger-print whorls swap heat, send
ripples of cool air between the coils
of light and shade. In the wavering
air of the Serengeti plain when thousands
of zebra migrate together, the shimmer
of stripes mesmerise and bewilder

predatory cats who grow headachy
in long grass and lose their appetites.
Nature sometimes protects her masterpieces.

Dermot read it a few times and then propped it up against the blue-and-white milk jug. He would read it again. It encouraged him that Maureen, at least, understood what it was that possessed him. He read it again before going upstairs; it helped him face the empty bed.

About three weeks from full term, Zoe showed signs of an early delivery. Not taking any chances, Dermot sent for Maureen who, after careful examination, said it was a false alarm.

"Are you sure?" Dermot asked anxiously.

"Yes. She may have had a little too much nitrogen from the clover, but she's fine. Let her back out in the field. Bring her into the stable in two weeks from now. That should be plenty of time."

"Thanks for the poem, by the way. Did you write it?"

She gave a brusque wave of her hand. "Oh, just a few jottings…"

"I liked it a lot. 'Nature protecting her masterpieces…'" He glanced from her to Zoe.

Maureen removed her goggles and looked closely at him. "How are you doing, Dermot?"

"Not so bad now. You?"

"OK…" She looked down at her green wellingtons for a while, then nodded towards Zoe. "She'll brighten the winter for you."

"Yes, she will." He smiled because Maureen understood.

On the following Wednesday morning Dermot set about milking the cows. Although he still missed Betty's singing, which used to carry from the house across the farmyard, he felt better than he had for some time. It was his practice to go and look at Zoe as soon as he finished the milking. He let the cows out of their stalls and started them on their way to the field. The dog would make sure they got there safely. He then walked down the lane to see the zebra.

The hedge was gapped here and there from the crush of onlookers, mercifully absent today. Maybe the novelty was wearing off at last. At first, he couldn't see the zebra, which was unusual, given her striking form. Then he saw her lying down, half hidden by the trough. The big old chaperone cow stood over her. As he got closer a bad feeling crawled through him. Her flanks were still, too still. She didn't seem to be breathing. Then he saw the massive wound in her side. The still-wadded buck-shot was lodged in the wound. The foetus was also dead.

He sank to his knees sick at heart, knowing that Jim had done it. The big cow's head lolled from side to side and her tail kept the flies away from Zoe's body. Dermot touched the striped hide and gently closed the eyes. A sharp breeze brought dark, slowly moving clouds down from the hills, and it began to rain, slowly at first, and then steadily and heavily as the sky closed in and formed a dark, unbroken canopy.

Local Ways and the Colorado Beetle

THE WRITING MAY have been on the wall for some time but John Keating was far from easy in his mind when he was summoned to the sickroom.

For weeks, waiting for this moment, he had pestered his sister, Rose, and on one occasion had followed her into the small pantry where she strained the milk.

"Has he asked for me?"

"No." She tried to soften the blow by adding, "Not yet." Rose, of course, could come and go as she pleased because she tended to the old man, fed him broth, emptied the commode, trimmed the oil lamp which he still used even though they had the electricity for over four years. The great thing about an oil lamp, he used to say, was that you could move it where you wanted, whereas a light bulb was fixed in one spot on the ceiling. Rose had never fallen out with the old man; maybe she lacked the power to offend him. For John it was different and as he crossed the flagstones of the kitchen to the bottom of the stairs, he hoped that he would have a chance to make peace with his father before he died.

He was under no illusion about his own failure. His father had signed over the farm to him five years ago. And how had John repaid this act of faith? Encouraged by a liberal bank manager, he had borrowed heavily to buy a tractor and beet puller and other machinery that they'd wanted for years. Sugar beet was the coming crop; everyone said so, including the Minister for Agriculture. It turned out to be a murderous crop. Between ploughing and pulling they slaved at it; during unseasonal rains they had to harrow the field three times. Hordes of youngsters from neighbouring farms were hired at a shilling a drill to help with the thinning. With sacks tied round their knees they crawled over the drills, up and down the hilly fields, as if tracing the curve of the earth. John Sr., who was still mobile though not capable of heavy work, would sometimes watch them and shake his head. Even the better shoots left after the thinning seemed wan and mildewed, and to cap it all, some strange insect – identified much later as the Colorado beetle – made its devastating appearance. So it was no surprise that the crop failed to pass muster with the man from the sugar company. To make matters worse the bank manager was replaced by a stickler, named Matterton, who, after several fraught 'discussions', moved to foreclose. As a gesture of goodwill the bank would leave them the house, but the land would be taken.

John removed his boots, trudged up the stairs in his woollen socks and entered the sickroom. He took some holy water from the china font nailed to the door jam and blessed himself. Over the years the sign of the cross had degenerated into a flurry of damp fingers in the general vicinity of the breastbone. The old man seemed lost in the middle of the bed – he had gravitated to its centre since his wife died. In the lamplight his face was old and tired. He had removed his teeth, probably for ever, and his jaws and mouth collapsed inwards. John had rarely seen him without his cap and was struck by the sickly proud flesh of his forehead. Only the head was visible, the rest of the body was sunk in the concavity of the feather mattress. The room reeked of paraffin and camphor and something else that could have been from a cow's placenta. Through the gaps in the rough floor boards came slivers of light from the kitchen below.

"How … are you?" John moved towards the bed in which he and Rose had probably been conceived. The silence underscored the stupidity of the question and was broken only when the major issue inevitably surfaced.

The old man raised himself slightly on the bolster. "You made a hames of it." The voice, though hoarse, had an edge to it and the watery eyes quickened. "How many times did I warn you about getting into debt?"

John nodded remorsefully. There was no point in fighting his corner or attempting to give his side of it. He had to humble himself to make peace; a dying man held all the cards. Anyway he'd had his chance and he'd failed. One wrong decision. The first and last.

"My father got forty-five acres from his father. I added forty-seven more, including the flat meadow.

And now it could all go."

John stood grimly and let the humiliation wash over him. His head was bowed in the shadow of a ceiling joist. He was vaguely conscious of a nail or a knot gouging his right foot, but the discomfort was not acute enough to make him move from the spot. He wasn't sure if a response was expected of him. What answer did he have anyway? Pests, rain, overproduction of cane sugar somewhere in the Gulf of Mexico? That he'd wanted to prove himself as a modern go-ahead farmer, to impress his father, to come out of his father's shadow before he lost whatever drive he had left? He was consumed by guilt. He wouldn't be adding his forty-seven acres. Instead, he had mortgaged it all and everyone in the townland knew about it. He felt weak and ineffectual standing there being reminded of his failings by the man he most respected in the world.

John Sr. stretched out a sinewy arm to turn up the wick in the lamp as if to see better how his big dope of a son was taking his medicine. John made a move to help but was stopped in his tracks by a gimlet look that seemed to say, 'You've helped enough already.' The brighter glow somehow made the silence more fraught.

"What got into you?" the old man demanded at length.

"I … don't know." John chafed his hands, picking at the welts that were almost as hard as spurs of bone. But the question eased his heart a little because it implied – or did it? – that his father might be prepared to accept a plea of temporary insanity from an otherwise dependable son. John remained standing, reluctant to sit in the bedside chair as if he hadn't earned the right.

"Well, I don't know either. Ah, I suppose it's that bloody bank's fault too. That citified gent, Matterton, or whatever he's called. Carrioners, the lot of them. All Freemasons of course. Freemartins more like." He gave a bitter cackle and made John's heart soar. "Bankers, God preserve us. Selling other people's money for profit. What kind of work is that?" It was a fair question coming from a man who'd worked all his life in the fields, one side of his braces hanging loose, the angled cap dark with sweat at the brim.

Both hands appeared from beneath the bedclothes; what once were smoked hams were now white and soft, half-open as if he lacked the strength to turn them into fists. A mineral glint came into his eyes. "They'll foreclose over my dead body."

John didn't know how to take this but he was relieved when the old man beckoned him to come closer and sit. Later, when he left the room, having been told about the old ways, a new burden of obligation replaced the old one of guilt. His father had made the peace, a conditional one.

Two days later the old man had the last sacraments and shortly afterwards slipped away, just stopped breathing, the mark of the holy oil visible on the waxen forehead.

"He's gone," John said unnecessarily, looking at the old face, grimmer than ever now that the eyes were closed. Rose wept into the hanky she normally kept in the sleeve of her cardigan. He didn't know what to say to her. They never conversed much and now with their father gone there was an awkwardness between them. The casement clock, still on old time, whirred and struck the hour. Rose glanced in its direction as if grateful for the sound, then looked out the window which her father always kept open on to the fields. What would become of them all now? She had looked after the men as she knew her mother would have wanted; she never flinched from the task and rarely complained because she knew how hard the men worked too. But she often felt that strange sort of frustration that came from being deprived of the right to complain at least once in a while. It would all be different now with just the two of them in the crumbling house, brother and sister, and no land to work. Maybe she could still keep a few chickens. And the kitchen garden, her preserve; surely the bank wouldn't take that? Maybe she could go to Dublin and keep house for some rich family, but what would be the point? – she was past the marrying age anyway. She was shocked that within minutes of her father's death she was thinking of herself, but by dying he seemed to have abandoned her. Despite the silent bulk of her brother she felt very alone.

The priest drove them into town in his Ford Prefect to call on the undertakers. Only when they were coming back with the undertaker did it dawn on them that they'd left the body unattended for almost two hours. It didn't seem right but they weren't sure why.

They put black crêpe on the door and waked him that night. The news that old John Keating was gone spread quickly and neighbours called to offer condolences. They came through the back door across the flagstones and into the parlour where the body was laid in the open coffin, surrounded by candles. Most of them touched the forehead, offered a prayer, then approached John and Rose with outstretched hands. Matt Feherty, a contemporary of the deceased, held John's hand in both of his and opined sadly that the bank had driven him to his grave. Any cause of death other than old age was preferable. More heatedly he added that Matterton didn't understand the first thing about farming. He was adamant that if the bank tried to sell the land from under them, no one would bid for it, none of the locals anyway.

The next day the neighbours turned out again for the funeral mass. The congregation consisted largely of farm people, although the local vet and a few merchant providers were also in attendance. Also making a token appearance was Tadgh O'Mahony, the bank porter, who sat in the last pew feeling a little out of place. He came from a small farm himself but, being the youngest of the family, had not inherited any land. Some years back he was about to emigrate to England to work on the buildings when the job of bank porter came up. It was the only stroke of luck he'd ever had in his life and he jumped at it, even though the job distanced him in more ways than one from his rural background. After the mass he waited outside the church for an opportunity to commiserate with John. Just before his chance came he heard John say something to the undertaker.

"The graveyard's the other way," the undertaker replied.

"I know," John said. "But we're going by the bank first."

Tadgh swallowed hard, got on his bike and cycled furiously into the centre of the town. Along the main street the housewives were out with yard brushes, sweeping dung off the pavements, complaining about the fair that had been held the day before. Apart from the manure, which smelled to high heaven in the morning sunshine, there was an abundance of litter and broken bottles, much of it the legacy of a Traveller fight. Tadgh located Mr. Matterton having his morning shave in the barber's shop across from the bank, giving instructions about how he wanted his pencil moustache trimmed. Breathing hard, Tadgh told him of his suspicions; it was his duty after all – or so he tried to convince himself.

"Oh, for God's sake," Matterton said dismissively. "I've never heard anything so stupid." Nevertheless he threw off the protective towel and put his long legs under him. A humourless man, he went by the book, lacking the imagination to do much else. He wore his Gonzaga tie almost every day, even though no one in the town would have recognised it as anything special. He kept very much to himself, partly out of choice but also because he had been sent to the town to improve the quality of the bank's loan book and that involved keeping a certain reserve. His predecessor had fraternised too much with the locals, was indeed constitutionally incapable of turning down an opportunity to play twenty-fives, and ended up approving some highly questionable loans. Matterton had no intention of falling into that trap. Anyway, he hated this posting and hoped that when he'd sorted out the bank's balance sheet, he would be recalled to Dublin and put in charge of a decent branch, maybe even in College Green.

The sight of the half-shaved manager and his porter rushing across the street to the bank did not go unnoticed by the townspeople, whose growing sense of expectancy seemed to rub off on Matterton. Foreclosures were a messy business, he knew too well, but collateral had to be realised. When would country people understand that fact of life? Uppermost in his mind though was the fact that, after the fair day, the vault was full of cash. Maybe he was being over cautious but he didn't want to leave anything to chance. Three of the four tellers were in already and had recorded, bagged and placed the cash on bogeys. Matterton ordered Tadgh to stand watch at the door while he phoned for a van. He also called the Guards.

Just as the funeral cortege came into view at the northern end of the main street the van left for Dublin with the cash. So far so good. Matterton began to breathe more easily. Three Guards stood with Tadgh at the entrance to the bank; they could see the hearse approaching slowly, followed by a battered Hillman, a few Fords and hundreds of people on foot, some of them trudging unconcernedly through the manure the housewives had swept into the gutters.

People came out of their houses, sensing that something was afoot. Guests of the Commercial Hotel appeared on the steps, some of them with breakfast napkins hanging from their collars. The editor of the local newspaper got out of a car, followed by his photographer equipped with camera and tripod. The windows of the school were filled with young faces. The only person who seemed uninterested was the schoolmaster, who had sent some of the senior infants out to shovel manure into a wheelbarrow for his rhubarb – but even he occasionally followed the example of his young work crew by glancing towards the slowly moving cortège.

"Close the gates," Matterton said grimly. The gates were made of wrought iron and bore the logo of the bank on both sides of the lock; between them and the oak doors was a sort of vestibule with a stucco ceiling and marble floor. Tadgh did as he was instructed, replacing the heavy keys, which were chained to his belt, in his pants pocket. He remained outside on the path with the Guards

The crowd parted to let the funeral procession through the main street. The photographer had already set up his tripod and disappeared under the black cloth, his eye glued to the viewfinder. John

Keating walked beside the hearse and when it drew level with the bank, ordered it to stop. Knowing what he had to do made him nervous, especially in front of the large crowd of onlookers, but he didn't falter. He walked towards the bank.

"We're … the bank's closed, John," Tadgh said with as much firmness as he could muster, but he involuntarily took a step backwards.

"Tell Mr. Matterton I want to see him." John's voice was calm and formal.

Tadgh hesitated, then fumbled for the keys. In the vestibule he looked out at John through the wrought iron and ruefully re-locked the gates against him.

Matterton was standing by a window when Tadgh delivered the message. His thin frame twitched in annoyance, the greying pencil moustache sat low on compressed lips. How had he fallen among such people?

"I'm not available," he snapped, not quite concealing the uncertainty that lay behind the angry tone.

Tadgh returned, embarrassed, forced into the role of a most unhappy go-between.

"He's awful busy right now, John." He spoke through the gates trying to soften the response.

"Tell him," John said, "that I have business to discuss with him before my father is buried." The words seemed to hang in the air for a long time, during which Tadgh stared wretchedly at him. There was no escape. He felt trapped, caught between two worlds, his earlier life giving him an intimation of what was on the cards.

"For God's sake, John," he whispered tersely. "I'm from Ballytogher too." His face twisted in a plea for understanding. "You know me … let it be." Out of the corner of his eye Tadgh could see the crowd forming more closely around the hearse.

"Go and tell him." John couldn't relent now. "We're not moving." His stolid shape and planted feet attested to this fact.

Miserably, Tadgh went back inside, where Matterton was sitting in the banking hall, seeming to be absorbed in a ledger.

"You'll … have to come out, Sir," Tadgh said, immediately regretting his choice of words.

Matterton looked up and removed his wire glasses in a slow curve. "Have to?" he queried. "Have to?" He squinted in the sunlight pouring through the Romanesque window on which the value of the bank's capital assets were sign-painted in assertive gold leaf. "Tell the Guards to move them on. They're blocking the main street. It's a funeral, Goddammit!"

"That's the problem, Sir … The Guards won't get involved in this…"

The manager glared at his mulish porter, clasped a hand to his uncomprehending forehead, then slammed the ledger shut. "Christ Almighty!" What stupid bucolic ritual was afoot? Matterton threw down his pen, adjusted his cuffs and went out. Was it his imagination or did he detect a hostile murmur rumbling through the crowd? The sight of the hearse squatting in the dusty street unnerved him slightly but he steeled himself against it.

Through the gates he rebuked John, "This is hardly the way to conduct business, Mr. Keating. It is most improper."

"What about taking our land?" John spoke with uncharacteristic authority. Maybe he'd finally inherited some of the cussedness for which his old man was justly renowned.

"You fell behind in servicing the loan. You were notified several times − I have the letters on file. Then you defaulted on the principal." Matterton wasn't making a moral judgement, simply reciting the facts of the case. To every action a reaction; default and forfeiture of security. There was no other way in his book. Some things were not negotiable. He lived his own rather lonely life along such fastidious lines.

John felt a momentary weakness in the face of these bald facts so well enunciated by this remote man, but he rallied. "Open the gates."

"Wh-a-at?" Matterton was nonplussed. Hadn't he just explained…?

"Open up."

"Certainly not. We've nothing further to discuss. The matter is closed." He glanced towards the Guards, who were studiously examining their boots.

"All right then." John signalled to Matt Feherty, who assembled the other pall-bearers. They opened the back of the hearse, removed the coffin and carried it towards the gates.

"Open up." This time John addressed himself to

Tadgh.

"This is … preposterous." Matterton recoiled; perplexity lay like cobweb on his thin features. It couldn't be happening, none of it. He thought he saw the porter move forward with the keys.

"No…! What on earth…? Guards…!"

"I'm sorry, Sir." Tadgh had no option. He sensed from the start it would come to this; he was just sorry that he'd got caught up in it. The Guards did not stand in his way; in fact they opened a path for him because they too had the same sense of what had to be done. One of them removed his cap as the pall-bearers passed; they had unquestioned right of passage, a right which went far back in time.

The coffin was brought through the gates and laid on the marble floor of the vestibule which suddenly took on the appearance of a mausoleum.

"What's the … meaning of this…?" Matterton demanded.

Tadgh took him literally. "The coffin on the doorstep," he explained, hoping that this would also earn him forgiveness for his insubordination in opening the gates.

The crowd pressed forward to get a better view, to satisfy themselves that the coffin had been placed on the doorstep. Matterton stood with his back against the inner oak doors as if he were the final bulwark. To his relief, no attempt was made to penetrate further into the bank.

John waited until all the mourners and several of the onlookers had a chance to witness what had been done; then he nodded judiciously and the pall-bearers took their cue. The coffin was removed from the vestibule, replaced in the hearse and the cortège moved back the way it had come, towards the graveyard.

"What the hell was all that about?" Matterton demanded of no one in particular. With a feeling of relief he went back into the bank to prepare for the day's business. Normality was returned, or so he assumed. But he was wrong, for the deed had been done and he had no understanding of it.

In the days that followed most of the country people and even some of the townsfolk refused to pass through the vestibule in which the coffin had lain on its last journey, and those who did felt obliged to withdraw their deposits. The story made the national newspapers, some of which tried to explain the odd customs which still held sway in remote parts of the country. The head office of the bank in Dublin, conscious of its image, assigned a nuisance value to the event and wrote off the Keating debt. Matterton reacted badly to the pragmatism of his superiors in Headquarters; he felt as if they had breached an important principle of banking and had also let him down. Realising also that his chances of a posting to College Green were now negligible, he took early retirement and devoted more time to his bridge club.

Some years later the branch was closed down and the building converted into a parish hall. Every Friday the Legion of Mary held Pioneer Socials in what used to be the banking hall and it was at one of those functions that Rose met the man she married in her middle years. Tadgh remained out of work but the bank gave him a modest pension and the local T.D. pulled strings to get him the dole as well.

John continued to farm the ninety odd acres along more traditional lines − mixed tillage and a few cattle − though he did, just to satisfy himself, bring in the odd sugar-beet crop when insecticides caught up on the Colorado beetle. He sometimes looked up from his work, tilted the cap back from his forehead, and thought about the plan hatched by the old man just before he died.

www.ingramcontent.com/pod-product-compliance
Lightning Source LLC
Chambersburg PA
CBHW022101240626
47154CB00012B/86